"THIS IS A MISTAKE FOR BOTH OF US."

Lenore's voice was flat, emotionless. "I won't see you again."

For once Mangas didn't know what to do. He only knew he couldn't leave her room. His fingertips moved to her throat, absorbing the silk of her flesh. An involuntary sigh escaped her. They merged like two drops of water on a pane of glass, ever so slowly. Tired of fighting a battle her body ached to lose, Lenore opened her mouth to receive his seeking tongue....

It was Mangas who pulled away. "This isn't what you want."

"Suddenly...I don't know anymore," she breathed. How she lied. She wanted him to leave—she wanted him to stay a lifetime.

Mangas felt her tremble, and was tormented by what he wanted. To love her—yet to protect her. From himself.

Books by Georgia Bockoven

HARLEQUIN SUPERROMANCES
82—RESTLESS TIDE
102—AFTER THE LIGHTNING

These books may be available at your local bookseller.

For a free catalog listing all titles currently available,
send your name and address to:

Harlequin Reader Service
P.O. Box 52040, Phoenix, AZ 85072-2040
Canadian address: Stratford, Ontario N5A 6W2

Georgia Bockoven
After the Lightning

Harlequin Books

TORONTO • NEW YORK • LONDON
AMSTERDAM • PARIS • SYDNEY • HAMBURG
STOCKHOLM • ATHENS • TOKYO • MILAN

To Margaret Carney—thank you seems so inadequate.

Published February 1984

First printing December 1983

ISBN 0-373-70102-0

CHAPTER ONE

MANGAS COLORADOS TAYLOR glanced at the raised white letters that spelled out Chancellor in one-inch block type on the door in front of him. He knew that behind the door would be a secretary, probably efficient, who would refuse to admit him to see the college director until the intruder answered a battery of questions first. The questions he could tolerate; the possibility that she might remember him later, he could not.

He reached up to rub the back of his neck, an unconscious action he had developed over the years. An action that indicated to the few who knew him well that he was deep in thought.

Suddenly his hand left his neck and his gaze traveled farther down the hall, seeking another door. He walked toward the door and tried the knob. As he had hoped, it was unlocked. Silently he eased it open a crack. As he had thought, it was a private entrance into the chancellor's office.

Mangas studied the man behind the desk. Dressed in shirt-sleeves with an open vest stretched halfway across his ample stomach, the man obviously wasn't expecting anyone. He looked to be in his mid-fifties, the years he had spent behind a desk evident in his rounding body and pale complexion. Judging by the slumped way he held himself and the unguarded look of depression on his face, Mangas surmised the chancellor's past year had been a difficult one.

He quickly looked at the rest of the room, further assessing the man by the mementos he chose to keep. Framed proclamations and plaques lined one wall; bookshelves another. There were no golf balls or unstrung tennis rackets given as a joke and kept as perpetual pieces to forever after collect dust. Instead the office was highly professional and rigidly impersonal.

When Mangas was satisfied that he would be able to deal with the man, he stepped into the room. He moved with a sureness and stealth that belied the awkwardness one might associate with a six-foot-four-inch man dressed in a proper three-piece pin-striped suit. He was standing in front of the broad mahogany desk before the chancellor was even aware another person had entered the room.

The chancellor glanced up. After the initial look of surprise had passed his face, a frown took its place. "Is there something I can—" he started to say.

"Yes, there is something you can do for me,"

Mangas interrupted. "And perhaps there is also something I can do for you." He purposely kept his voice low, nonthreatening. "Give me a few minutes of your time, and we shall find out."

Warily the man stared at Mangas. After a slow, assessing perusal, he dropped the pen he'd been holding, folded his hands and rested them on top of the paper-strewed desk. "You have managed to pique my interest," he said. "I have a few minutes if that is indeed all you want."

Before beginning, Mangas pulled his coat aside and shoved his hands into his pockets, ruining the perfect line of the expensive custom-tailored suit. "I learned late last night that Winchester College is in financial trouble. Trouble so severe that there is a possibility the school will close. Is that right?"

The chancellor's eyes narrowed. He nodded. "It hasn't exactly been kept a secret," he said, a trace of sarcasm in his voice.

"But it's hardly the kind of thing to make headlines beyond southern Colorado, wouldn't you agree?" Mangas countered with a cutting edge to his voice. His immediate and defensive reaction was an indication of the sleepless frustrated hours he'd spent since discovering late the previous night that financial problems were causing Winchester College to close its doors forever. That he might be too late to do anything about it had been a realization that had deeply disturbed him ever since. With conscious effort Mangas controlled his voice, again making it even toned and businesslike. "When is the deadline for securing the needed funds?"

Chancellor Bingham leaned back in his chair and snorted. "You *have* been out of touch, haven't you? The deadline was yesterday. Last week. Last month." His voice grew more agitated with each pronouncement.

Mangas stared at him for a moment before reaching into the breast pocket of his jacket. He withdrew a piece of paper and handed it to the man sitting in front of him. "Does that mean it's too late to give you this?"

Before reaching out to take the parchment-colored rectangle from Mangas, the chancellor ran his hand over his bald pate. He swallowed and with seeming reluctance accepted the check. He looked at the figure written on the paper, blanched, then glanced at Mangas. "Is this some kind of joke?"

Mangas ignored the question. "Is it enough to keep the school open?"

"Of course it is!" he spat. "If it's real, that is." Charles Bingham tossed the check aside. He started to rise. "I don't know what kind of game you're indulging in—" he glanced at the signature on the check "—Mr. Taylor, but I'm not amused. This school has been my entire life for the past seven years, and I did not give it up easily! Your last-minute, grandstand play is not appreciated. I suppose you thought you were safe. That you could make this grandiose gesture, and because time was so limited, it would be refused and you could get a pat on the back for trying.''

The chancellor's fists were jammed into the top of his desk, balancing his body as he leaned aggressively toward Mangas. ''Well, I have news for you, Mr. Taylor. It is not too late.'' Fire shot from his eyes. ''If you are unable to cover this check, I will personally see to it that criminal charges are filed against you.'' He started to press the button on the intercom on the corner of his desk, but Mangas reached out to stop him.

''There is a condition,'' he said.

''Isn't there always.'' The chancellor laughed mirthlessly as he sat back down heavily in the black leather chair. He glared at Mangas. ''Get out of my office, Taylor.''

Mangas ignored him. ''*No one* is to know where the money came from.'' While he waited a moment to give the chancellor time to realize there were no other strings attached to the money, he walked to the window and stared down at the small stand of aspen directly below. When his gaze left the shimmering trees, it quickly swept over the campus. A flood of memories made him turn away from the sight. He leaned his back against the sill.

''Should my identity become known through any source directly traceable to the college, all remaining funds will revert to me. I have had an agreement made up stating this condition. When you sign it as the legal representative of the college, the money will be yours.''

''Why are you doing this?'' Bingham said slowly, his voice betraying a glimmer of hope that the money might be real, after all.

Mangas smiled. Deep clefts appeared in the flesh under the high cheekbones that marked his strong Indian heritage. But the smile didn't reach the blue depths of his eyes. Eyes that had told him over and over again when he was a young man and desperately seeking roots, that although he carried the name of a great Apache chief, his blood was not pure Indian. He had been one of the world's lost children. Without a parent to guide him and help him feel comfortable about who he was, he had been forced to create a place for himself. Over the years Mangas had become a nation, a people, a homeland, of one.

Those eyes remained as cold as the ice buried inside a glacier as he answered the chancellor's question. ''My reasons are personal and hardly germane. The only two things that concern you are the money and the knowledge that I want nothing in return except total anonymity.''

''May I see the agreement?''

Mangas withdrew a thin envelope from the same pocket that had held the check and handed it to the chancellor.

After reading the simple one-page document, the man looked at Mangas as though the answer to this riddle might be hidden somewhere in the stranger's enigmatic features. Bingham glanced at his watch. "I'm sure you understand my hesitation to believe that the college has been saved at the proverbial last minute."

Mangas nodded slightly and waited for the chancellor to go on.

"Before I spread the news, I feel it would only be prudent for me to make a few phone calls to verify the authenticity of this check."

Assuming the man would make such a request if he were competent—and not the reason the school was in trouble in the first place—Mangas had had the funds transferred to his personal account earlier that morning. He had awakened his California banker, Bob Gallardo, at home to be sure the process would be started as soon as the man arrived at work.

"I anticipated as much," Mangas said evenly.

The chancellor's hand shook as he reached for the receiver. Within minutes he had contacted the San Jose, California branch office of Mangas's bank. It was verified that there were indeed sufficient funds to cover the check. Slowly Chancellor Bingham replaced the receiver. Without looking at Mangas, he took his pen and signed the statement that swore him to secrecy. With careful precise movements, he refolded the paper and slipped it back into the envelope.

"You're not going to tell me anything else about this, are you?" he said as he handed the paper to Mangas.

"Having doubts?" Mangas said softly.

"If there were any other way to keep the school open, I wouldn't accept your money. Something tells me I will someday regret what happened here this afternoon."

Mangas met his gaze unflinchingly. "Perhaps you will."

The chancellor leaned forward, resting his elbows on his desk. "Will you be staying the weekend?" When it became obvious that Mangas didn't know what he was talking about, he went on. "I'm sure the article you read must have mentioned somewhere that this weekend was to be the big farewell for the college...the official turning over of the grounds to the Winchester family. Scores of people have been invited." He chuckled suddenly, as though he had just realized what effect Mangas's check would have on the celebration. In a conspiratorial tone he said, "I can promise you one hell of a good time."

The chancellor's eyes sparkled when he again looked at Mangas. "Frankly, Mr. Taylor, right this minute, I don't give a damn what your reasons are for saving the college."

Mangas smiled. That time some of the warmth reached his eyes. He turned his head slightly to look through the window and reached up to rub the back of his neck. Although the like-lihood of anyone connecting him with the scrawny Indian who had haunted the classrooms on this campus more than twelve years ago was remote, it would be dangerous to remain. Yet . . . it would be a sweet victory to witness. One that had been totally unanticipated, yet one he had waited for for a long time. He looked back at the chancellor. "You said this weekend was going to be an official ceremony? I assume that means the principals involved will be here?"

"Yes. . . ." The chancellor hesitated, as though trying to figure out the reason behind the question. "I was going to represent the college, and Adrian Winchester, of course, would represent the Winchester family."

Mangas's eyes narrowed almost impercep-tibly. "Why do you say, 'of course'?"

Bingham laughed derisively. "You must not know Mr. Winchester very well to ask that. Adrian wouldn't miss this kind of show on a bet, even if he weren't the beneficiary. It has turned into the social event of the season. He will cry his crocodile tears over the school's clos-ing, and go home to count the fortune that will now be his alone because of it."

Mangas felt a sudden sense of apprehension, which made it almost impossible for him to keep his voice on the same conversational level. "His alone?" he finally managed to say. "I thought there was a sister."

The chancellor's brow furrowed in puzzlement. "Could you possibly mean Jacquelyn Winchester?"

Mangas nodded, afraid to trust his speech.

The chancellor hesitated before answering. When he did, his voice had dropped, indicating he realized the question hadn't been one of idle curiosity. "She died more than eight years ago. I understand it was a particularly sad death. Did you know her?"

"How did she die?" Mangas said woodenly.

The chancellor seemed reluctant to go on. Nervously he began to gather up the papers on the desk. Finally he looked up and said, "The family and close friends tried very hard to keep it a secret, but it was commonly known that she took her own life." He ran his hand across his forehead and sighed. "Such a waste. Some say she was so filled with grief over her father's and mother's deaths on a plane crash the year before that she couldn't go on. Others have said that a desperately unhappy marriage was the cause. But as she didn't leave a note, it's all just gossip, isn't it?" He went back to gathering the papers, then stopped again to look at Mangas. "It is gossip I would prefer not to explore further. Anyway, Jacquelyn and Adrian were the only children, the last of the Winchester line. Now there's only Adrian...."

Mangas's thoughts whirled without order or pattern. Jacquelyn dead? Eight years? Somehow it seemed sad that he hadn't known. Sad yet fitting that he hadn't been among those who had mourned her.

He felt numb. He needed time to think. The almost fifty hours since he had last slept suddenly seemed like a hundred. Mechanically he reached for the chancellor's hand. "I think I'll pass on the invitation," he said absently. "If it becomes imperative that you get in touch with me, you can leave a message with my bank. They'll know what to do."

"I would thank you for what you've done, but there aren't words or time enough to express what your gift means." Chancellor Bingham's handclasp was firm, his eyes warm. Softly he said, "Besides, I have a feeling it wasn't thanks you were after when you decided to do this. Whatever your motivations were, I heartily approve of your actions."

Mangas left the chancellor's office the same way he had entered. He quickly strode the long hallway to the stairs, the leather soles on his shoes making a soft squishing sound against the asphalt tile. Late-afternoon sun streamed through a large plate-glass window at the end of the hall, and in the distance, Mangas could see the mountains where he had gone hiking to try to work out his seemingly insurmountable problems when he had been a student here. He knew those mountains as well as he knew any place on earth. They had provided an uncritical home and haven when he had none other.

As though drawn by invisible hands, Mangas went to the window and stared at the mountains he had only just then realized how desperately he had missed. He had never shared the love he felt for this place with anyone else. Not even Jacquelyn.

Jacquelyn. What flaw was it in his personality that had permitted him to love someone so completely, who had later so effortlessly denied that love? How could he have been so blind not to see her weaknesses? The softness, lack of aggression and utter femininity that had so enchanted him in the beginning had, in the end, been the reason their love hadn't survived. Her malleability, under the guise of sensitivity, had been wrought by her family with ''reasoning,'' until she had agreed that it was indeed best for everyone involved if she never saw Mangas again.

Her farewell to him had been tucked into his box with the other mail. Only that and a flyer announcing a local company's going-out-of-business sale had arrived that day. Couched in loving words of goodbye was the message that Jacquelyn could not marry him because of the irreparable social harm that would befall the Winchester family. Perhaps, she had said, if they had lived somewhere else or in another time, things might have been different. But there was no denying how people in the southwest felt about Indians, and no matter how strong their love for each other was, Jacquelyn and Mangas could never change public sentiment.

A flash of bright red caught his eyes, and Mangas glanced from the forest-covered mountains to the walkway below. Struggling with a large, awkward artist's portfolio she had tucked under one arm and an overnight case she carried in her other hand, was a woman that even from this distance made Mangas catch his breath. Her light brown hair, coiled in a twist and caught at the back of her head, glistened with golden highlights in the afternoon sun. She was coltish looking, almost as tall as the man who walked beside her. She moved with a grace and ease that radiated self-assurance. And she stirred something in Mangas that was exciting and challenging. She was precisely the kind of woman he went out of his way to avoid. The type of woman he knew could lead to complications and involvement. Even this far from him, she managed to make his heart beat a little quicker.

He smiled in commiseration when she dropped the unwieldy portfolio and it popped open, letting papers slip out the sides. Her companion shook his head in irritation and set his own burden of suitcases down to give her a hand, gathering the papers that were being ruffled in the light breeze. When the man turned so that he again faced the building, he glanced up to where Mangas stood. And for the first time Mangas was able to distinguish the man's features.

Mangas's smile froze. His heart beat heavily against his chest. He knew a hatred that was as pure and untainted as the love that had once coursed through his veins. The man who stared at Mangas, but who couldn't possibly see him through the one-way glass, was Adrian Winchester III.

Mangas glanced back at the woman. He watched her interaction with Adrian. Even though she carried the paraphernalia of an employee, it was obvious she was more than that to Adrian. There was an easy familiarity between them, almost as if there were.... But the chancellor hadn't mentioned that Adrian was married. Then again, why should he have?

Mangas watched the scene below for the few more seconds it took Adrian and the woman to regather their belongings and leave. He was convinced as he watched them go that if the woman wasn't Adrian's wife, she was still someone very special to him.

Seeing Adrian had made Mangas realize that the unexpected taste of victory over his nemesis, the bailing out of Winchester College, had only whet his appetite. There were so many wrongs Mangas could never right, so many wounds that had never, would never, heal. Slowly he turned and walked away from the window.

Without realizing he was doing so, Mangas started to walk back to the chancellor's office. As he moved along the corridor, a plan formed in his mind. A plan that would pay Adrian back in kind. A love for a love. Even though revenge against the man hadn't been the motive for giving the money to the college, it had been a sweet bonus. By keeping the college from Adrian, Mangas was thwarting his love of money.... Now he would take the woman.

Mangas went into Chancellor Bingham's office to tell him he would be staying the weekend, after all.

CHAPTER TWO

LENORE RANDOLPH'S BURGUNDY HEELS tapped out a forlorn hollow sound as she slowly, reluctantly walked across the wooden footbridge on her way to the amphitheater. With the campus now nearly deserted, it seemed impossible that only a month ago this gracefully arched bridge had been overrun with students rushing to class. She looked down at the path her feet followed. Seventy years of students passing this way had worn the massive center timbers smooth, while those who had lingered a while had left the railing and struts rough with their carved initials, hearts and graduation dates.

Lenore leaned against the railing, resting her elbows between "J.T., class of 1924" and "M.R., class of 1975." Absently she traced an arrow-pierced heart with her fingertip. Did the occupants of this slightly lopsided heart ever get married, she wondered. Did they have children? Did they plan to send them to Winchester College?

"Well." She sighed aloud and flicked a triangle-shaped pebble into the stream with a manicured nail. ''If they did, they were tough out of luck.'' As always, the thought made her wince.

She knew she was being unprofessional, sentimental and rather sloppy about the whole thing. After all, Winchester wasn't even her college. She had received her Master of Architecture degree from UCLA, really had no ties to Winchester College beyond the fact that it was another job.

But as she looked over the beautifully landscaped campus, she had no doubt that if she had discovered Winchester earlier, she would have been a student there. Academically, it was one of the most respected small colleges in the west. Scenically, it was a Rocky Mountain jewel. Nestled in a valley at the foot of some of Colorado's most spectacular slopes, it had managed to remain uncorrupted, isolated and pristine, much to the credit of a long line of hardheaded, incredibly competent administrators.

But not any longer.

After today, Adrian Winchester III planned to see to it that thousands of people were drawn to this lovely valley each winter. Under his direction, Winchester College would become a flashy rival with Aspen, Steamboat Springs and Sun Valley for a portion of the multimillion-dollar ski business. It was her job to help redesign the college's conservative ivy-covered walls into the ''flash'' Adrian insisted the skiers would expect.

Lenore moved languorously along the railing, letting her hand lightly caress the human history traced there. Seeking the flimsiest excuse to tarry and thus avoid the group now gathering at the amphitheater to listen to the university's eulogy, she paused to watch a hitchhiking beetle float by on a leaf.

When the leaf disappeared around a rock, her gaze swung up to the stand of aspens behind the sports arena. She tried to visualize a wide swath cut through their rippling grace, a planned scar to accommodate the beginner's ski run. The thought made her ill.

As she stared at the trees and imagined their destruction, she was surprised to see a runner emerge from the trail head and swing onto the track surrounding the practice soccer field. With all the students gone for the year and the summer session canceled, she hadn't expected to see anyone on campus who wouldn't be at the meeting.

The runner glided around the field with a sense of freedom that belied the effort he expended. His movements were executed with a natural grace and rhythm that made his running look effortless.

Lenore continued to watch as the tall, dark-haired man, clad only in running shoes, shorts and a bright red headband, finished two more laps. He was too far away for her to discern much about his face, beyond the fact that his features were prominent and angular and that he was clean shaven. She judged him to be in his early, perhaps mid-thirties.

He ran the laps as if he were in a hotly contested race, then slowed to a cool-down walk. He traveled the far side of the track with his hands resting lightly on his narrow hips, his head thrown back as if in ancient ritualistic supplication to the sun. His arm and leg muscles were pronounced from the exertion; his skin glistened like grass spangled with early-morning dew.

Lenore caught her breath. Something primitive stirred inside her. He was the most ruggedly, sensuously healthy man she could ever remember seeing. A shiver of deep, unbridled attraction stripped away a lifetime of rigidly civilized thoughts. She found she was drawn to him in ancient fundamental fascination.

When she realized where her thoughts were leading, she laughingly chided herself. *Lenore, you have just lost the right to complain about construction workers who stand around and ogle women.*

Still she continued to openly stare at the runner, unable to withdraw her gaze. She felt compelled, almost as if he had willed her to look at him. She tried to convince herself she was only admiring an exceptional work of art, much as she would have done at any gallery. That this particular piece of sculpture happened to be moving around shouldn't make any difference.

Nice try, but no prize, Lenore. This time she laughed aloud, amazed at her feeble reasoning, intended to cover her lustful thoughts. She'd had no idea her long self-imposed celibacy would eventually reverse itself so dramatically, turning her into a panting frustrated female.

The clock tower struck ten and startled her out of her reverie. She was embarrassed anew to realize how long she'd been staring at the runner. . . and she quickly glanced around, grateful she hadn't been caught. She would have hated to have someone come along and ask her to explain her strange behavior.

Just as the last chime struck, Lenore stepped off the bridge and broke into a run of her own. She held her burgundy skirt high above her knees, sprinting as fast as her two-and-a-half-inch heels would allow. Adrian would be furious if she was late. She groaned. The last thing she needed this weekend was a lecture on professionalism.

To say that Adrian was anxious to have the college land returned to the Winchester family was a gross understatement. He was like a quintessential hard-luck gambler who had finally won the Irish Sweepstakes and New York lottery rolled into one. Which really didn't make any sense. The Winchester wealth was legendary, so it couldn't be the money he needed. But, then, perhaps it could. Insidious rumors about Adrian's foolish investments had started almost immediately after his parents' plane crash nearly twelve years ago.

Lenore pushed open the back door that led to the amphitheater stage and listened for sounds of a speech. Only the low hum of a crowd in conversation greeted her. She had made it.

As she worked her way to the front of the stage, she glanced at Adrian. As always, he looked as though he'd just stepped out of an ad in a slick men's magazine. Cool, composed and impeccably dressed, he was the epitome of the fashion world's idea of a business executive. Yet real executives were infrequently blessed with Adrian's blond good looks and rarely had the time to acquire his year-round tan Lenore was positive that ten years from now, at forty-eight, the Winchester heir would be every bit as handsome and every bit as shallow. She had come to know him better than she had wanted to the past year and a half. Long meetings at the office had turned into social evenings that were always somehow tied to business and therefore impossible for her to avoid. His actions at these meetings were never overt enough to call them passes, yet she constantly had the feeling she was being subtly maneuvered into a position where she and Adrian were being accepted as a "couple."

As unobtrusively as possible, Lenore crossed the stage and took her seat beside the podium. She answered Adrian's concerned glance with her most convincingly innocent look. She smoothed her skirt as she fought to bring her breathing under control.

"Cut it rather close, didn't you?" Adrian asked, coolly.

She smiled. "I had to stop to get something out of my eye." *And out of my overly active imagination, too.* She glanced out at the audience and was surprised to see the five-hundred-seat theater was nearly full.

"Were this many people expected?" she asked, trying to bring the conversation to neutral ground.

Adrian snorted. "It would seem our dear Chancellor Bingham has a streak of showmanship in him. Not only has he invited every alumnus in the area who ever contributed a dime, he has convinced some die-hard press people his little ceremony is worth covering. He must have decided it would be advantageous to go out with a bang. I understand many of the people were only invited last night." Adrian plucked a miniscule piece of lint from his navy blue serge pants.

"Perhaps it's just the chancellor's way of thanking the campaign workers after a losing election," Lenore said. "I understand there were quite a few people who were involved in the effort this past year." She fought to keep the distaste she felt for Adrian's comments out of her voice.

She glanced at him again. This time she noted he was wearing his Phi Beta Kappa pin and Winchester College class ring. The ring was something she had never seen on his hand before. Mentally she groaned. She wondered who he was trying to impress with such spurious fidelity.

"Perhaps," he absently agreed. Then, as if unconsciously speaking his thoughts aloud, he almost growled, "But if it's not—if Bingham has some grandstand, last-minute stunt up his sleeve, I'll...." He left the threat dangling.

Lenore shuddered. She had tried a dozen ways to avoid this weekend, knowing beforehand what was in store. But the elder Mason of Mason, Langly and Mason, the firm that employed her and commandeered a great deal of her spare time, had insisted she was the ideal person to accompany their star client on this, his triumphant weekend. After all, Mr. Mason had reasoned, she was the major designer for the project and had worked more closely with Winchester than anyone else. Besides, and most important as far as they were concerned, he had specifically requested she be the one to attend.

Careful attention to clients, both their needs and their wants, was one of the things that had catapulted Mason, Langly and Mason to the forefront of architectural firms. This added part of her job had been carefully outlined when Lenore had first applied to the firm; a socially acceptable style of behavior was one of the conditions of advancement. She was grateful she didn't have a spouse, as many of the other young architects did. It would have been nerve-racking for a husband to be constantly watched for his slightest social faux pas. Still, there were some occasions, like the weekend before her, when not even the prestige and opportunities that came from working for M., L. & M. seemed worth it.

While she waited for the chancellor to appear to start the proceedings, Lenore went over, one more time, the short speech she was to make. As briefly as possible, she was to describe the changes that would be made at the college and how long they were expected to take, ending with a pleasant, "And we hope to see all of you here again—only next time come dressed for the slopes." Ugh! She hoped she didn't choke on the words.

Lenore looked at her watch: ten-fifteen. She murmured a silent prayer of thanks that Chancellor Bingham was uncharacteristically late, allowing her own tardiness to go unnoticed by everyone but Adrian.

A flutter in the curtains to her left drew her attention. Coming out of the opening in the royal blue drapes was the beaming chancellor. He paused a moment to adjust his tie before he fully emerged to make his way to the podium. Wild spontaneous applause greeted his appearance.

Dressed in an ancient tweed jacket with leather patches on the sleeves, the rotund man looked typecast for the role of the absentminded professor. Shortly after meeting him, Lenore had discovered he cleverly used his benign appearance to his full advantage. Those who were foolish enough to prejudge him were often stung by his rapier wit and brilliant mind. Lenore tilted her head in wonder and quickly studied the man she had come to think of as a friend, despite their seeming professional differences.

He looked harried, yet strangely happy. The taut skin separating the wild puffs of gray hair sticking out over his ears shone in the bright stage lights with a thin coating of perspiration. He stopped for a moment to catch his breath and to acknowledge the on-going applause. When finally he was able to quiet the outpouring of love and respect the audience seemed intent on giving him, he began.

"The feeling is mutual, my friends. I applaud each and every one of you for the superhuman effort you have made the past few years to keep this school open. However, as most of you already know, and the rest of you have guessed, even our combined money-making energies could not bring in enough additional finances to keep pace with double-digit inflation."

The room grew eerily quiet. It was as if five hundred people were collectively holding their breath, hoping the bomb the chancellor was there to drop would be disarmed in time.

In the shadows behind the last row of seats, Lenore saw a door ease open. For an instant an outline of a tall man appeared. She had a fleeting sense of recognition before the door closed and there was only darkness again.

"Finally," the chancellor continued, "all of us were forced to accept the inevitable...that after seventy illustrious years, this school would cease to exist. As most of you know, Adrian Winchester I, the founder of Winchester College, was very specific in his instructions, should this deplorable occasion arise. The grounds and buildings were to revert to any living Winchester heirs." He paused, waiting for complete silence before he dropped his voice slightly lower and continued dramatically. "It seemed for a while that this would indeed happen...."

Lenore saw Adrian tense at the unanticipated direction the chancellor's speech had taken. The knuckles of his folded hands grew white. She could see a muscle twitch at his temple. She could almost *feel* the change in his mood. It was as if a peacefully lounging house cat had suddenly turned feral.

Chancellor Bingham paused once more to let his words take effect. When the room quieted he began again. "It is with deep pleasure that I inform you, my dear friends, that in the nick of time, funds were secured. It is virtually guaranteed Winchester College will remain open not only this next year, but for many many years to come—'' Wild applause and shouts of joy made it impossible for him to continue. After several unsuccessful attempts to finish his speech, he laughed and stepped from the podium, waving his arms at the jubilant crowd.

As stunned by the announcement as everyone else around her, Lenore wondered how and where the funds had been found. She knew every source had been tapped, every appeal made. She secretly suspected some of those sources had dried up because Adrian had surreptitiously informed donors they were throwing away their money on a lost cause. No one had openly suggested Adrian was responsible for contributions dwindling, but the pattern had become all too familiar—attend a party at Adrian's penthouse one day, withdraw support for the college the next.

The unanticipated news caused deep conflicting emotions inside Lenore. She was acutely disappointed that some of her finest work would never be seen, and at the same time, delighted that there was no longer a reason to use her designs. She felt as though a constricting band had been cut from her chest. She could breath freely again.

Lenore saw Adrian's hands shake as he forced them to unclench. Always in control, he rose stiffly and approached the chancellor to offer his congratulations. Lenore saw the men exchange a few words. Then Adrian turned to the jubilant crowd, smiled and gave a quick wave before he disappeared behind the curtain.

When she was sure he was gone, Lenore rose and went to the chancellor. "I can't imagine how you accomplished it," she said, "but please accept my sincere congratulations. I couldn't be more pleased for you."

"Thank you, my dear. I appreciate—" The rest of his words were lost in the confusion of people rushing on stage to share the ecstatic moment.

Making her way through the crowd, Lenore returned to her room in the women's dorm. Assuming Adrian would want to return to Colorado Springs as soon as possible, she began to repack the clothing she had unpacked the night before. She was closing the last lock when she heard the harsh ring of the pay telephone down the hall. Positive the call wasn't for her, she grabbed a pencil and piece of paper to take down a message for one of the other, still-absent dorm occupants. She ran into the corridor.

Adrian's clipped voice answered her friendly, "Hello," making her wish she had let the phone ring.

"Be ready for the party by seven. I'll pick you up in the dorm lounge."

She started to protest, but her words were met by the hum of a dead line.

"Damn!" She slammed the receiver on its cradle and stomped back to her room. Angrily she shoved her suitcase aside and sat on the bed. She couldn't imagine why Adrian would want to stay. He'd never shown himself to be the type to pour salt on his wounds. Now that the tone of tonight's party had changed so dramatically, it was sure to be torture for him to sit through. But then, Lenore reconsidered, perhaps the torture was nothing compared to the prospect of how it would look if he didn't attend. There were still some people who sincerely believed Adrian was unhappy about the college closing and the land reverting to him.

Lenore was amazed to realize that in a perverse way, she felt sorry for him. Over the past six months she had learned how much the ski resort meant to Adrian. Tonight was sure to be incredibly painful to him.

Briefly she considered calling a taxi, going into Crowley to rent a car and heading back to Colorado Springs by herself. After all, the job she had been hired to do was over. Holding Adrian Winchester's hand while he bemoaned his loss was above and beyond the call of duty.

Lenore sighed, disgusted with herself because she knew she wouldn't carry through with her plans. She could no more leave Adrian than she could leave a puppy out in the rain. As much as she would like to, she had known all along she wouldn't leave. No matter how tough hearted she talked or thought, the toughness never seemed to reach the center part of her where the final decisions were made.

Lenore would stay to see the weekend through and file a complete report on the happenings for Mason, Langly and Mason on Monday morning, whether she really wanted to or not. So why not make the best of it?

When her few things were put away, she walked over to the cafeteria, talked the cook out of an orange and a banana, which she ate for lunch, and spent the rest of the afternoon wandering around the campus. She returned to her room early to take a shower before the rush of party goers claimed the community bathroom.

She took her time, lingering in the warm spray of the shower until she saw the skin on her fingers had begun to pucker. Afterward she worked with her long, golden brown hair until it lay glisteningly smooth around her shoulders in a style that looked natural and free and belied the half hour it took to create.

The sea-green-and-mocha dress she chose to wear was one of her favorites. Long and slinky, it looked daring, but in reality covered more of her full breasts than was currently fashionable. The full skirt was topped with a swatch of matching messaline that attached to the waist and looped over her neck to cover her breasts like two wide suspenders. She started to pull the dress's deeply fringed shawl over her bare shoulders, then decided to leave it behind. That way if the party grew too uncomfortable, she could claim she was cold, then easily and gracefully excuse herself.

ADRIAN WAS SMOKING HEAVILY and pacing the dorm lounge when Lenore arrived. She could almost follow his path through the long room by the cloud of smoke he'd left behind. She paused to stare at him before he had a chance to see her. If blatant handsomeness had counted for anything in the battle for Winchester College, he would have won hands down. Even though he was cast in the role of villain tonight, Lenore doubted he would lack eager female companionship at the party.

Adrian bent over to press his cigarette into a pot of sand. He glanced up to discover Lenore staring at him.

"Where the hell have you been?"

Lenore gritted her teeth, biting back the immediate retort that came to mind. Purposely she looked at the wall clock before she coolly replied, "It's ten minutes to seven. I believe I'm early."

He reached inside his tuxedo jacket and withdrew a gold cigarette case and lighter. "I'm sorry," he mumbled, obviously sensing her anger. "It's been a hellish day. I didn't mean to take it out on you." He lit the cigarette and inhaled deeply. "Shall we go?"

Lenore sighed. "Apology accepted." The evening was going to be uncomfortable enough without added animosity. She nodded and forced a smile.

Once outside, she took his proffered arm. They walked down the steps, maintaining an awkward silence. They were almost halfway to the party before either spoke.

"By the way, I meant to tell you earlier that you look stunning this evening. There won't be another woman at the party who will hold a candle to you." Adrian spoke mechanically, as if reciting a page out of a book on appropriate dialogue.

Lenore was positive that if she was to ask him to close his eyes, he wouldn't be able to tell her what she was wearing. She didn't bother to thank him for the generic compliment. Instead she asked conversationally, "How was your afternoon?"

It was the wrong thing to ask, she knew immediately. Adrian threw his cigarette onto the lawn as if he were hurling a weapon.

"My afternoon stunk. Bingham refuses to say where he acquired his mysterious funds or how much money is involved." He reached for another cigarette. "I know the bastard is just stalling for time. He thinks he can invite a crowd to witness his dramatic farce of a Hollywood production, and fresh money will come flowing in. Then at the right moment he will disclose the fact that the original funds were

really rather meager, but thanks to a new outpouring, the college will survive the crisis.''
Adrian mimicked the chancellor's speech in
a whiney falsetto that set Lenore's teeth on
edge.

She shuddered and mentally congratulated
the mysterious benefactors, whoever they might
be. They had freed her from spending the coming year with Adrian as effectively as if they had
slipped her a key to the jailhouse door. After the
weekend was over and she had fulfilled her duty
to her firm, she would do everything in her
power to make sure she never saw Adrian Winchester III again. The thought brought a spring
to her step.

A secret smile played at the corners of Lenore's mouth, while Adrian brooded as they
continued along the narrow twisting path to the
large patio area where the party was to be held.
As soon as they reached a point where they
could be seen by others, Adrian assumed a
proper smile, one Lenore was sure would remain fixed throughout the evening.

She endured two hours of being an unwilling
participant in Adrian's charade before she
began to actively seek an escape. She had started
to feel like she was caught in an earthquake
fault, the two plates constantly ramming against
each other. She felt suffocated in her role as
Adrian's ''date'' and had to constantly remind
herself not to reveal how delighted she was that
the school wasn't closing. At the first oppor-

tunity, she maneuvered over to him and lightly touched his arm.

"It's getting cold," she murmured. "I'm going to return to the dorm to get my shawl. I won't be gone too long."

Adrian turned to her, his face still frozen in a smile. "Would you like me to go with you?"

"That isn't necessary."

"I don't think it's wise for you to be walking around after dark by yourself."

"For God's sake, Adrian, I'm only going to the dorm."

"Still. . . ."

Lenore bit back an angry retort about his feigned interest in her safety on a virtually crime-free campus, forced herself to smile sweetly and said, "I appreciate your concern, Adrian, but I assure you I can make it to the dorm and back without incident." She turned and left before he had a chance to say anything more.

CHAPTER THREE

LENORE, SHIVERING, retraveled the winding path and stepped onto the wider walkway that lead back to the dorm. Without the crush of humanity at the party to provide warmth, it had indeed turned cold.

Hugging herself and quickening her pace so that her heels clicked hard and loud on the concrete surface, she almost missed the faint sound of a piano. The fragments of music drifted with the light breeze like errant fingerlings of fog. Lenore stopped to listen, straining to blend the notes into a recognizable melody. They seemed hauntingly familiar, yet unlike any other she could recall. It was as if she was tasting a favorite food while wearing a blindfold, a food that was tangy and sharp but kept short of bitterness by the addition of a few quick swirls of golden honey.

Forgetting the cold, Lenore abandoned the walkway and followed the trail of music. It led her over a mound of grass, then to a rectangular, two-story building. She peered through the glass doors at the main entrance. A dim light around a portal of the end of the hallway was the only physical evidence that the building was inhabited. She tried the doors in front of her but found both securely fastened.

Without stopping to wonder about her unorthodox behavior, she began a determined search for another entrance, finally finding a side door unlocked. She got the full impact of the music now and was as drawn to it as the children of Hamelin had been to the Pied Piper's.

As quietly as possible, she made her way down the hall to the partially open door. She paused and slipped out of her shoes, hooking the thin leather ankle straps over her fingers. She peeked around the corner and into the room.

Only a low-wattage light placed over the keyboard illuminated the interior. In the glow of that light, Lenore could see a man sitting at the piano, intent on the music he made. Lying on the bench beside him was a discarded tuxedo jacket. The cloud-white, pleated shirt he wore was open at the collar, and the sleeves were casually folded back, making him look as comfortable as though he was in his own living room. He seemed lost in the world he was creating with his haunting melody.

Feeling like a sneak thief but unwilling to halt the exquisite performance by announcing her arrival, Lenore crept into the room and eased into the shadows.

The music drifted into a light staccato rhythm that reminded her of children at play. She leaned against the cool cement wall and closed her eyes. Quick photographic visions of her own happy childhood spent in the rich farmland of Salinas, California, brought a smile to her lips.

Abruptly the music changed. The quick tripping notes disappeared, replaced by hesitant fearful chords. Lenore frowned. A strange transition had just occurred in the man before her.

She couldn't tell if his face reflected his shift in mood; she had maneuvered herself into such a position that he was poised at the ebony grand piano with his back to his unknown audience. Forgetting the music for a moment, she studied the man. His hair was black and full, lying in natural waves, curling softly and starkly against his white collar. He had wide powerful shoulders and a lean narrow waist. His posture and his ease with the keyboard, as well as his obvious talent, made Lenore wonder if he'd been hired to entertain at the party.

Without warning, the music stopped. Only an echo lingered in her ears as slowly, deliberately, the man turned and looked directly at her.

"What do you want?" His voice cut the air like a knife. Even in the dim light, she could see his features were set in a scowl. She pressed her bare back tightly against the cement, subconsciously trying to blend into the background to escape the piercing eyes that had found her in the dark room as easily as if she was standing under floodlights. Seconds ticked by, controlled by the hands on a Salvador Dali clock.

Mentally Lenore tried to form an apology for her seeming rudeness, but before she could open her mouth a thought came to her. She gasped. Although she had never seen his face clearly, she knew without question this man at the piano was the runner she had watched that morning. Twice now she had been guilty of covertly watching him. She could feel a flush of embarrassment warm her cheeks.

Finally, after what seemed like hours, she managed to stammer, "I—I'm sorry. It was rude of me to intrude. I should have let you know I was here." She turned to leave.

"Wait."

Lenore glanced up to see the man's look of anger disappear, replaced by one of curiosity.

Recognizing that he no longer had a choice in the matter, Mangas gestured toward her with an outstretched hand. He forcefully swallowed the irritation he felt at being discovered. After almost running into her on the fringes of the party, he had purposely shut himself off in the music room to avoid any accidental encounter. He wasn't ready to make contact yet. He hadn't observed her long enough—didn't know enough about her for that. "I didn't mean to bark at you. Did you want something?"

His deep voice felt like a caress, the way it

tugged at her. "No." She tried to smile. "That is, nothing other than to listen to you play. It was very beautiful."

Lenore saw the man's eyes narrow. His gaze never left her face. She had an uneasy feeling she was being inspected. Then subtly, in a way she couldn't pinpoint, his rigid posture changed. He seemed to become less guarded.

"Thank you," he said slowly, at last acknowledging her compliment. Then as though none of the previous tension had existed between them, he said, "Would you like to come down here to listen? The acoustics are probably better than up there against the wall."

Lenore hesitated. A sudden shiver of apprehension brought goose bumps to her arms. Absently she rubbed the raised flesh and chided herself for suspecting that there was more to the invitation than a simple act of friendliness. While she was still trying to make up her mind whether she should join him or go back to her room, he indicated a spot next to him on the bench. "You are sincerely welcome to join me."

His voice filled her with an ache to hear more. "Are you sure I wouldn't be interrupting?"

He smiled warmly, revealing deep indentations in his cheeks. "Not at all. I would enjoy your company."

Scarcely aware that she'd made a decision, Lenore returned his smile and walked toward the small platform. "Sorry about the cloak-and-dagger business. I really didn't mean to spy on you. I just didn't want to interrupt your playing to ask you if you minded if I stayed."

"And I apologize for the angry looks. I was deep in thought about something and not prepared for visitors."

"Your playing certainly didn't suffer. I would have guessed you were totally absorbed in the music."

He acknowledged her second compliment with a slight nod. "Playing the piano is a hobby I find little time to indulge in lately. I'm afraid I've gotten rather rusty."

So he wasn't a professional, after all, simply a gifted amateur. What a waste! Lenore stopped beside him and offered her hand. "I'm Lenore Randolph, struggling architect, and as you've already discovered for yourself, very bad spy."

Strong artist's fingers closed warmly around her hand, lingering longer than propriety dictated, yet not so long that Lenore felt uncomfortable or sought to break the contact.

"Mangas Taylor, Ms Randolph." He gave her a lopsided grin. "I'm sure the CIA's loss is architecture's gain."

Smooth, Lenore thought. *Very smooth.* He had offered her a compliment, but no information about himself. She propped her elbows on the piano and leaned forward, her hair falling over her shoulders like twin shimmering waterfalls.

"And music's loss?" she prodded.

"Electronic's gain. I think the expression is that I'm 'into computers.' "

"Designing, building or repairing?"

"A little of all three."

"You wouldn't happen to work for Lowell's, would you?" She had designed the offices for Lowell Electronic Company, Colorado Springs's newest industrial complex. It had been a plum assignment, and the clients had not only been satisfied—they had also been generously grateful. Her success at Lowell's was the major reason she'd been considered ready for the work at the college.

"No. I'm with Apache. We're based—"

"In the famous, or perhaps I should say infamous, Silicon Valley. You'd have to be a hermit not to have heard of Apache Computers." Lenore's mind skipped to what she knew of industry gossip. Several electronics and computer firms were thinking of relocating, out of California into cheaper areas of the country where less pirating of staff and ideas occurred. "Apache isn't thinking of moving, is it?" she asked, unable to keep the excitement from her voice. Possibly she could recruit a new client.

He laughed aloud. It was a wonderfully uninhibited and happy sound. "If they are, I'm sure it's a closely guarded secret."

She grinned sheepishly. "Subtlety has never been one of my virtues. I do design terrific offices, though.'' She pulled her hair back over her shoulders in an unconscious gesture that emphasized the fullness of her breasts. Mangas's eyes unabashedly noted the motion, and she fought an urge to glance down to make sure she was still modestly covered.

As though reading her thoughts, he said, ''You carry it off very well.'' At her confusion, he said, ''The dress, I mean. Not many women could wear something so blatantly enticing and still look so elegant.''

She swallowed. His compliment had been as intimate as a kiss. She didn't know whether to thank him or be irritated by his forwardness.

He didn't wait for her to decide. ''You weren't by any chance the one responsible for the office design at Lowell's, were you?''

''As a matter of fact, I was.''

''I had a chance to see the work you did earlier today. The way you combined privacy and space with a sense of opulence in the office section was brilliant.''

Lenore was at a loss for words. His astute observation pleased her immensely. Suddenly feeling shy, and unable to think of anything to say in reply beyond a flustered thank-you, she purposely changed the direction of their conversation, away from herself.

''Mangas...'' she murmured, letting the name roll off her tongue. She savored the unfamiliar feel as she looked at the way his hair dripped over the top of his ears. "Is that a family name?"

"I'm sure it must have been," he said slowly, wondering what she would say if he told her the truth. He moved his jacket to a chair to make room for Lenore to sit beside him. When she was settled, he leaned his arm against the piano top and turned his body so that he could look directly at her. "I come from a very large family," he said with an expressive shrug, deciding a lie would create fewer complications. "I suppose it would be hard not to be named after someone."

Lenore studied his face. It was a compilation of angles and planes with high prominent cheekbones and a strong wide jaw. His eyes were large and blue, the color of a clear, deep mountain lake. She found herself as drawn to them as she was to fireplaces in stormy weather.

Studying him, she decided that if "taciturn" could be used to describe eyes, she would use it to describe his. As captivating and warm as they were, they stopped far short of mirroring his soul. That, she somehow sensed, he kept carefully veiled. She guessed him to be a private person, someone few people were allowed to know too intimately.

"And Lenore?" Mangas asked. "Is that a family name?"

Lenore laughed. "I'm sure it is in someone's family, but not in mine. I have the questionable honor of being named after a young woman Edgar Allan Poe loved and wrote poems about.''

Mangas closed his eyes and thought for a moment. Softly he began to quote, ''For the rare and radiant maiden whom the angels name Lenore. . . .''

Lenore was stunned and strangely flattered. ''You must have had an English teacher who was as fond of Poe as my mother was. Did yours make all her students memorize 'The Raven,' too?''

Mangas's expression grew closed, guarded. ''No. . . .'' He hesitated. ''It was something I did on my own.'' Abruptly he changed his manner and the subject, making both less personal. ''Are you staying the entire weekend?''

Lenore felt her stomach tighten. She had almost forgotten her reason for being at the college. ''Yes,'' she finally said. ''I think so. At least until after breakfast tomorrow.''

''You don't seem too happy about it,'' he said slowly, his finger lightly tapping against an ivory key.

''Not terribly.''

''I take it you weren't pleased, then, to hear the school would be remaining open, after all?''

Lenore frowned. It seemed such an odd question for him to ask. How, why, would he think she had wanted the school to close? Then it dawned on her. He must have seen her with Adrian and assumed she would feel the same way he would. "I—" She started to explain her position.

Mangas stopped her. "Never mind. It was an unfair question."

Lenore started to answer, anyway, but paused. She didn't want the college to intrude on this tiny island of refuge, too. There had been enough of that today, not counting what she was bound to have to listen to on the way home tomorrow. She decided to change the subject entirely. "It seems I've done exactly what I said I didn't want to do. I've interrupted your playing. Would you please continue?"

He smiled. The deep clefts in his cheeks gave him an almost boyish appearance. He stared at her a moment while an inner battle raged. His love affair with the piano was private. A part of himself he had never shared with anyone. From somewhere in the back of his mind, a soft voice urged him to make an exception, before he had time to reconsider, he bowed slightly and said, "How could I possibly refuse so appreciative an audience?"

When he turned to the piano and adjusted his position to begin playing, their legs and shoulders touched in an easy familiarity. The contact was electrifying, yet as natural and as comfortable as if they were old friends. She could feel his warmth along her bare arm, on her thigh through the thin material of her dress. She had to consciously keep herself from snuggling into his side to capture more.

She glanced over to Mangas's shoulder. She calculated it was just far enough above her own that if he was to raise his arm, she could slip comfortably into his embrace, something she could rarely do with a man because of her own five-foot-nine-inch height. She smiled. It was a private wondering expression of amusement at her remarkable reactions to this man, this Mangas Taylor.

She hadn't contemplated such fantasies since... since when? She couldn't remember the last time a man had made her feel like this. She thought of him as she had seen him that morning. Tall and lean and clothed only in shorts and running shoes. She was suddenly very grateful Mangas Taylor worked and lived a thousand miles away. She sensed he could disrupt her well-ordered life as easily as a tornado moved across a wheat field.

Mangas drew her attention back to her immediate surroundings when he began to play a song from that year's Academy Award winning movie. Lenore felt a quick stab of disappointment, and without thinking, reached out to touch his arm, stopping him. He turned, a questioning look in his eyes.

"Changed your mind about my playing already, have you?" He laughed. "I warned you I was out of practice."

"I'm sorry. I should have waited for you to finish. My enthusiasm often overrules my manners. I just wanted to ask you to play the piece you were playing earlier. I would love to hear it all the way through." As she spoke she could feel the muscles tense in his arm where her hand still rested lightly on his sleeve.

"I would rather not," he said with rigid politeness. A steel door had closed between them. Dumbfounded by his unexpected, almost angry reaction to her request, she was at a loss for words.

Mangas let out a deep breath. His voice had returned to its earlier caressing timbre when he said, "Surely there is something you'd like to hear more than that self-indulgent piece I was massacring earlier. A little Bach? Perhaps something from the Rolling Stones?"

Tentatively Lenore smiled. Teasingly she said, "You can't possibly be as out of practice as you claim if your repertoire ranges from classical to rock."

Mangas winked at her conspiratorially. "It does sound impressive, doesn't it? The trick is to memorize one of each."

Lenore laughed. "I *was* impressed." She shivered. The room had grown colder.

Finally noticing the way she hugged herself for warmth, Mangas reached for his jacket and gently draped it around her shoulders. Where his hands brushed her bare flesh, she felt touched by a glowing ember.

The jacket was huge and bulky, disconcertingly intimate. Lenore snaked her arms into the sleeves and smiled her thanks. As she pulled the jacket snugly around her, she was enveloped in a pervasive scent that made her catch her breath. It was the natural unaffected essence of the man beside her. A scent redolent of sunshine and pine forests and the air after a fierce summer storm.

Mangas smiled at the obvious way she burrowed into the jacket. "You should have said something earlier...." Then more softly he added, "Or perhaps I should have been more observant."

He reached over and slipped his hands along the nape of her neck, pulling her hair out of the jacket to let it lay smoothly against the black material like tawny-colored strands of silk. He left his hands on her shoulders and stared at her. Lenore could see turmoil in his eyes and wondered about it.

Mangas felt as though he had been artfully cornered. How could he refuse her without making a ridiculous scene that would blow the whole thing grossly out of proportion? It would be far easier to simply run through the rambling personal catharsis as if it was merely another piece of music than to try to dissuade her with half-thought-out excuses. Still, the thought of playing his piece for another person struck in his throat like aspirins taken without water.

When at last he met her eyes with his own and said, "It's a very long and I'm afraid, hackneyed, piece of music," her heart jumped. Strangely, she felt as though he had just given her a gift.

As a form of compromise to his wildly protesting mind, he said, "It's far too long to play again tonight. How would it be if I just picked up where I stopped?"

"If you don't mind, I would rather hear the part. . . ." Not knowing anything about music, she sought a nontechnical way to describe the passage she had found particularly beautiful. "The part where the children were playing."

Mangas's eyes narrowed speculatively as they gazed into hers. How could she possibly have guessed the reason behind that particular section? He wasn't so foolish to think it was good enough to be obvious. "Did you really know that, or was it just a lucky guess?"

Suddenly Lenore understood why he was reluctant to play the music for her. It was his. He had written it. Playing it for an audience would be like letting someone read a personal journal. "It's something I know because the music is so beautifully—" she sought a better word "—so expressively written, that listening to it touches a universal feeling. It made me think of my own childhood." She smiled coaxingly and pulled his jacket closer around her shoulders. "If you don't mind, I would very much like to hear that part again."

Mangas shook his head slowly, again amazed with himself for so easily agreeing. He turned to the piano and began to play.

The happy staccato sounds filled the room with a joy and hope that were the birthright of every child. For Mangas, the music expressed a brief span of time when the world had indeed seemed laden with promise. It was a time before he had realized who and what he was—a time that sparkled in his memory like a sliver of gold lying in the black mud of a miner's pan.

Then, as before, came the fearful hesitant chords that destroyed the happy mood. The gaiety was replaced by confusion and turmoil. The sliver of gold had so easily slipped from the miner's pan and fallen back into the wildly running stream. Mangas's ensuing years had been filled with the agonies of a boy becoming a man, but had held none of the joys that come from experiencing the process within the cocoon of a loving family. It had been an incredibly lonely time, one he seldom looked back on, but one that frequently guided the man he had become.

After several minutes the music changed again, gradually growing peaceful and even, like the smooth surface of a lake on a windless day.

Lenore thought of the long hot lazy summers she had spent in transition between childhood and womanhood. How on some days she would desperately fight to be considered "all grown up," and then on others, privately fear she would be. The daylight hours had been spent in barefoot exploration along the Salinas River; the nighttime had been spent trying to curtail some young man's explorations of her budding female form.

Mangas had composed this particular segment as a student at Winchester College. Then he had felt the trauma of his past was behind him forever, that he would be able to slip into a happy and fulfilling future as easily and as rightfully as each day slips into night. Then there had been Jacquelyn and whispered promises and foolish daydreams.

Lenore did not, could not, follow where the music traveled next. The tranquil secure episode ended, replaced by hauntingly confused and private refrains that sought escape on each octave of the piano. She caught her breath, stunned by the abject loneliness she felt in the music. She had never known such sorrow or loss. She had never experienced such pain.

Like a storm that pounds against a tree until the trunk lets go of its life-giving earth, the music lashed against her heart until tears slid unheeded down her cheeks.

Finally the agony ended and a hesitant exploring mood began, flowing into a bright modern piece of music. Slick...commercial...brittle. For reasons she couldn't understand, she hated it.

This was the part of the music Mangas liked

the least but received the most satisfaction from playing. It represented his recovery. It reminded him he had come through the worst life could offer and that he had not only survived, he had prospered. Jacquelyn, Adrian, his desperately lonely childhood—all of them had been conquered. He might have become a "nation of one" in the process, but it was an exchange he had never regretted making.

And then it was over.

Mangas turned to her. The moment was electric, hushed, fragile. He looked at her, and for the briefest instant Lenore saw the lonely young man he had been. Then the youth was gone, in his place the magnificently free and self-assured runner she had watched that morning. The same man who sat beside her now.

"Thank you," she whispered, realizing how special the performance had been and how privileged she was to have heard it.

Mangas stared at her for a long time before he reached up to touch her cheek with his fingertips. Lightly he wiped away the lingering trail of tears that had spilled so easily from her deep brown eyes. He cupped her chin in his hands and held her. Slowly he lowered his mouth to her temple and touched the delicate skin in a kiss that was as gentle, as fleeting, as the touch of a butterfly's wing.

"You're welcome," he breathed lightly into her hair.

Lenore tilted her head back, bringing her lips up to his. She waited, willing him, wanting him to kiss her with a need that frightened her. For an instant their breath mingled warmly, his tickling the sensitive flesh around her mouth with an aching intimacy. At last his lips pressed into hers. The kiss, tender and hesitant at first, as if both of them were unsure of their welcome, soon deepened.

When Lenore parted her lips to let his seeking tongue explore the velvet interior of her mouth, she felt a rush of desire sweep over her that was so intense, it left her stunned. Panic gripped her when she realized how much she wanted Mangas to go on making love to her. What had happened to her carefully cultivated control? How could one kiss from this man make her lose what she had worked a lifetime to gain?

When Lenore tried to pull away, she realized Mangas's hand held the back of her head. She could feel her panic growing and put her hands against his chest to push him away. After she had exerted only the slightest pressure, he released her. They stared at each other, and Lenore could see in the depths of Mangas's blue eyes that something unfathomable had happened to him, also.

"Lenore," he whispered. "I'm sorry."

All she could think about was getting away from him as fast as she could. He was the very man she had been afraid she would meet someday. The man who would do to her what her father had done to her mother. The man who would be able to gain control of her thoughts and her actions and make her lose the essence of her individuality. The man she could grow to love so desperately that she would no longer be Lenore Randolph. She would be the person his love dictated she become, her identity so intermeshed with his that it was lost. With his music and the force of his personality, he had stripped away her protective armor and reached in to touch her soul. And she had responded as readily as a rose bud opens to the coaxing of the warm summer sun. Lenore moved away from him. He had suddenly become a fearsome creature.

She fought for control, thought she had succeeded until she saw the look in his eyes and knew he understood her fear. "I—I have to get back to the party," she stammered. "My friend will be looking for me."

"Your friend?" The power of Mangas's voice brought her to a halt as she moved toward the aisle.

"The man I came with."

"What is he to you?"

There was no time to answer. She must get away. She thought she shouted, "Nothing," as she fled from the room, but the word came out as a choked whisper.

Seconds later she was once again in the cool

night air, gasping for breath. She needed time to think about what had just happened to her. Time alone. She glanced at her watch. "My God," she said aloud, "I've been gone for almost two hours. Adrian will be frantic."

She had started back toward the celebration, which was still quite obviously and noisily in full swing, when she remembered she still wore Mangas's jacket. How would she ever explain a stranger's coat to Adrian? She had no choice. She would have to go to the dorm first, get her shawl and hope she could think of a convincing reason for her absent before she had to face Adrian.

WHEN SHE ARRIVED back at the party, she almost laughed with relief when she confronted Adrian and learned he hadn't even noticed how long she'd been missing.

CHAPTER FOUR

Mangas sat at the piano long after Lenore had left, his hands unconsciously curled into clenched fists. The unanticipated and undesired confrontation had been difficult for him. He hadn't wanted to make contact with Adrian's woman yet. Had, in fact, carefully avoided running into her several times earlier that day as she wandered around the campus. He wasn't ready. His plan of attack was still in the embryonic stage, not yet the precisely thought-out path to success it would have been, should have been before connecting with her. He had needed more time to study her from a distance. Now all that had changed.

Now the not-yet-completed plan was suddenly useless. He would have to start again. Using their unforeseen encounter to his advantage wouldn't be difficult, though. Actually it had probably been a far more convincing way for them to come together than anything he could have manipulated.

No, their chance confrontation wasn't going to ruin everything. Lenore might decide to tell

Adrian about a piano-playing stranger, and that was the danger. If Lenore was only partially accurate in her description, it wouldn't take Adrian long to figure out it was Mangas she had met. He had made the mistake of underestimating Adrian once—he would never do it again.

The possibility that he would be unable to exact this final bit of revenge on Adrian ate away at him. It weighed him down like heavy snow on a fir tree. He couldn't move or shake himself free from the oppressiveness. In less than three days the focus of his life had irreversibly changed. It was as if a puppeteer, ruled by the bitter taste of vengeance, had somehow gained control over him. His thoughts, his drive, his actions were finely focused on only one thing. Adrian. And Lenore was the vessel that would make it all happen.

Wearily Mangas closed his eyes. Unbidden, an image of the woman appeared. Impatiently he raked his fingers through his hair. His forehead furrowed in troubled thought; his conscience nagged him.

Lenore didn't seem to be Adrian's type. Certainly not someone Mangas would ever have pictured him with. She seemed too open, too naive, too intelligent, too—

Mangas crashed his hands against the keys of the piano, creating a discordant sound perfectly in tune with his mood. What in the hell was the matter with him? He had learned a long time ago that people were rarely what they tried to make themselves out to be. Hadn't experience taught him that? Bitter experience. Beneath the open trusting facade Lenore had shown him, Mangas was sure there beat the heart of a conniving bitch. Someone who was the female equivalent of an Adrian, only someone who was more adept at keeping the baser side of her personality hidden. Why else would she be with him?

But what if she wasn't the perfidious person he assumed her to be? Did he have the right to use her? What did using her make him?

Mangas closed the piano, stood and twisted the knob at the base of the light. The room became as black as his mood. Thoughtfully he made his way to the faintly outlined doorway. If indeed Lenore was the person she appeared to be, she would undoubtedly be hurt if Mangas proceeded with his plan. But which pain would be the kindest? Surely, Mangas reasoned, it would be better if she was to discover Adrian's true nature now. Quietly he slipped from the music center, walking in the building's shadow toward the still-noisy party.

Without his tuxedo jacket, he no longer blended in with the celebrants, so he stood at a distance where he was unlikely to be seen, and watched. He had no trouble finding Lenore in the crowd. His eyes were drawn to her as readily and as surely as if they were old friends. . . or

new lovers. Mangas frowned in irritation, then
inwardly laughed at himself. It had been a long
time since he'd played the games of the flesh.
Lenore was a beautiful woman—obviously he
was looking forward to their tryst more than
he'd been prepared to acknowledge.

Forcing his thoughts back to the original reason he had followed her, Mangas noticed, as he
had anticipated, his coat was missing from her
shoulders. In its place she had donned a lux-
uriant shawl that matched her dress. Mangas
stared at her, at the way she held her slim champagne glass. His eyes followed her hand when she
absently brought the glass to her mouth. In his
mind he could see her full bottom lip press delicately against the glass as she sipped the bubbling
liquid. Vividly he remembered the feel of that lip
against his own, and it made him catch his
breath. He was stunned at the intensity of feeling
the simple memory brought to his loins.

His eyes narrowed in anger as he abruptly
turned and strode away from the party. His
lapse into adolescent behavior infuriated him.
As he crossed the campus and bounded up the
stairs to the men's dorm, he didn't even bother
to vow that it would not happen again. The possibility was unthinkable.

SEVERAL HOURS LATER, after patiently waiting in
his room for the last of the revelers to retire,
Mangas left the dorm. The full moon shone

high overhead, casting a light, detailed shadow. Dressed in jeans and a navy blue turtleneck, Mangas walked across the hushed campus as though he was an integral part of the scene. His footsteps were quick and sure as he moved toward his destination.

Nearing the women's dorm, he slowed and stepped off the path, into the concealing shadows of the trees. Finally he reached the shelter of a neatly trimmed privet hedge. He began carefully counting the windows of the small balconies strung across the second story. When he found the window he sought, he crossed the courtyard and climbed to the top of the fence that went around the tiny patio of the first-floor room. Reaching overhead to grab the balcony railing of the second-floor room, he pulled himself up onto the small landing. The maneuver had taken only the time required for three quick breaths, had been accomplished in virtual silence.

Mangas hesitated a moment to listen to the sounds around him before he tapped lightly against the sliding glass door. After several seconds had passed he tapped again, consciously keeping the sound at the same muted level. This time there was a stirring at the window. The curtain was pulled aside. Lenore peeked out at him, her hair in the tumbled disarray of sleep, her face devoid of makeup.

"What are you doing here?" she whispered as

she opened the door wide enough for her to see out.

"I've come for my jacket...."

Still with a confused look on her face, she started to turn away as if to get the jacket for him, but Mangas's voice stopped her.

"And to talk to you."

"Now?"

He smiled. It was a lopsided grin meant to charm, to acknowledge his unorthodox behavior and ask her to bear with him. "I'm leaving in an hour," he said simply, and shrugged.

Lenore bit her lip. Mangas could see her indecision plainly reflected in her eyes.

"Please," he added softly. "It will only take a minute."

She sighed. "All right. Wait here."

Mangas could hear her quickly moving around the room. When she reappeared at the sliding door, she was wearing a floor-length satiny bathrobe loosely belted at the waist. She was combing her long golden brown hair with her fingers.

"My father would disown me if he ever found out about this," she said as she opened the door farther and held the curtain aside so that Mangas could enter.

"For any besides the obvious reasons?" The light from a small lamp beside the bed softly illuminated the tiny room.

"He's a retired policeman." She smiled nervously, obviously uncomfortable with her decision to let him in. "This—" she motioned toward him "—is rather like the fireman's kid playing with matches."

Mangas studied her for a moment. The simple tailoring of her emerald-green robe accentuated her lanky body and full unbound breasts. Without the sophisticated clothing and makeup she had worn earlier, she looked younger than the twenty-eight or twenty-nine he had guessed her to be. He was caught off guard by the change and found it difficult not to stare.

Lenore smiled nervously and went to her closet. She removed Mangas's jacket, lying it across the bed, carefully smoothing away a wrinkle. She then straightened and jammed her hands into the pockets of her robe. Letting out another deep sigh, she said, "I wish I had an explanation for the ridiculous way I behaved earlier, but try as I might, I can't seem to come up with one."

Mangas sat down, leaning his back into the chair, resting his elbows on the metal arms and folding his hands across the flat of his stomach. He was surprised Lenore had decided to bring up the awkward moment that had passed between them. He had expected her to dismiss it with a blasé shrug of her creamy shoulders or by simply, arrogantly pretending it had never happened. Readily acknowledging a lapse of control didn't fit the mental image of her that he had created.

Quickly picking up on the surprising direction their conversation had taken, Mangas said, "That was one of the reasons I came to see you before I left, rather than leaving a note telling you where to send my jacket. I wanted to apologize." He smiled. "Mauling someone I've just met is not my usual style."

Lenore leaned against the dresser and crossed her arms over her chest. She glanced at the wall opposite her, at Mangas, then glanced away again. A tiny smile played at the corners of her mouth. "I would hardly call it 'mauling,'" she said. Her dark brown eyes warmed as she looked at him once more. "And even though you really don't owe me one, I accept your apology. It's much easier than wondering whether or not it's me who owes you one."

"Friends?"

Lenore laughed. "Oh, I hope so. I would hate to think I had invited someone who wasn't a friend into my room in the middle of the night." She shook her head in wonder. "I still can't believe this is happening. If you really knew me, you would know how inconsistent—"

"That's why I've come."

Lenore turned so that she faced him directly. Her eyebrow quirked in puzzlement. "What?"

"I want to get to know you. That's the other reason—the important reason I've come here.

I've spent the past several hours thinking about it, and I've decided I can't simply let you walk into my life, then out of it again as if you were just a passing storm." Mangas leaned forward. His voice dropped to a low caress. "Besides being disconcerting, what happened between us back there in the music room was. . . ." His gaze met hers, and he saw a look of wariness suddenly, subtly change her features. No longer was her expression open and friendly. Mangas saw anger there. Or could it be fear? He decided to go ahead with what he'd planned to say, even if it meant risking her derision. "How can I put into words what happened between us in a way that won't diminish it?"

Lenore swallowed. With obvious difficulty she tore her gaze from Mangas's and glanced down to the floor. She reached up to tuck her hair behind her ear. Barely above a whisper, as if admitting a crime, she hesitatingly said, "I know. I felt it, too."

Her words hit him like a physical blow. They made him acknowledge that what he had thought of as mere rhetoric intended to seduce a possibly reluctant woman was in reality a painful truth. By simply agreeing with him, she had penetrated his veneer, as easily as though it were a thin layer of dust instead of the coat of armor he had worn for a lifetime. Subtle warning signals penetrated his mind, made his heart quicken as, unbidden, he once again remembered the sensation of Lenore's lips pressed to his.

The air between them grew heavy with tension. The silence became a palpable thing that neither seemed able to maneuver in. Mangas forced himself to stop looking at Lenore. He needed time to absorb what had just happened.

Quickly he glanced around the room, automatically seeking and finding tiny clues to Lenore's personality while trying to regain control of his emotions. His eyes settled briefly on a thick paperback book left carelessly open on the stand beside the bed, before they went on to the large artist's portfolio standing against one wall. One part of his mind absorbed and catalogued all he saw with the precision and coolness of a computer, taking in such minor details as a small atomizer of perfume on the dresser and lacy lingerie lying neatly folded in the open overnight bag.

But when reason gave way to emotion, he found a deep sense of pleasure in knowing that the book he had discovered on Lenore's nightstand was one that he, too, had recently chosen to read, that the perfume she wore was a highly feminine floral one. He liked the fact that she had enough pride in what she did to carry her work in a fine leather case, and enough casualness about both her work and the case that she left it sitting on the floor propped up against a wall.

When his gaze came back to Lenore, Mangas was stunned at the intensity of his desire to cross the short distance separating them and take her into his arms. A physical ache coursed through him as he imagined the feel of her against him. The firm mounds of her breasts pressed into his chest, her hips snuggled into his own. He had never known, never felt such desire for a woman. It was as if the reservoir of hatred he had stored up throughout the past ten years for all that had happened to him at the hands of the Winchesters had suddenly, inexplicably been funneled into a craving for this woman who stood, unsuspecting, across the room from him.

With profound sureness, he knew that if he chose to do so, he could take her now. He knew that although she would deny it should he ask, she wanted him with the same longing he felt for her. Her eyes and the way her breath came in short gasps through her slightly open mouth told him of her desire, despite the way she held her arms protectively over her breasts. Oh, he knew he could have her body, that she would make love to him with little coaxing, but he wanted more than her body. He wanted her soul. He wanted her so completely that there would be nothing, not the smallest corner of her being, left for Adrian.

"I want to see you again," Mangas said softly.

Lenore's gaze never wavered. "No," she breathed.

"No?" Her answer caught him so much by surprise that it was almost impossible for him not to shout the word.

"I don't think it would be a good idea."

Mangas's eyes narrowed speculatively. He forced himself to lean back in the chair, his casual, carefully controlled action belying the turmoil that raged inside him. "Why not?" he asked as calmly as he could manage.

A flush spread from Lenore's neck to her cheeks. Mangas could see she waged a fierce inner battle as she sought the words with which to answer him. Finally, softly, she said, "I don't know why. It's just something I feel."

Desperately searching for a concrete reason for her refusal, something he could argue with, use to convince her she was wrong, Mangas said, "You're not married, are you?"

"No," she whispered.

"Engaged?"

"No...."

"Then why?"

"I told you, I don't know why. I only know that it would be a mistake...for both of us." Lenore reached down to pick up Mangas's jacket. She held it out to him. "I think you had better go now."

Slowly Mangas rose from the chair. For once in his life he didn't know what to do. Reason abandoned him. He only knew he couldn't let it end this way. Instinctively he reached his hand out as if to take the jacket but took her arm instead and gently pulled her to him. She came to him reluctantly but without resistance, as though she realized as well as Mangas now did that this moment had been inevitable. He felt her tremble as he enfolded her in his arms, and an overwhelming desire to protect her came over him. But protect her from what—from whom, he fleetingly wondered.

She fit against him as he had known she would, their bodies molded as naturally as if they had come together a hundred times before. "This cannot be the end," he whispered against her hair. And as he said it, it became poignantly true. He could not let her go. He must see her again.

His hands left her shoulders and slowly traveled over the smooth emerald satin lying across her back. He pulled her closer, breathing in the intoxicating scent of her. Still she held herself rigidly against him, her arms stiff at her sides.

"I cannot see you again." Lenore's voice was flat, her words emotionless.

Mangas held her away from him and looked into her eyes. His heart thudded heavily in his chest. He searched her face and was devastated by what he saw. It was as if she knew. As if somehow she had been able to reach inside him and read his soul.

"All right, Lenore," he said, regretting what he would say before it was spoken. "I won't force you to do something you don't want." Each of the words felt as if it had been torn from him. "Perhaps it's for the best."

He touched her cheek with his fingertips, absorbing the feel of her flesh. His hands traveled down her jaw to cup her chin, then moved on to the silkiness of her throat. He felt a gentle warmth on his face as a silent sigh escaped her lips. Slowly, ever so slowly, they moved toward each other as though two drops of water on a pane of glass, drawn together by an invisible compelling force. Their lips touched in a kiss that was filled with a timeless knowledge. It destroyed all that had gone before.

Mangas held Lenore in an embrace that shouted his need for her, and she responded to that need with a pent-up sob of release. She would not fight him, nor herself, anymore. Her arms, until then heavy weights at her sides, now reached around his neck and pulled him closer to her.

Lenore let herself be pulled into the vortex of her out-of-control emotions. Tired of fighting a battle her body ached to lose, she pushed her fears into a dark corner of her mind, knowing they would surface later to haunt her, but not caring. All she knew, all she wanted to know was how supremely right it felt to be in Mangas's arms. To revel in the hard length of his body pressed against hers. To sense that whatever force controlled her held him as tightly in its grasp.

What she felt, *how* she felt inside, were unfathomable. Right and wrong were opposite sides of a wildly spinning coin. She was afraid of the man who held her, terrified of the ease with which he controlled her racing heart. Yet she had gone to him as readily as a moth to the flame. Was this how it had been with her mother? Had her father held this kind of power over her? Was this the way her deepest fears would come true? *Why*, her mind railed. Where was it written that a woman had to become less than she was when a man entered her life? Couldn't one woman—her—and this man be the exception? Did she have to wind up like her mother, a woman whose potential in life had only been half realized because she had loved a man?

Lenore pushed the ancient lifelong fears to the back of her mind, and without coaxing opened her mouth to receive Mangas's seeking tongue. He kissed her with infinite gentleness, afraid she might flee if he was to express the true depth of the desire that burned in his loins. Lenore responded by opening her mouth wider, urging him to caress the softness he so delicately sought.

But instead of deepening the kiss, Mangas pulled away, catching his breath in surprise. His hands reached up to hold her face, his palms pressing against her cheeks. He stared into her eyes. Lenore's body swayed toward him, seeking respite from the almost painful yearning she felt.

"Is this truly what you want?" Mangas searched her face as though probing for her answer there rather than in the words she would use.

"I...don't...know," she breathed. "I can't tell what I want anymore." How she lied. She knew what she wanted, just not how to tell him. What would he think if she were to say she wished he would leave, that she truly never wanted to see him again? Would he believe her words when her body denied everything she would say? She knew that no matter what, he would see in her eyes that she desperately wanted him to stay, not just tonight but tomorrow and the next day and for endless days after that. Yet how she feared him.

"Let me see you again, Lenore."

She studied his face, wondering at the incredible blueness of his eyes, so startling because the rest of his coloring indicated they should have been brown. She sought her answer in the curve of his mouth and the fine lines at the corners of his eyes. If she was to offer this man the greatest gift she possessed, would he cherish or destroy it? Would her heart become a symbol of conquest or a rare flower to be held closely and nurtured? She had decided long ago never to give love to a man. The price women had to pay for the commodity was just too high. But then did she really have a choice? Somehow she knew, if she didn't give her heart to Mangas, he would simply reach out and take it.

Lenore turned and walked over to the dresser. She reached inside her purse, withdrew a silver case. Taking a card from the case, she wrote her home address and phone number on the back and handed it to Mangas.

He glanced at the card, then at her. His free hand grasped the back of her head, pulling her to him. The kiss was a promise that they would meet again. Without uttering a word, saying goodbye by softly pressing his lips to her forehead, Mangas left.

CHAPTER FIVE

LENORE SLAMMED HER PENCIL down on the drawing board and propped her chin in her hands. She had just botched her third attempt to come up with an "unorthodox" yet highly conservative design for the new head offices of San Juan Savings and Loan. A virtually impossible task her boss, David Mason, had set her. Five days earlier, before she left for the weekend at Winchester College, submitting the design that would catch the eye of the San Juan Board of Directors and being given a shot at the chief architect's job on the project had been the most important things on her mind. Now she could hardly concentrate.

She stifled an urge to visit the offices of the two other architects who were competing for the project, sensing that not even knowing they were way ahead of her would give her back the tunnel vision she needed to finish her work.

She sighed heavily and slid off the stool, wandering over to stare out the window. Usually just spending a few minutes watching the work being done on Colorado Springs's rapidly rising skyscrapers was enough to stimulate her into delving back into her own work with a vengeance. But not today. Not even her intensely private and passionate desire to someday have her name inscribed on a brass plaque as architect of one of her adopted city's skyscrapers prodded her back to her drawing board.

The plaque was a dream she'd never shared with anyone, knowing she was incapable of expressing the true motives behind her goal. It wasn't that she wanted the fame; that was laughable in itself. No one paid any more attention to the raised letters of a brass plate stuck on a building than they did to most writers' by-lines in magazine features. No, public attention had nothing to do with her dream.

The inscription would be more like a tiny signature on a painting. A painting that had been created to give pleasure to those who beheld it, not to bring glory to the painter. She would know, even if nobody else did, that what she had created would live beyond her to be enjoyed by generations yet unborn.

Lenore had sacrificed much to work toward the realization of her dream. Things she knew the men who accused her of trading on her femininity for advancement would never have to sacrifice. There were times when she had sincerely believed she was the loneliest human being on earth. Times when the whole world seemed to be composed of people in laughing intimate pairs.

She had thought those painful periods were over, that she had learned to accept and to live with her decision. That her goal in life was more important than any personal relationship could ever be. Until. . . .

Damn! What magic web had Mangas Taylor spun around her? The strands were so fine they seemed to be invisible, yet Lenore felt them as though they were chains weighing down her every thought.

She leaned against the cool glass and watched the traffic move along Union Boulevard, her mind and her passions eighty miles away in a nondescript room in a college dorm, focused on a man who had pleaded to see her again. . .and then failed to call.

Realizing how easily she had once again slipped into daydreaming, Lenore shook her head in irritation and glanced at her watch. "It can't be eleven-thirty!" she gasped. But a quick check confirmed her watch hadn't stopped, and that she had indeed let the morning go by without producing one workable idea.

Lenore glanced out the window once more before determinedly turning away from the view she loved so much and climbing back on to her stool. She had worked hard for the right to look out from that particular vantage point. She wasn't about to let some man she hardly knew play head games with her that might result in its loss.

Windows and the direction they faced were symbols of success at Mason, Langly and Mason. The firm occupied the entire top floor of the Wright Building, one of the most prestigious addresses in the city. Beyond an opulent reception area, the floor had been divided into offices that subtly bespoke each employee's rank in the firm. Those who had windows facing east toward Colorado's undulating high prairies were the draftsmen, secretaries, bookkeepers, as well as architects who were new and unproven. To attain an office with a window that faced north, toward the lush green hills surrounding the Air Force Academy or south toward the flatlands of Fort Carson and Pueblo, meant you were one of the "up and coming." An office on the west side of the building, with a window that commanded a spectacular view of Pikes Peak, meant you were one of the chosen.

Lenore had become one of Mason, Langly and Mason's "up and coming" architects. She had been moved into her own office after a grueling, two-year view of the plains, where in reality she had rarely ever taken time to look out the window.

Remembering how hard she had worked for recognition, she never failed to bristle when one of the architects still laboring on the east side of the building made a comment about the firm's "token" woman, implying she was where she was as fast as she was because of her sex, not her talent. Although it pained her to do so, she kept her mouth shut, convinced that actions would speak louder than any words she might use to defend herself. She would design and see built the finest, most innovative buildings in Colorado Springs. Then someday she would throw a banquet for all the skeptics, and at that banquet she would serve them their words on a silver platter.

"Boy, I sure hope I'm not the subject of your thoughts right now!"

The commanding male voice shattered Lenore's private world. She jumped as though someone had popped a balloon behind her. Swinging around to face the door, she let out an audible sigh when she saw it was Paul Shaughnessy and not a wandering Mason or Langly or "west window" man who had caught her daydreaming.

"You just aged me ten years," Lenore grumbled.

Paul rested his broad shoulder against the polished oak of the doorframe. A mischievous gleam lit his eyes. "Mmm.... Everyone should look so good at thirty-nine." As usual, Paul refused to be intimidated when Lenore's anxiousness displayed itself in gruffness. He closed the door and sauntered into the room. "I've been doing a little spying," he said conspiratorially. "And as long as you turn in your usual excellent stuff, Abbott and Crossfield don't stand a chance of winning the San Juan project.''

Lenore groaned. She knew Paul Shaughnessy's sole reason for coming into her office this morning was to bolster her confidence. As her best friend and strongest supporter, he took a personal interest in everything she did. He was going to have a fit when he discovered her ''usual excellent stuff'' consisted of a few scrawls across an otherwise clean piece of paper. She tried to distract him while she hid the paper from his inquisitive gaze, but she didn't move quickly enough.

''What in the hell is that?'' he nearly shouted. Although he was a full two years younger than Lenore, Paul had treated her like a combination father and older brother since they'd met. He had bulldozed into her life, completely ignoring her usual shyness when making friends with his indomitable humor and insistence that they were ''made to be friends, so why fight it?'' She calmly accepted from him what she wouldn't have tolerated from anyone else. Not only was he a perfect alter ego, easygoing where she was uptight; he was incredibly talented. And more than anyone else ever had, he understood what drove her to succeed. At twenty-seven, he was already on his way to making a distinctive mark on styles and trends in the housing industry. She was an ardent admirer of both his personality and his talent.

As one of the "east wall" men, he was fully utilized, but his work wasn't yet individually recognized. Instead, everything he did, as with all the other apprentices, went under the firm's heading. Lenore was confident he wouldn't remain where he was much longer. Paul was highly skeptical. It was an old argument between them. Paul saw the heirarchy of M. L. & M. as a group of dangerously pompous, priggish and prejudiced bastards who were only a means to an end for his career. Lenore saw them as slightly stuffy old men.

When Lenore didn't immediately answer, Paul went on, none of the fire gone from his voice. "Where are the preliminary sketches you were working on last week?"

Lenore tilted her head in the direction of the wastebasket. Paul looked at the steel-gray container, then slowly turned back to look at Lenore. "You mean you have nothing?"

"Not even a decent idea to work from."

Paul unbuttoned his jacket and shoved his hands into his pants pockets. He stood and stared at Lenore until she had to forcibly resist the urge to ask him to stop. Finally he said, "You want to tell me what's wrong?"

She started to ask him what made him think anything was wrong, but decided it was an exercise in futility to try to fool him. "No," she said simply instead. "I don't want to talk about it."

"All right." Paul reached over and snapped

off the light over the drawing board. "If you don't want to talk, let's go to lunch."

Lenore smiled. She knew she would probably be telling Paul all about Mangas Taylor before they'd eaten half their lunch, whether she wanted to or not. Without pressing or prodding, she would share her details of her strange weekend with him because she needed someone to talk to about it, and Paul was the perfect someone. "Let me get my coat and I'll be right with you." Lenore slipped her arms in her russet jacket as Paul held it for her. "Where are we going?"

"I've already sent out for sandwiches. It's such a beautiful day, I thought we would eat on the roof."

"Great idea," she said, following him to the stairs. "It seems like ages since we've been up there."

Lenore and Paul had accidently discovered their private dining room the previous year, when during a particularly hectic month they had wanted to get away from the office yet needed to be near. Since then they had sometimes gone to the roof for coffee breaks, as well as lunch whenever the weather and their schedules permitted.

The janitor had given them a corner of the storage area for their portable chairs and umbrella. The table they had purchased at a summer clearance sale the previous year now stayed outside permanently. Although in the beginning they had been concerned about the rest of the office discovering their rooftop haven and wanting to join them, they soon learned they had nothing to worry about. Everyone else thought they were crazy and so needed no encouragement to stay away.

Once they were settled in, but before Lenore had a chance to unwrap her sandwich, Paul was back to the San Juan assignment. "I sure hate to see you let this one go, Lenore. You know that's exactly what everyone's been waiting for. They would love to see you fall on your face."

Lenore bit into her pickle. She waited a minute before she looked up and smiled at Paul. "I think you're even more paranoid than I am. Surely not everyone is waiting for me to lose an assignment."

"Don't be naive. Your failure would give half of them a chance to say 'I told you so,' and the other half fresh hope that they could fill your shoes."

Lenore looked down at her black leather high heels. She had a frown on her forehead and a mischievous twinkle in her eyes. "I can't think of one of them who would look good in them."

"Cute, Lenore. Real cute. Are you going to be this flip when you hear the assignment has been given to Abbott or Crossfield?"

The thought made her sick. She tossed her uneaten sandwich on the table. "You must have lettered in fencing in college. I've never known anyone better at bloodletting.''

''What do you want me to do, leave you alone and pretend that by some miracle you'll snap out of whatever's bothering you? What are you going to do, slip into your Wonder Woman costume and manage to produce two weeks' work by Friday?''

''Hey, isn't that kind of strong, even for you?''

Paul's sandwich joined Lenore's on the table. ''Sorry.'' He let out a frustrated sigh. ''It's just that I get so damn mad whenever I— Oh, never mind.''

''Whenever you what—listen to the locker-room gossip?'' Lenore leaned over and caught Paul's hand between her own. ''I love having you as my champion, Paul, but you really shouldn't get an ulcer over this.''

Obviously already impatient with what he knew Lenore would say next, Paul started to interrupt. Lenore stopped him.

''Like it or not, Paul, you're going to hear me out—even if it's not fresh material. No matter what you or I do, we're not going to change the minds of those who think I'm where I am because I walk and dress differently than they do. When your protective streak comes out, you always seem to forget that the number of people around here who would like to see me fail are no larger than the people who fear you and would like to see you gone because of your talent."

Paul grinned sheepishly. "Saying it out loud sure makes it sound stupid, doesn't it?"

Lenore grinned back at him. "Thank God no one can hear us." Just then she looked up at the open doorway, and saw Mangas Taylor standing there.

"Your secretary said I might find you here," he said.

Lenore forced her gaping mouth closed and struggled to overcome an almost overwhelming urge to get up and run. She let go of Paul's hand, started to rise only to bump into Paul as he, too, started to get up from his chair. Lenore was forced back into her seat while Paul struggled to regain his balance, knocking over his folding aluminum chair in the process.

Lenore groaned inwardly. She and Paul were behaving like a couple of teenagers who had been caught fooling around. She glanced at Mangas, who filled the doorway, standing with his shoulder pressed against the frame, his arms folded across his chest. He studied her, an unspoken question in his eyes. She passionately wished she could disappear into her surroundings and start the day over again. Instead she shrugged, and indicating Paul, said, "Mangas Taylor, this is an associate of mine, Paul Shaughnessy." She turned to Paul. "Paul, this is Mangas Taylor, a friend." The two men shook hands.

Paul glanced at Lenore as though seeking a clue to what he should do next. When neither Mangas nor Lenore broke the silence, he opted for discretion. "Well, I guess I'd better get going. I still have several things to do this afternoon." He turned to Mangas. Lenore could see the rapid assessment Paul made in the seemingly casual glance he gave him. "It was nice meeting you," he said.

Mangas stepped from the doorway to let him pass. When Paul had gone, Mangas strode the short distance to where Lenore sat, pulled Paul's collapsed lawn chair open and sat down beside her. "I hope I passed," he said.

"He wouldn't have left if you hadn't."

A slow smile deepened the clefts in Mangas's cheeks. "You're obviously someone quite capable of taking care of yourself, yet you seem to have a knack for attracting men who want to protect you. Quite a feat."

How did he know what kind of men she attracted, Lenore wondered. "It's totally unintentional, I assure you," she said. "I take care of myself quite nicely."

"I have no doubt." Mangas leaned forward, reaching out to take Lenore's hand. Suddenly serious, he changed his tone of voice and manner when he said, "I didn't come here for a casual visit, Lenore. You've haunted everything I've tried to do since I left you three days ago. I finally had to give up trying to get any work done and come back to Colorado Springs to see if you could possibly live up to my imaginings.''

''And. . .?'' Her half smile reflected her skepticism that she had indeed disrupted his life to such a degree.

''If my memory had been more accurate,'' he said softly, ''I could never have stayed away as long as I did.''

A warning bell sounded in Lenore's mind. While the words were fresh, the delivery smacked of a dozen men she had known who could use words as seductively and meaninglessly as a politician looking for votes. She couldn't deny something had happened between her and Mangas that she had never experienced before, but her pragmatic nature kept her from believing it was anything more than the age-old urge that had kept mankind from disappearing off the face of the earth long ago.

As usual, Lenore's eyes mirrored her thoughts. Mangas looked at her quizzically. ''What is it? Do you doubt my sincerity, or that I find you so beautiful that you haunt my dreams?''

Lenore stared at him. Could he possibly discern her feelings so effortlessly, or was he merely an astute guesser? ''I don't think we should put fancy labels on what passed between us.''

Mangas let go of her hand and leaned back in his chair. ''I see,'' he said slowly. ''I take it, then, that you've had the experience before?''

"No, but I can't see—"

"Can't see what? That something strongly physical could also be unique?"

"Unique?" Lenore scoffed. "I hardly think—"

"Did it ever occur to you that it's possible to kill something special by analyzing it too carefully? I don't want to see that happen to what we have going for us. Believe it to be what you will—I suppose that right now it really doesn't matter what we call it—but to me it's rare, and I don't want to see it destroyed." More softly he said, "Give it a chance. Give us a chance."

Did she dare? There was still time to get out, to keep her life the well-ordered cocoon she had constructed. All she had to do was to tell him she wasn't interested and refuse to see him again. She would be safe. Her life would go on as before—stable, predictable, comfortable. Mangas could, and probably would, shatter her. Could anything, even the fulfillment of the provocative promise she saw shining from his eyes, be worth the possible carnage?

Mangas sighed deeply. "Now is obviously not the time to talk about this. I'll pick you up at your place at eight, and we'll work it out then."

"All right," Lenore murmured, unable to tell him no despite her mind's demand that she do so. "But I think it would be better if we met somewhere."

Mangas smiled. "Why don't *you* pick *me* up?

We'll spend the evening doing whatever you decide.''

Lenore studied his face before answering. That he was willing to give her control over the evening to make it easier for her did little to reassure her. It wasn't Mangas and what he might ask of her that she was afraid of, she suddenly realized. It was herself.

"That sounds fine," she finally said. "Where are you staying?"

"At the Broadmoor. Have the desk ring me when you arrive, and I'll meet you in the lobby. If you like we can eat dinner there. I understand the Charles Court Restaurant is excellent. Or we can go somewhere else if you have a favorite. It doesn't matter." A grin deepened the cleft in one cheek. "Just don't stand me up. I would hate to get all dressed up and then have nowhere to go."

Afraid to trust her legs to hold her, Lenore remained seated, brushing imaginary crumbs from her lap while Mangas rose to leave. When he reached the door, he turned.

"Tonight?" Myriad meanings were contained in the lone word.

Lenore nodded.

When she returned to her office, she purposely cleared away the physical evidence of the rambling journeys her mind had taken during the past three days and started anew. The final details of the building she had been trying to design for San Juan Savings and Loan had miraculously jelled and now flowed from her rapidly moving pencil almost faster than she could put them on paper.

As always when she was deep in work, the hours disappeared without her noticing. A light tapping on the door, quickly followed by Paul's head peeking around the corner, brought Lenore back to awareness of her surroundings.

"Are you mad at me for some reason?" Paul ventured.

"What makes you think that?"

"Well, when I saw your friend leave and I went up to finish my lunch and found it in the garbage, that gave me the first clue. Then when I tried to get in to see you this afternoon and your secretary barred the door, I was pretty sure I was on the right track."

Lenore laid her pencil on the board and turned on her stool. "Sorry about the lunch. I figured you were off somewhere, never to return, and I was anxious to get back to work. I just swept the whole mess into the trash and took off. As for the barred door, it wasn't personal. I told Jackie to keep everyone out."

"Speaking of Jackie, she said to tell you that someone named Samantha Baxter called while you were incommunicado."

"Samantha called? From California?"

"She didn't say from where she called—only that she called."

"Damn...." A quick smile lighted Lenore's

eyes. "I haven't talked to Samantha in ages. She's one of my very favorite people. You'd love her Paul.... She's not like me at all."

"Then I wouldn't love her. You are definitely my type. Someday you'll come to your senses and run off to Madagascar with me. But in the meantime...."

"Yes?"

"Was it worth it?"

"Was what worth it?"

"Your afternoon of isolation?"

"Come in and see what you think."

Paul moved over to Lenore's drawing board. Wordlessly he flipped through the sketches. When he came to the end his face broke into a huge grin. A shouted "Yee haw," a reflection of Paul's western roots, told Lenore all she needed to know.

"I take it that means you approve the preliminary sketching?" She couldn't contain her own smile of pleasure.

Paul threw his arms around Lenore and squeezed her in a breath-catching hug. "Looks like all you needed was another dose of the same medicine to cure you."

"Am I supposed to understand what you mean by that?"

"That Taylor guy. I knew it had to be a man Nothing else could have destroyed your concen tration." A sly gleam made Paul's eyes twinkle "Must be serious. I've never seen anyone man· age to shake you like this before."

A denial almost spilled from her mouth be

fore Lenore realized there was no way she could lie to Paul. She laughed. Not only couldn't she lie to him because she never had before—she knew he wouldn't believe her if she tried.

"I don't know how serious I am, but you're right about one thing. No one has ever interfered with my work before." Lenore began to straighten the sketches. "I'm not sure I like it—No, let me amend that. That is one thing of which I am sure. I don't like it. My work comes first."

"You want to tell me about him?"

Lenore began to roll the papers. She glanced at Paul. "What would you like to know?"

"Whatever you want to tell."

"His name is Mangas Taylor, he lives in California and he works for Apache Computers."

"You *are* miffed about something, aren't you?"

Lenore laughed. "No, I'm not. I've just told you everything I know about him."

"I hope you're kidding." When Lenore failed to reassure him, Paul went on. "Are you seriously planning to go out with a man you know nothing about?" he asked, his eyes wide with disbelief.

Lenore sighed. "Paul, when my father was at his overprotective worst, he was *never* as bad as you are. Please keep in mind that I'm twenty-nine years old. Sometimes you have to use judgment when you begin a relationship.

This happens to be one of those times. And I do think I'm old enough to do that." After all, Lenore mentally added, ignoring a twinge of guilt, what could possibly be wrong with a man who could sneak into a second-story window in the middle of the night with the ease of a cat burgler. God forbid that Paul should ever find out about that. She shuddered at the thought.

Lenore slipped a large rubber band around the rolled-up drawings and sat them beside her briefcase, planning to work on them at home after her date with Mangas. "Besides...." She started to add another argument in her favor but saw that Paul had stopped listening.

"I know I've seen him somewhere before, and the name is so tantalizingly familiar," Paul mumbled to himself, barely loud enough for Lenore to hear. "Wait a minute," he said snapping his fingers. "I'll be right back."

Lenore had finished clearing her desk and had her jacket on ready to leave when Paul came bursting back into the room. "Look at this," he said, thrusting an old issue of *Time* magazine under her nose. "Your Mr. Taylor doesn't work for Apache Computers—he owns it."

On the top left-hand corner of the page, Lenore saw a small black-and-white picture of Mangas Taylor. Although it wasn't a very good shot, taken while he'd been getting into a car, there was no doubt it was he. Stunned, Lenore took the magazine from Paul. She glanced at the caption under the photograph. It read: M.C. Taylor, president and owner of Apache Computers, is rumored to be in Colorado looking for a new plant site.

LENORE ANXIOUSLY SKIMMED the rest of the page. She discovered the article was about the severe pirating of employees that had become a way of life in the Silicon Valley region of California and the problems this was causing the highly technical industries located there. The information about Mangas was included in a section about firms looking for new locations to establish branch offices away from the already densely populated region, where the cost of material and equipment was also spiraling out of control.

Staring out the window, she tried to assimilate the news that the M.C. Taylor in *Time* was the same man who had insisted he must see her again because of some magical attraction they shared. She found it impossible to reconcile the two images.

It didn't fit. It didn't fit at all. Lenore felt as though a cold hand had reached into her chest to wrench her heart. What kind of game was Mangas Taylor playing?

With the total concentration she normally devoted to her work, Lenore searched her memory for the scraps of information she'd picked up over the past few years about the elusive M.C.

Taylor and Apache Computers. As the most notably successful small-computer company started, owned and operated by an individual, Apache was frequently mentioned in publications as diverse as Sunday supplements and major financial-planning magazines. Lenore had followed the stories on Apache for a special reason. It was a means, however remote, of receiving information about an area close to where she'd been raised. An area where several old friends, as well as aunts, uncles and cousins still lived, many of whom were involved in the burgeoning computer industry.

M.C. Taylor had long been the mystery man of the Silicon Valley, that very real area south of San Francisco named after the tiny silicon semiconductors first produced there in the early 1960s.

Despite the reams of material on Apache—it's phenomenal growth, its unique profit sharing that had made millionaires out of several of its employees, its think tank of engineers—the man behind it all had somehow managed to stay out of the limelight. Lenore realized with a start that she knew more about the colorful executives and designers who worked for Apache than she knew about its founder.

She glanced up at Paul, who stood watching her with an expression of concern on his face. "What can you tell me about him?" she asked evenly.

"You mean beyond the obvious?"

Lenore nodded.

"Rumor has it he's being forced into a position that will either make Apache one of the largest companies involved in personal computers in the world, or else destroy it. Several large corporations are after Taylor. They want to get rid of him by buying him out, but from everything I've read, it appears he doesn't want to sell. It could be he's just playing with them until they up the ante, but personally I don't think so. He's earned a reputation as a street fighter, and I'll bet he's not going to let them run him out. But if he's not, he's going to have to expand to the point of ruin and hope he isn't undercut so much he can't make a profit."

"He'll sell," she said softly. "He's no different than anyone else. He's just angling for more money."

"I don't think so," Paul insisted.

Lenore leaned back in her chair. "What else?"

"Huh?"

"What else can you tell me about Taylor?"

Paul thought a moment before he shrugged. "That's about it. I only know that much because of an article I read last week at the dentist's office."

Lenore glanced at her watch. If she was going to keep her date with Mangas Taylor, she was going to have to leave right away. Something held her back. "Why do you suppose Taylor would be interested in me?"

Frowning, Paul cocked his head. "Aw, come on, Lenore," he grumbled. "Fishing for compliments is a little out of character for you, isn't it?"

"In other words, you don't know, either."

"How does beauty, brains and personality sound?"

"Like a chauvinist's shopping list—except for the brains, of course."

Paul let out an exasperated sigh. "Why don't you ask *him* what he sees in you?"

Lenore reached for her purse, her decision made. "I plan to. As a matter of fact, that will be the first thing I ask him when I see him tonight."

CHAPTER SIX

LENORE DROVE UP to the portico at the Broadmoor Hotel and handed her keys to the attendant. Still irritated and grudgingly admitting a deep disappointment at the unexpected way things had turned out, she reasoned she should have guessed that Mangas Taylor was more than just an ordinary employee of Apache Computers. Few average company employees had expense accounts that covered the cost of a five-star hotel.

Making her way to the front desk past small groups of people gathered in the lobby, Lenore wondered what other subtle clues she'd missed. What other surprises were in store for her? More importantly, did she really want to stick around to find out?

"May I help you? A middle-aged man in a dark blue suit leaned toward Lenore, resting one hand peremptorily on the counter, while with the other he signaled a bellhop to pick up some luggage.

"Would you please ring Mr. Mangas Taylor's room and tell him Ms Randolph is waiting for him in the lobby?"

"Certainly."

Lenore smiled her thanks and wandered over to look at a display case holding several pieces of porcelain. A small card discreetly tucked in the corner of the window stated that they were for sale in one of the gift shops. The central piece immediately drew her attention, and in her fascination with it she ignored the others. There was a strange familiarity about the lone Indian figure standing beside a horse, looking longingly at something in the distance. A haunting sadness marked the Indian's stoic features, drawing Lenore into a game she had played since childhood. She imagined herself as the Indian and tried to see what he was seeing and feel what he felt. Something she had once memorized came back to her, a quote from Back Elk of the Oglalas, who had survived the massacres:

A people's dream died there. It was a beautiful dream...the nation's hoop is broken and scattered. There is no center any longer, and the sacred tree is dead.

Lost in a world of missing buffalo and disappearing plains, Lenore didn't at first hear her name being called. When the discreetly spoken words finally penetrated her consciousness, she jumped in surprise and whirled around to see that the concierge who had called Mangas's room for her was now standing beside her.

"Ms Randolph, Mr. Taylor has asked me to inform you he will be slightly and unavoidably delayed. He suggested you might like to wait for him in the Tavern Room."

"Did he say how long he would be?"

"No, I'm sorry, but he didn't."

"All right. Thank you." Lenore turned back to the window. With time on her hands, her nervousness returned. She had an overwhelming urge to get in her car and leave, to forget she had ever met anyone named Mangas Taylor. She grasped at the thought, a kind of life preserver. But as drowning victims sometimes do in their panic and confusion, she discarded the very thing she felt might save her. She would stay.

Staring at her image reflected in the glass, she saw herself superimposed over the image of the porcelain Indian. It was as if they had somehow become one, still both distinct, yet somehow inexplicably locked together.

Lenore caught her breath. She suddenly realized why the figure looked familiar. The resemblance to Mangas Taylor was so strong, he could have posed for the sculptor. Everything was there, the lean hard muscled body, the strong angular features, the thick black hair. Only the eyes were wrong. Instead of the intense blue of an early-summer sky, they were deep brown.

No longer able to patiently await the answers

to her questions, Lenore turned from the window and walked back to the front desk. "Excuse me," she said, fighting to keep her voice steady.

The concierge looked up from the papers he held. "Yes?"

Lenore knew a direct approach would never get him to reveal Mangas's room number, so she smiled her most convincing smile and said, "I've decided to meet Mr. Taylor in his suite, after all. Could you please direct me?"

His directions were so precise to help her through the maze of hallways that Lenore could have found Mangas's room even without knowing the number. She walked through the lobby and out the back door to the wide walkway that went around the lake. Coming to the end of the ground-floor suites, which were located in the old section of the hotel, she followed the short path to the small front porch.

Chewing on her lip, she stopped and stared at the shiny silver numbers, delaying the moment when she and Mangas would meet again while wanting it with an intensity that kept her rooted to the spot, unable to go forward or retreat.

Behind her, the Broadmoor's lake shimmered in the reflected sunset, bathing the cream-colored walls of the old hotel in a soft orange. The staid formality and richness of her surroundings helped to soothe her frayed nerves, and she reached up to knock on the door.

Before her hand met the wood, the door swung open.

In answer to Lenore's exclamation of surprise, Mangas said, "I saw you through the window." He stepped aside, motioning her to enter.

Lenore didn't move. She simply stared at him. His hair was in damp disarray; he must have stepped from the shower a few minutes earlier. His unbuttoned shirt lay loosely against his chest, revealing a narrow patch of the bronze skin beneath. Unbidden, Lenore recalled the glistening image of an almost-naked Mangas walking around the track at the college, his head thrown back to catch his breath, his hands resting on his hips. That living image became tangled with the one of the porcelain Indian, and she felt them become intertwined in her mind as the raw strength of the man in front of her reached out and surrounded her like a near-suffocating wave of heat.

Lenore fought the sensual tug she felt pulling her toward Mangas by frantically seeking the anger and doubt she had felt earlier. The anger and doubt swelled out of all proportion.

Her confidence restored, Lenore stepped into the living room of Mangas's suite. She walked toward the marble fireplace, turned and leaned against the cold stone, using her hands as a brace. "Why didn't you tell me you owned Apache Computers?" she said with deceptive calm.

Mangas quietly closed the door. He could see by her posture and the way she held her head cocked at an aggressive angle that there was more behind the question than she wanted to reveal. Fleetingly he wondered how she had found out about him, but dismissed the question as unimportant. Deftly closing his cuffs with a pair of turquoise-and-gold cuff links, he moved toward Lenore. He stopped inches away and paused a moment to breathe in the light traces of her perfume. "Does it matter?" he asked.

"Answer my question first. Then we'll move on to yours."

Mangas reached out to caress the filmy silk material of Lenore's dress where it lay against her neck. Angrily she stepped away from him. "Please don't touch me. I didn't come here to play games. I came for some answers."

"Don't you think it would have been a little ostentatious of me to announce I owned Apache?" he reasoned.

Lenore glared at him.

"All right, dammit. I just didn't think it was any of your business. A chance encounter in a college music room didn't give you the right to my life story."

"If it had stopped there, I would agree, but it didn't. When you decided to pursue the relationship, you gave tacit approval for me to know more about you, especially something as basic as your occupation." Unconsciously Lenore's hand went to her neck, rubbing the flesh Mangas had brushed with his hand. "The more I think about it, the more I find it impossible to believe the M.C. Taylor that *Time* describes— cool, calculating, inscrutable were some of the adjectives used, as I recall— Anyway, I just can't buy the idea that that kind of man has either the inclination or the time to chase reluctant women. Why me?" Lenore's voice rose in anger. "Just what in the hell is going on?"

She was so incensed she didn't wait for his answer. "Not only are money and power incredible aphrodisiacs in themselves to some women, but any man who looks like you do could work in a barnyard and women would still chase him." A humorless laugh punctuated her words. "And you would have me believe that after one chance encounter I've moved to the forefront of those hoards of women."

Mangas wondered if she really knew how close she was coming to the truth, or if she was just acutely uncomfortable with the intensity of the feelings that had already passed between them and was trying to reason those feelings away. "I'm not sure," he said easily. "But in a perverse way, I think I've just been complimented."

"No, you haven't. I was simply stating the obvious. Are you going to stick to my questions, or am I wasting my time?"

Mangas reached up to rub the back of his

neck. He walked over to the burgundy sofa and sat down, propping his stocking feet on the table in front of him. It was obvious Lenore wasn't going to let go until she was satisfied with his answers. Glibly telling her what she wanted to hear would be as easy as it would be to find someone to buy Apache from him. But for some reason the lies wouldn't come. He found himself telling her what he could, as long as it was the truth.

"Contrary to the image you've created of me, I lead a very quiet social life. I go out of my way to avoid situations where I might meet the type of women you mentioned, and I have very little time for any other. As for not clarifying my connection with Apache, an opportunity never presented itself.

"Now it's my turn to ask a question," he went on. "Why in the hell is it so damn important?"

"I...I don't know." Lenore sank into a chair nearby. Softly she said, "I don't believe in fairy tales, and everything that's happened lately has the markings of a Brothers Grimm classic."

"Are you always so rigid in your thinking?"

"You see, that's precisely what I mean. You know nothing about me and yet you'd have me believe I've become vitally important to you."

Like a curtain being pulled aside, Lenore's words revealed to Mangas what he doubted she knew herself. "You're afraid of me, aren't you?" he said incredulously. For an instant before she could hide it with a derisive laugh, Mangas could see the truth of his accusation flash through her eyes. She reminded him of a young desert fox he'd once chased and cornered, all spit and fire and fear.

Lenore rose from the chair and went to the fireplace, where she retrieved her purse from the mantel. "What I really came for was to tell you I can't make it tonight. I should have mentioned it earlier, but I have another date I was unable to get out of and...."

Reluctantly Mangas contracted his lanky frame and rose as if to walk her to the door. He intercepted her midway across the room, placing his hands on her shoulders. "You don't for a minute think I believe you, do you? I haven't changed my entire week around in order to be with you, to let you walk out of here with such a flimsy excuse. I don't care what name you want to put on it, Lenore. There is something happening between us, and I'm not about to let it go without knowing what it is." He lifted her chin with his hand, forcing her to look at him. "Tell me you don't feel it, too, and I'll back off," he demanded.

Mangas didn't need to hear the words; he saw the answer in her eyes. For an instant, somewhere in a corner of his mind where there was still a fragment of the innocent man he had once been, he ached for what they had experienced to be true. The lies he had spoken to manipulate Lenore soured his mouth and almost made him turn away from her. Instead he pulled her to him and gently touched her lips with his own. Quickly the kiss deepened as he tried to drive away the reality of what he was doing to this woman, who only asked that there be trust between them.

He would have let her go had Lenore not uttered a small cry in the back of her throat and reached up to put her arms around his neck. She pulled him closer, and where she touched him, he wanted more. Where his tongue sampled the flavor of her lips, he ached to feel the warm welcoming interior of her mouth. Desperately he wanted to feel her respond to him, for her tongue to seek his mouth, for her body to arch against him in the ancient universal signal of desire. But stronger than wanting, was needing. Nipping at his consciousness was the knowledge that he needed this woman to be a part of him more than he had ever needed anything in his life.

Suddenly, overwhelmingly he wanted to share a morning with Lenore. He wanted to sit on the side of a mountain with her, her back pressed into his chest, and watch as the sun began to lighten the sky to a soft purple. He wanted to breath in the perfume of her hair mixed with the surrounding smell of cedar and pine. In his mind's eye he could see her walking toward him, silhouetted by a brilliant morning sun against a stand of shimmering aspens. Until that moment, he hadn't known how desperately he had missed the refuge and peace he had once found while wandering through the mountains of Colorado. Now, somehow, in unlocking that secret corner of his heart, Lenore had become a part of it.

Mangas broke the kiss so he could look at her. He let his hands follow the firm contours of her chin before they moved on to the pliable softness of her lips. "To say I understand what I'm feeling would be a lie, but to tell you I've never felt this way toward another woman would not be. I don't know what this means or where it will lead. I only know I can't let you disappear from my life."

Lenore felt as though she were swimming on the edge of a whirlpool, frantically trying to keep herself from being pulled into the center. Slowly, as his hand tenderly caressed her arm and then her back, she stopped struggling and let herself be carried into the sensations his touch aroused. In answer to his quiet plea not to leave him, Lenore meaningfully kissed the finger that brushed against her lip.

The moment was as fragile and precarious as a glass ornament that had been placed on the highest branch of a Christmas tree. Neither wanted to break the wonderous thing they shared for fear they would never be able to regain it. With the power of his gaze that spoke so eloquently of his longing, Mangas drew Lenore to him. She leaned against him with a soft sigh that indicated her surrender more poignantly than words could have expressed.

Her arms closed around Mangas's neck as she fit her body into the welcoming niche of his. As his mouth took hers, Lenore felt the sting of tears against her closed eyelids. They were tears that expressed the joy she had finally allowed herself to feel now that she had stopped waging a fierce inner battle against her emotions. The doubts and fears weren't gone. They had been forced into a corner of her mind where they didn't rear their ugly heads at every thought of how deeply she wanted this man.

When Lenore sought to taste the heady nectar of Mangas's mouth, she felt him shudder and heard a soft moan in his throat. Tentatively she slipped her arms inside his open shirt to explore the rigid plains of his back.

Mangas could feel himself slipping. Soon he would no longer have control over himself, let alone be able to gain the control he sought over Lenore. To let things go too far now could easily destroy everything. He must stop their lovemaking. As his hands went to Lenore's waist to gently ease her away from him, they brushed the sides of her breasts, and his resolve nearly evaporated. God, he wanted her. More than air to breathe or food to eat, he wanted this woman.

Breaking their kiss and burying his face in the shimmering mass of her hair, Mangas reeled in the unbridled chaos of his senses. The feel, taste, sight, smell of her intoxicated him. If she would only pull back or tell him she didn't want him....

When Lenore's lips pressed against his neck and he felt her tongue delicately touch the hollow at the base of his throat, he knew he could stand no more.

"Lenore," he breathed against her hair, "you know where this will lead if we don't stop." Her answer to him was a soft sigh that contracted his stomach until it felt as though it were tied in knots. Roughly he held her away from him. "My control is gone. We either finish this or we leave."

Before she could answer him, Mangas abruptly turned and started toward the bedroom. "I'm going to get dressed. Think of someplace you'd like to go for dinner."

Lenore was dumbfounded. She couldn't believe he was letting her go. It was certainly not what she had expected. She had given him every indication she wanted him to make love to her, and yet he had refused. Was it really possible, after all, that her fears and doubts were unfounded?

She wanted to follow him and tell him about

her frustration and her awakened passions. But years of rigid training were not so easily discarded. She found she couldn't speak the words to bring him back into her arms.

Forcing her voice to sound normal, she said, "I suppose you're right." She almost choked on the inanity of the sentence after what they had just shared.

THEY WENT TO A QUIET RESTAURANT, dark and intimate, known for its exceptional service and discreet waiters. Mangas ordered a Cabernet Sauvignon from a small exclusive winery in the Salinas Valley, and they discovered they had a mutal friend in the winery's owner.

"I went to school with his oldest son," Lenore said.

Mangas smiled. "He now works in Apache's accounting department. He and his wife are expecting their third child."

Lenore felt herself pale. How could it be possible? "I've been away too long," she said slowly. "It's hard to imagine my childhood friends with children of their own."

"You're welcome to come back with me when I leave next week." It was meant to be a lighthearted invitation, the kind so easily made and then ignored, but its implications were painful beyond measure.

"I didn't realize you would be leaving so soon," she said.

Mangas reached for her hand. "I have this weekend free.... Spend it with me."

"Yes." Lenore was surprised at how quickly and how easily she answered.

"Where would you like to go?"

"It doesn't matter."

"It's been a long time since I've walked in Colorado's mountains. I didn't realize how much I'd missed them...."

Catching his enthusiasm, Lenore said, "It's been two years since I've gone backpacking, but I know some trails that would be perfect for weekend trips. Or if you prefer, we could take horses. Better yet, there's a place I know of where we could go ballooning when we get tired of walking."

Mangas laughed. "I suppose you hang glide, too?"

"Not as much as I'd like to." Lenore grinned. "I have a friend with the soul of an adventurer who hates to do things alone. I'm the only one crazy enough to let him talk me into going along."

He wanted to ask her about her friend—someone who sounded so unlike Adrian that Mangas was sure it wasn't him—but he knew the twinge of jealousy he felt would be impossible to keep from his voice. Instead he asked for time to consider her suggestions and switched the subject to questions about her job and why she had left California to be an architect in Colorado.

"At the time I was engaged to an Air Force Academy cadet. It seemed reasonable to use him as an excuse to move, so I followed him here. When he graduated, I stayed behind. I guess you might say I traded one love for another." Lenore laughed. "The second has been far more faithful."

"And since then?" When it became obvious Lenore didn't understand him, Mangas elaborated. "Has there been another man?" He regretted the question before he'd finished asking it. He didn't want to know if there had been other men in Lenore's life. More importantly, he didn't want to hear her speak of Adrian or to have her words bring to his mind images of them together. There would be time enough for that later.

Before she could answer, Mangas stopped her. A smile warmed his eyes. "No, don't answer. I had no right to ask you that. There was more than casual curiosity behind the question."

"This is the second time you've asked me if there was or is a man in my life. Why?"

Mangas ran his finger around the edge of his wineglass. "Perhaps I find it difficult to believe you're free."

"Or. . . ."

"Perhaps it's just my desire to know everything about you."

"Maybe we could work something out," she said.

"Meaning?"

"A friendly exchange of information."

Mangas laughed. "What would you like to know?"

"Hmm, let's start with your favorite food."

"Meat loaf—it's adaptable and forgiving. I can put just about anything into it, and it's still edible. But best of all, I can make sandwiches out of the leftovers. Sometimes it will last me for days."

"You do your own cooking?" Lenore couldn't keep the surprise from her voice or her face.

"How else would you suggest I eat?"

She shrugged. "I guess I just assumed you would probably have a cook or eat out most of the time."

"If you recall, I told you I lead a rather quiet social life."

She believed that like she believed her apartment had suddenly become ocean-front property. Unless of course he was comparing his social schedule to that of a Hollywood starlet looking for her first part, who believed it wasn't what she knew but who she knew that would bring her success. Lenore had been away from home for several years, but not long enough to believe the women in California had gone blind or lost their touch. "Okay, let's forget about food—how about your favorite color?"

"Honey brown. Coincidentally, the exact shade of your hair and eyes."

"Imagine that!" Lenore laughed.

"Is it my turn?"

"I will yield, but only temporarily."

"Your favorite flower?" he asked.

"That's easy. The California golden poppy. It's such an intergral part of my childhood that I can't see one without smiling."

"Place?"

"That's harder. I have several. There's a beach in California near Big Sur...a mountaintop in Colorado near Independence Pass... Carmel in the winter...the Salinas Valley in the spring...." Lenore smiled. "Shall I go on?"

Mangas caressed her with his gaze. In a husky intimate whisper he said, "Where do you like to be touched when you make love?"

Lenore caught her breath. His words sent such warmth through her that her ears burned. "I suppose after a question like that, I'm expected to calmly take another bite of sole and ask you about your favorite indoor sport?" She realized her mistake the minute the words were spoken.

Mangas laughed. It was a deep infectious sound that echoed his obvious delight. He winked conspiratorially at her. "My *second* favorite indoor sport is chess. But you haven't answered *my* question."

"Would you believe me if I said I didn't know?" Lenore tried to convey a disinterested dismissal of the subject and not the ignorance that was the truth. Other than the obvious places, she had never been made aware that one area of her body was more sensitive than another. The brief frustrating affair she had experienced hadn't led to any wild awakenings or indicated to her that she was one of the current generation's sensual creatures. Somehow she couldn't imagine an elbow or a knee suddenly becoming erotically exciting, at least not *her* elbow or knee.

The smile faded from Mangas's face. He wondered about Lenore's answer. He had wanted something carefree and easy and intimate to pass between them; instead she had given him a deeply revealing glimpse of herself. Was it possible that someone who looked as she did, who radiated sensuality in the very way she held her head, could be sexually naive? Impossible! He was an idiot to even think it. Lenore only knew how to play the game of enticement better than most.

In answer, Mangas drew her hand to his lips and lightly kissed her fingers. "Then we can find out together," he murmured, willing to go along with her game.

Lenore almost choked. Had they not been in a public restaurant, she would have forgotten her earlier shyness and urged him to begin the experimenting then. She was stunned at her abrupt departure from her usual reserve. As she took a sip of wine, she looked at Mangas over the rim of the glass. To pretend that if she became involved with this man, he wouldn't change her life, would be to say the earth would remain the same if suddenly placed in another orbit. Then again, to say she could even now walk away unscathed would be as preposterous.

Mangas touched her hand. "I believe it's my turn?"

Lenore nodded.

"Your favorite outdoor sport."

Lenore was grateful he seemed to have noticed her discomfort and had so smoothly changed the direction of their conversation. "Tennis."

"Perfect." He leaned back, a satisfied smile on his face. "I haven't played in years, but I would love to. How would it be if I pick you up tomorrow after work and we use the courts at the Broadmoor? Bring a change of clothes. We'll go somewhere for dinner afterward." He gave her a wicked grin. "Loser pays!"

Lenore smiled sweetly, confident she could leave her money at home. "You're on," she said innocently.

CHAPTER SEVEN

MANGAS STOPPED TO CATCH HIS BREATH as Lenore ran to retrieve an out-of-bounds ball. A low chuckle accompanied his smile as he thought about their previous two games. While he had managed to score enough points so as not to lose by too great a margin, he'd done so only by playing better than he'd ever played before—while Lenore had made her game look effortless.

She had easily returned balls Mangas thought out of her reach. Then, using the volley to her advantage, she'd had him running all over the court. She was magnificent, he acknowledged with an admiration that came from a deep appreciation of excellence. He was grateful he hadn't been stupid enough to bet more than a dinner on the outcome.

Mangas watched as Lenore tucked a strand of hair behind her ear and prepared to serve. She was clothed in bright yellow shorts and a sleeveless top that left her long arms and shapely legs bare. For the past hour he had been captivated, watching her every move. Each motion revealed a strength and grace akin to that of a dancer. Watching her bend to pick up a ball or move across court to regain position had given him a pleasure foreign to him until he had met her.

In five minutes their third game was over. Lenore met him at the net, a twinkle in her eyes. "Do you want to make it six out of ten?"

"You might have mentioned you were on hiatus from the pro circuit before you suckered me into this." Mangas draped a towel around her neck and quickly kissed her on the forehead.

Lenore laughed. As naturally as if they were long-time friends, she reached out to take his hand as they walked from the court. "It's the only exercise I seem to be able to find time for lately. I've discovered it's a marvelous way to work out my frustrations."

"The way you play is a little more than that," he said, refusing to let her make light of her talent. "Want to let me in on your secret?"

"Self-defense. When my brother and I were growing up—long before he went pro—whenever he needed someone to practice with, he would haul me onto the courts. I finally grew so tired of chasing balls, I learned to hit them back."

"Mark Randolph is your brother?"

"Yes." She looked at him in surprise. "Do you know him?"

"We've met several times at charity functions."

"I thought you shunned that type of thing."

Mangas held the gate as Lenore passed through. "The ones I attend are usually very quiet, low-profile affairs where there's as much business transacted as coffers filled for charity."

"How altruistic," she needled.

Mangas glanced at her, a look of amusement on his face. "And realistic," he said. "A prosperous business can keep hundreds of people from needing charity."

"Touché." Lenore bowed lightly.

They continued to hold hands as they walked past the ice arena toward the lake. It was the quiet time before dinner, and the cooling breeze had attracted joggers and strollers alike to the path that meandered around the Broadmoor's sprawling lake.

Mangas stopped to pick up a small piece of bread lying beside the walkway. He tossed it to a mallard swimming lazily beside them. The motion attracted several keen-eyed observers from the groups of other fowl close by, and Mangas and Lenore were soon accompanied by an assortment of loudly squawking swans, geese and ducks.

"Remind me to save them bread from dinner," he said, laughing at the menagerie as he opened the door to his suite. "I assume, by the way, you have decided where it's going to be?"

"I'm working on it," Lenore said, tossing her

racket on the couch. Actually what she had been working on since Mangas had taken her home the night before was some way to tell him she wanted him to make love to her. How did one go about such a thing. Should she just blurt it out? Say something like—"Hey, Mangas, how about finding out where I like to be touched by you?"

Lenore could feel a flush of embarrassment crawl up her neck. She moved to the window and pulled the curtain aside. Unseeing, she stared at the iron post that stood next to the walkway, at the flower-filled baskets suspended from it. She knew she was handling it all wrong.... Oh, if she could only look and sound as sophisticated as he seemed to think she was.

Finally, still staring out the window, barely above a whisper, she said, "I understand the hotel has excellent room service...."

Silence fell between them while the implication in what she had said seemed to grow until it became almost a physical thing separating them. Lenore swallowed, unconsciously clutching the curtain in a grip that twisted and wrinkled the delicate satin fabric. Why didn't he say something, she agonized, unable to turn around to see what effect her words had had on him for fear she had gone too far, too fast.

Mangas stood spellbound. Again she had caught him off guard. With the merest hint of her willingness to spend the night, she had ignited a fire that had robbed him of coherent thought or speech. Where he had walked a sure path, he now stumbled in darkness. Unconsciously he lifted his hand to rub his neck as he stared at Lenore's back.

God, she was so achingly beautiful. Whether dressed in jeans and sweater, as she had been when he'd watched her wandering around Winchester College, or in a gown that teasingly covered her breasts with only wide suspenders of fabric, she took his breath away. With a start he realized she was the woman who had frequented his dreams, the unobtainable creature he had thought a figment of his imagination, assured, challenging, erotic—and, he rigidly forced himself to remember, even if not Adrian Winchester's current lover, obviously still his intimate friend.

Wordlessly Mangas moved across the room. He came to stand behind Lenore, his hands resting on her arms. She trembled at his touch. A deep sigh escaped her lips. She now readily acknowledged that she had waited for this moment for a lifetime. Even before she met Mangas she had dreamed of him, longed for him. Yet how she had feared him and the upheaval he would bring. No longer. Never again would she scoff at fairy tales and love stories; how could she?

Lenore eased her back against Mangas's chest, and he folded his arms over her breasts. She could feel his chin nestle against her hair and his warm breath caress the tip of her ear. It felt so right for them to be like this. It was as if their coming together had been predestined, as though all that had gone before had been in preparation for this moment.

Gently Mangas turned her to face him. He reached for the pins in her hair, deftly removing them with unhurried ease until the dark honey tresses tumbled free to lie on her shoulders. Lenore started to reach for him, but he caught her wrists. Taking her hands in his, he slowly brought them to his mouth. Lenore held her breath as he kissed the tip of each finger before tracing a moist circle with his tongue on the center of each palm.

When at last he looked at her, his blue eyes dusky and filled with desire, Lenore meaningfully whispered, "It seems I like to have my hands touched...."

A tiny smile curved his mouth. He reached up to brush her hair from her face. As gently as a feather borne aloft by a breeze, he kissed the hollow below her ear, his mouth moving on to follow the curve of her throat, tasting the saltiness of her skin with his tongue as he pressed his lips to her eyes, her temple, her nose. When at last he took possession of her mouth, she welcomed him with a little cry of pleasure.

Mangas moved his hands to the curve at the base of her spine and guided her closer to him. He stroked her back, then slowly moved on to her sides, where, in sure teasing motions, his touch came tantalizingly close to her breasts but failed to reach its goal. Lenore fought an urge to reach for his hands and place them on her breasts. Unsure of her role, she stood passively.

Obviously sensing but not understanding her reluctance to become actively involved in their lovemaking, Mangas reached up to grasp the sides of her face. He held her, forcing her to look at him. "Lenore, tell me now if you don't want this to go any further," he urged. "If you've changed your mind, it's all right. We don't have to make love now."

Dammit, she knew so little, ached for so much. How should she react to let him know she wanted him? What should she do to please him? For the first time since she had made her decision to avoid emotional entanglements, Lenore sincerely regretted it. That choice had left her impossibly, sexually naive for a twenty-nine-year-old woman. Who would believe such a thing was possible in the era in which she lived? How could she not know how to make love to a man, when at any given moment for the past ten years, a book telling her how had been somewhere on the best-seller list?

Lenore tried to avoid Mangas's gaze, but he persisted in holding her. Their faces were inches apart. She groaned inwardly. It would be so much easier to tell him what she wanted to if she could only bury her face in the curve of his neck, not have to witness the reaction she feared.

With a catch in her throat she answered him. "I want you to make love to me, but I'm not sure what I should do. I don't know—" The skeptical look on Mangas's face stopped her from trying to explain further. Obviously he didn't believe anything she had said or would say.

"Are you trying to tell me you're a virgin?" he asked, undisguised doubt making his question more of a barb than a query.

"No!" she breathed, caught off guard by his attack. Immediate and defensive anger covered her mortification. She pushed Mangas away and glared at him. "I was *trying* to tell you that I've had very little experience in making love, and that what experience I have had taught me nothing. I wanted it to be different this time. I hoped it would be different. But I can see I was wrong. Underneath you seem to be made of the same self-centered, egotistical stuff as the last man I thought I could have a relationship with. Thanks, but no thanks." She tried to step past him, but he reached out and stopped her. "Let me go," she demanded through tightly clenched teeth.

"Not until this is settled."

"Settled?" Lenore cried. "What's there to settle? I made a mistake in coming here. I'm about to rectify that mistake by leaving. Now let go of me."

"What I said was unforgivably insensitive and I can understand your anger, but not why wanting to make love to me is suddenly a mistake."

"I've changed my mind, that's all."

"Have you?" Mangas dropped his hands to his sides. "If you have, I won't keep you here—but I don't believe you. I think that under your ruffled feathers, you want me as much as I want you. I think even as you're standing there denying it, your breasts yearn to be touched... your body burns with the same need I feel in mine."

She would be an idiot to try to deny what he said. Every fiber of her being ached with the intensity of wanting him.

"Lenore?" he gently coaxed.

She turned and walked the few steps back to the window. It was so hard for her to just let go. Why did she insist on using a simple misunderstanding as a platform for a fight that would remove her from a situation she might not be able to control? She truly longed to reach out to him, yet a perverse part of her personality was bent on destroying something that could be so wonderful before it had even had a chance to begin.

Determined not to let fear rule her actions, Lenore took a deep breath and forced the words she really wanted to say past her cowardice and doubts. "Mangas, please make love to me. Make love to me before I find a way to reason my way out of it.'' Barely above a whisper, she went on. ''Take me on the journey your eyes have promised since we sat alone together on a piano stool. . .a lifetime ago.''

He sucked in his breath. Lenore's vulnerability and her quietly spoken words hit him with the impact of a fist. She had opened her soul to him, asking only his honesty in return. The enormity of what he had planned to do to her, how he had planned to use her, settled over him like a black cloak, making him shudder in revulsion.

Suddenly knowing he would never see her that way again, never see the look of complete trust shining from her eyes, he stared at her, forcing himself to memorize the smallest detail of the way she looked, silhouetted against the early-evening sun. ''Lenore, I don't know what to say to you. I've been so wrong. . .about so many things. You won't understand this, but I'm sorry. I'm so very sorry.''

She turned to face him. A new fear made her heart beat quicker. ''You're right. I don't understand.''

Thank God, Mangas wanted to cry. He gazed at her, sorrow in his eyes.

''Mangas?'' she said tentatively, a nervous smile playing over her lips. ''Are you trying to tell me that now it's you who has changed your mind?''

''Lenore.'' He sighed, his voice edged in pain.

"I want you beyond reason—beyond what is right and wrong."

"How can what happens between us be wrong?"

Mangas moaned softly, and the distance separating them disappeared. He crushed her to him, burying his face in her hair. "I should stop this," he breathed, "but I can't. Forgive me, Lenore...." His words were cut off by her seeking mouth.

Coherent thought disappeared in the rush of feelings that crashed through her senses. Mangas met the fire in her kiss with a hunger that demanded she hold back nothing. He coaxed and encouraged her until she boldly returned his passion. Her natural sensual instincts that had been buried for so long finally surfaced and were ruling her every action. She eagerly explored the honeyed recesses of his mouth and gloried in the groan of pleasure that greeted her quest. She knew at last the heady feeling that giving pleasure could bring.

"Tell me again that you want me, Lenore," he demanded. But as he sought her mouth, his lips found the answer in the force of her response.

"Help me..." he whispered, pulling away to stare down at her, his hands holding the sides of her face as his tortured eyes looked into hers.

"Make me forget," he pleaded.

Although she didn't understand why he had

said what he had, she understood the message in his eyes. She reached for his arms, running her fingers along their tightly muscled lengths until she touched his hands. Her gaze never wavering from his, she brought his hands to her breasts.

Mangas caught his breath. Even through the thickness of the confining material, he could feel the heat of her desire. His hands moved to the hem of her top, and she raised her arms to help him to remove the garment. He eased the straps of her bra from first one shoulder and then the other, letting his lips trace the faint lines they had left behind. Moving lower, he nudged the lacy material from her breasts with slow lazy kisses. His assault on her senses was controlled and deliberate. He chipped away at what little reserve remained with the skill of a diamond cutter. She held her breath and waited for him to reach the throbbing flesh of her nipple, suffering a torment that was edged with ecstasy.

At last he took the hardened peak into his mouth, to caress it with his tongue and gently nip it with his teeth. Moaning in pleasure she grasped the back of his head and pulled him closer to her still.

Mangas moved his hands to her buttocks. Effortlessly he lifted her, holding her tightly against him as he began to kiss the sensitive skin beneath her breasts. She arched to meet his demanding mouth as a wave of sensual pleasure washed everything from her consciousness except the man who brought her that pleasure with his touch, his feel, his fire.

"Wrap your legs around my waist," he huskily commanded.

When she did so, the contact was as natural as it was intimate, erotic in its implications, breathtaking in its promise. The texture of his shirt chafed against her inner thighs. Hungrily her mouth sought his, delving into its depths, caressing, tasting, teasing.

She locked her arms around his neck, and his hands moved from her hips to the smooth skin of her back, then on to the tangle of her hair. Cradling her head, he pressed her closer into the claiming depth of his kiss. He shuddered, his fragile control nearly disappearing with her eager answer.

Her newfound sense of power had taught her much. Unerringly she now knew that by simply touching the tip of her tongue to the hollow of his ear, or her lips to the base of his throat, he would sigh his pleasure. She also knew beforehand that when she whispered her request to let her remove his shirt, to let her feel his bare chest against hers, she would hear him catch his breath.

A deep moan escaped Mangas's lips as he lifted her and carried her to the bedroom, where he knelt to set her on the edge of the bed, then slid between her legs. Lenore slipped her arms from around his neck. Slowly she trailed her hands down the rigid plains of his chest, stopping to feel the heavy beating of his heart, before she went on to the waistband of his shorts. He held his breath as she moved her hands past the constricting band and gently began to pull the material free. When at last she had separated shirt and shorts, she reached beneath the material and touched him, luxuriating in the taut feel of his bare back against her splayed fingers.

His skin was so smooth, the flesh beneath it so firm. She could feel his muscles work as he ran his hands along her thighs. Rather timidly she began to explore his waist, then his chest, noticing his nipple had grown rigid as she neared it, wondering if he could be as sensitive there as she was. The soft sigh that greeted her caress and the tightening of his grip on her upper arms was her eloquent answer.

Impatiently, lithely he drew the shirt over his head. He reached for her again and pulled her to him. The contact was everything Lenore had known it would be. The feel of her breasts yielding and molding to the firm contours of his chest, while her thighs burned against his waist, ignited yet a new, more demanding flame.

"Mangas," she whispered over and over again, hardly aware that the calling of his name became a plea to fulfill the promise his touch whispered. Gently he laid her back and then joined her on the wide bed. When his leg possessively moved over hers and his hand touched her hip before moving on to the flat of her stomach in slow deliberate circles, she was enticed yet further into a world she had only dared to imagine. . . .

The rest of their clothing soon joined Mangas's discarded shirt. Lenore began to discover even greater fulfillment in touching and being touched. She learned the insides of her elbows and the back of her knees were indeed highly responsive, almost unbearably so when it was Mangas's mouth or tongue that did the caressing.

Slowly, poignantly he made love to her as though the act were a precious gift, something to be remembered and cherished over a lifetime. Gently he stroked her almost painfully sensitive thighs, moving higher and more intimately with each motion until she eagerly opened for him, wantonly forgetting her earlier shyness. She moved against his exploring touch with an urgency that quickened her breath and almost destroyed his control. Their need swelled inexorably beyond control, and at last they moved as one in the ancient dance of love. . . .

With loving caring movements he led her in a fascinating journey to a place she had never been until then. She was deeply shaken by the waves of sensual delectation that swept over her, by the ecstasy. A cry of surprise escaped her lips as she clung tightly to him.

When finally her breathing no longer came in tiny gasps, when he could no longer feel her heart beating against his chest, Mangas raised Lenore's chin so that he could look into her eyes. "That's never happened to you before?" he inquired softly.

"Not like that. . . ." Before he pulled her back to him and laid his cheek against hers, she saw a flash of pain in his eyes.

"Dammit, Lenore," he breathed into her hair. "Everything about you is such a contradiction. . . . If only I had known. . . ."

She nudged him away and looked into his eyes. "You're not making much sense, you know. Perhaps I could understand your complaining if I had been the only one who enjoyed what just happened." A smile tugged at the corners of her mouth. "But even in all my naiveté, I know that it just isn't so." With her tongue she traced the rigid line of his collarbone, smiling triumphantly when she heard his sharp intake of breath.

"What happened to the shy creature who didn't know how to please a man?" he laughingly demanded.

"Hmm. . . . She must have been left somewhere back in the living room with a few pieces of clothing. I think it was about time I got rid of her, don't you?" Squirming lower, Lenore lazily covered his chest with light kisses until she came to the dark brown flesh surrounding his nipple. Again his reaction to her gentle nip and caressing tongue told her everything she wanted to know.

Mangas rolled over onto his back, grabbing her shoulders and bringing her with him. "I think I've created a monster," he growled, pulling her head down and capturing her mouth in a ravishing kiss.

Lenore matched his rekindled passion, moving against him in unmistakable invitation. She uttered a welcoming cry of pleasure when he grasped her thighs and guided her so that they were once again joined in the ultimate expression of love. The final release was as explosive as before, but this time Lenore saw only contentment in Mangas's eyes as he slowly returned with her from their erotic journey.

Cradling her head on his shoulder, Mangas tenderly kissed away the tiny beads of perspiration on her forehead.

Suddenly serious, Lenore looked up at him and whispered, "Thank you."

His thick brows arched in question. "I guess it's my turn not to understand."

She struggled for the right words. "My life was everything I wanted it to be before I met you...at least I thought it was. Now I know there was something missing...." She felt him stiffen and inwardly cursed her clumsiness. Moving out of his embrace, she propped herself up on her elbows and stared down at him.

"What I'm trying to tell you is that you've made me feel like a woman—a grown-up, mature, sexual woman for the first time in my life, and I love it. Just as I—"

She choked back the words that had nearly tumbled out as naturally as the rest. She had almost told him she loved him. Shaken by both the realization of her feelings and the near confession to Mangas so soon in their relationship, Lenore sat up, swinging her legs over the edge of the bed.

"I'm getting a little hungry," she said hurriedly. "Maybe we should—" She caught her breath in surprise when she felt Mangas kiss the hollow at the base of her spine.

"What happened to room service?" he asked between nibbling kisses.

"Nothing. . . it's just— Mangas," she gasped, "if you don't stop that . . . ."

"Yes?"

Gathering what little strength she had left to resist him, Lenore stood up and headed for the door. "I'll tell you later. For now, I'm going to take a shower."

"Need company?"

She laughed. "Like I need another leg."

It wasn't until she had stepped from the shower and was wiping the moisture from her legs, thinking what she would do with a third one, that she realized she had left her change of clothes in the bedroom. Wrapping the fluffy white towel with the embroidered *B* snugly around her, she stepped into the short hallway that joined the suite's three rooms.

The aroma wafed in from the living room. Like a magnet, the delicious smell drew her into that room instead of the bedroom. There she saw Mangas, fully dressed, standing beside an elegantly set table lighting a candle. He looked up and smiled. "You look fetching," he gently teased.

"How did you manage to get a meal here so quickly?" she asked, ignoring his comment.

"There are some things that should remain shrouded in mystery, sweetheart."

Laughing at his poor Humphrey Bogart imitation, she moved over to the table. "Can I peek?"

"Be my guest, m'lady."

Under the pewter-colored warming canopies she found a huge cut of prime rib, baked potatoes and asparagus spears. Unable to deny her rumbling stomach any longer, Lenore reached for one of the spears and bit off the end. "Scrumptuous." She closed her eyes and sighed. Opening them a second later to see Mangas staring at her with a broad smile curving his mouth, she added, "Is something funny?"

"What do you think you would have said if I'd told you three hours ago that you would be nonchalantly prancing around my hotel room wearing nothing but a towel?"

"I'd have told you that you were crazy—" she grinned "—but then I'm not prancing. I'm standing still." She popped the rest of the asparagus into her mouth. "Just give me five minutes...."

"Fat chance," he growled, reaching for her. "Pleasant scenery aids the digestion," he murmured against her neck.

She felt the towel slowly slipping from her breasts and made a halfhearted attempt to catch it before it fell. "Let it go," he huskily urged, a new hunger commanding his actions.

After all that had gone before, he was dumbfounded at how easily she had again aroused him. And he knew it wasn't the seductive way she wore the towel that made him feel as he did; she could have come into the room wearing a floor-length flour sack and he would have reacted the same way.

"This is insanity," he grumbled, untangling her arms from around his neck and setting her away from him. But the look in her eyes told him she wanted him with the same urgency he wanted her. His resolve disappeared. He pulled her back into his arms, and their worlds once again shrank to the sphere of each other.

Despite the hotel's meticulously thought-out safeguards against delivering a meal less than "fresh from the kitchen," Mangas and Lenore's food was cold by the time they once again investigated the offering. When, unable to accept the waste of throwing everything away, she refused to let him reorder the meal, they dined on cold meat and warm chocolate mousse. She knew Mangas didn't believe her when she told him, but Lenore sincerely thought it was one of the best meals she had ever eaten.

Their immediate hungers satisfied, they sat together on the burgundy sofa, content for the moment to luxuriate in the comfort of holding and being held in a satiated intimacy. When finally it came time for her to get ready to go home, she realized with a start that her life had been abruptly turned inside out. The thought of returning to the apartment she had spent years painstakingly turning into a much-beloved haven was now no more inviting than the prospect of closeting herself in a cave filled with bats.

Later, as she wriggled into the dress she'd brought to go out to dinner in, a secret smile played on her lips. In less than a week her life had turned into one big cliché. Almost at first sight she had fallen like a ton of bricks for a total stranger. *Oh, if my journalism instructor could only read my thoughts,* she laughingly chided herself. *He would destroy every school record showing I had taken his class. No marks for originality.*

A light tapping on the bedroom door broke into her musings. "Ready?" Mangas called.

"Yes—at least I'm almost ready. Come in.

I've a few more things to do." She shook her head slowly in wonder as she stepped into her shoes. How strange that the act of dressing was considered more private than lovemaking. And how thoughtful of him to realize she would feel a trace of shyness, and so insist she use his bedroom while he dressed elsewhere. A shiver of pleasure passed through her. It was going to be such a joy to discover life anew with this man. To learn the intricacies of sharing, of caring for someone who held such a special place in her life. To have, in time, all of her lingering shyness dissolve as surely as her fears about becoming involved with him had dissolved. Like a kitten whose eyes had just opened, she was eager to explore this new role they shared. She looked up to see Mangas leaning against the doorframe, his navy gabardine jacket carelessly open, his hand resting on his hip.

"Taking you home is not something I really want to do. Are you sure you don't want to stay?"

More than she could tell him. "And show up for work tomorrow like this?" She indicated her clinging dress. "My ears would be burning for weeks."

"Would that bother you—to have people talking about you?"

"No. At least it hasn't up until now."

Mangas looked at her quizzically. "That sounds interesting. Want to tell me about it?"

She squeezed past him, playfully pinching his waist. "There are some things that should remain shrouded in mystery, sweetheart."

His laugh echoed through the hallway as he turned to join her.

On the way to Lenore's apartment, they discovered they had yet another mutual friend in one of the engineers who worked for Apache. Mangas told her Barbara Arden had started with Apache directly out of college, when the company was little more than an all-consuming idea and a rented corner of a warehouse. Barbara had been steadfast even through the rough months when none of them had taken home a paycheck. Now she and her husband, another engineer at Apache, owned a home in Blackthorne, the Beverly Hills of the San Francisco Bay area.

"At least I think she still works for Apache," Mangas grumbled. "The last time I saw her she was nursing her new baby daughter and threatening to stay home for the next five years to take care of her until she starts school."

"Somehow it's easier for me to picture Barbara with a slide rule in her hands than a baby."

"She handles both of them as easily as she does me when she wants things done her way."

"Now *that* sounds like Barbara," Lenore laughed.

As they drove into the apartment complex's parking area, the headlights outlined Lenore's neighbor, Ruth Swanson, getting out of her car. When the neighbor saw it was Lenore, she waited for them to leave their car.

"A man named Adrian Winchester came to my place around ten o'clock looking for you. He said he'd been trying to reach you all night and that he was terribly worried something might have happened to you. I assured him I'd seen you this morning, but he insisted I check your apartment anyway, so I did. I hope you don't mind. I had a feeling that either I did or the police would."

Lenore sighed in exasperation. She had forgotten tonight was the night she'd promised Adrian she would look at the sketches the New York interior decorators had come up with for his Aspen condominiums. Damn! Why couldn't he have dropped them by the office tomorrow instead of insisting she look at them as soon as he got back in town? But she knew why. While she had never encouraged Adrian, she hadn't done everything she should have to discourage him, either. She had allowed their relationship to progress past the point where she wanted it to out of laziness. There was no easy way to extricate herself from this situation.

"No, it's all right," she finally said to the waiting neighbor. "I'm sorry you were put to so much trouble. I forgot I had an . . . an appointment with him, and he has a tendency to get a little excited at times. I appreciate your taking care of it."

"Oh, it wasn't any real trouble," she said with a dismissing wave. She smiled broadly and started toward her apartment. "See you tomorrow."

When she was gone, Lenore turned to Mangas. She was startled to see the change in his expression. Where his eyes had been warm and inviting, they were now hooded and unfathomable. He closed the car door and walked up beside her. "Trouble?" he asked softly.

Talking to Mangas about Adrian was the last thing she wanted to do. "No. Just a forgotten appointment. I'll take care of it tomorrow."

Mangas forced himself to swallow the immediate retort that had come to mind. He didn't want her to misinterpret his reasons for asking her how often she made evening "appointments" with men like Adrian Winchester. Jealousy was one emotion he'd never been accused of displaying. "What you really mean is you'd rather not talk about it."

"Do you mind?"

He stared at her, fighting the urge to shout just how terribly he minded. "No, not if that's the way you want it."

She took his hand. "I'd rather talk about where we're going to go this weekend. Have you made up your mind?"

"Not yet," he answered slowly.

"All I ask is a little warning so I know what to pack," she said, taking her key out and turning to face him. "Other than that, I'm yours—do what you will with me for two and a half days."

"I'll let you know."

Lenore fought an urge to reach up to his face and smooth away the strangely haunted look that had so dramatically altered his features. Instead she stood on tiptoe and chastely kissed him, hoping he would lengthen the quick meeting of their lips and that the look in his eyes would change to one of dusky passion—a look she now felt she knew how to handle.

But Mangas remained closed to her, shielding his troubled thoughts by retreating behind the closed facade reporters so frequently wrote about. He took her keys and unlocked the door, then quickly guided her through.

She started to reach for the light, but his hand caught hers. "I can't stay, Lenore." He dropped the keys onto her palm as he briefly touched his lips to her forehead. "Goodbye."

"Good night, Mangas," she softly called as he walked away from her and into the shadows of the courtyard.

THE DRIVE BACK TO THE HOTEL was a journey through a private hell for Mangas. For an evening he had allowed himself to feel again, and while the joy had been breathtaking, the pain was now devastating.

Why had the one person in twelve years who had been able to make him feel alive again turned out to be someone Adrian had found first? Damn her! So briefly, she had made him forget, made him believe that perhaps his bad-luck charm didn't matter. But Adrian did. Mangas tried to swallow the hostility that burned his throat like bile, but it would not be denied.

How easily his plan for revenge had backfired. As easily and effortlessly as a lanky beauty had asked to enter his life and he had unwittingly let her in.

My God, he silently gasped, *could I really have fallen in love with her?* With dreaded certainty he knew it was true. He was somewhere he had vowed never to go again, the fool's paradise populated by lonely people looking for companionship on life's one-way journey. Thinking of the woman with the honey-brown hair who had taken him there, he cursed himself for being the biggest fool of all. No one could have fallen harder than he had.

CHAPTER EIGHT

LENORE CROSSED THEN RECROSSED her legs, futilely trying to hide her impatience. What should have been a moment of triumph, earning the right to design the San Juan Savings and Loan Building, had turned into a painfully long delay in getting out of the office to start her weekend with Mangas. Her properly humble smile of appreciation for all the glowing things being said about her design had begun to feel as though it had been pasted on.

Finally finding an opportune moment to excuse herself, Lenore hurried to her office, almost colliding with Paul Shaughnessy as she rounded the hall corner. "I understand congratulations are in order." He beamed. "How about letting me buy you dinner?"

"Thanks, but I've got a date." She slipped her arm through his as they walked. "How about a rain check?"

"Saturday?"

She shook her head.

"Sunday, then."

She laughed. "Maybe one day next week."

Paul followed her into her office, grinning as he watched her put things away. "Well, it's about time."

Lenore stopped long enough to give him a quizzical look.

"We've been friends for three years, and this is the first time you've ever gone away with a man for a weekend."

"How could you possibly know that?"

"What—that this is the first time or that you're going away?"

"Either. . . both!"

"I have a keen sense of observation, painstakingly developed over twelve semesters of intense study at the Dick Tracy Correspondence School."

As she passed him on her way out the door, she tugged on the end of his tie and quickly kissed his cheek. "Want me to tell you where you can put your diploma?" she whispered sweetly.

"No!" His laughter followed her to the elevator.

The traffic was even worse than usual, with the crush of summer vacationers now using Colorado Springs as a crossroads in their travels While normally a patient and courteous driver, this evening Lenore honked loudly at two men who hadn't been immediately aware that a light had changed to green she glared threateningly at several people who looked as though they weren't going to let her merge in front of them. Still the trip took over a half hour. Even if Mangas had chosen to go somewhere fairly close, they were almost sure to arrive after dark.

Pulling up to her reserved parking area, she jumped out of the car and hurried to her apartment. A pleased grin softened the determined line of her mouth when she saw an envelope with her name on it wedged between the door and the frame. The distinctive Broadmoor logo printed on the outside told her immediately who the note was from. Wanting to savor Mangas's message in privacy, she tucked it under her arm as she let herself into the apartment.

Tossing her purse in a chair and stepping out of her heels, she moved to the bedroom while impatiently running her finger under the envelope flap and ripping it in her haste. She held the note in her teeth as she shrugged out of her linen jacket and reached back to unzip her skirt. Letting the skirt fall to the floor, she caught it with one foot and brought it up to her free hand, opening the precisely folded paper with the other.

She stopped her frantic activity and smiled when she saw her name written in a bold script.

Lenore—I tried to find a way to tell you this that would make it sound more diplomatic. I failed. Therefore I will do it the only way I know how—straightforwardly.

We both know what happened between us last night was out of character.
We seem to affect each other in ways that
are not necessarily good for either of us. I
know that once you think about it, you'll
agree that for this reason, it really is better
if we don't let it go any further by continuing to see each other.

I wish you all that is good in life.

Mangas

As the words merged in indistinct blurs on the
light brown parchment, lines of confusion appeared between Lenore's brows. Then, as
though she were compelled to complete the motions of a prerecorded program, she walked to
the brass bed and carefully laid her skirt across
the patchwork spread. Mechanically turning
from the bed, the note still clutched tightly in
her hand, she went into the living room. Subconsciously seeking the comfort that someone's
arms around her might have brought, she curled
up in the corner of her high-backed, overstuffed
sofa. Only then did she try to reread and understand the note Mangas had left.

"Lenore." How boldly, with such sure
strokes he had written her name.

"I tried to find a way to tell you this that
would make it sound more diplomatic." How
hard had he tried? How long? An hour? Two?
Would he have tried harder if he had known

how deeply he was going to hurt her? Did it even matter to him?

"I failed." *My God, how miserably you failed, Mangas,* she wanted to scream.

"Therefore I will do it the only way I know how—straightforwardly." As an archer would fire an arrow from an eighty-pound bow.

"We both know what happened between us last night was out of character." For whom? And how?

"We seem to affect each other in ways that are not necessarily good for either of us." Again she wondered, how? She didn't understand, couldn't conceive what he meant. Was it "not necessarily a good thing" for her to feel such happiness? For her to feel such joy in the pleasure she had shared with him last night? To know for the first time in her life what it felt like to be more excited by the prospect of going home than the thought of going to work?

"I know that once you think about it, you'll agree that for this reason, it really is better if we don't let it go any further by continuing to see each other." "Dammit," she softly swore aloud. "I don't agree—I don't understand." But then, he hadn't really given her a chance. Her cries of protest were to an empty room.

"I wish you all that is good in life." She wiped away tears that threatened to spill over. She needed anger to kill the pain. Where was her righteous indignation.

A long-forgotten quote came to mind. The harder she tried to bury it, the stronger it returned to taunt her. Echoing louder and louder in her thoughts, it soon picked up a tempo of its own, a steadily beating drum she was forced to acknowledge.

> 'Tis better to have loved and lost
> Than never to have loved at all.

What kind of man was Tennyson to have written such a thing, she wondered. How deeply could he have loved? For a day? For a week, as she had?

Lenore pulled her legs to her chest, encircling them with her tightly clasped arms. She leaned her forehead against her knees, only subliminally feeling the silky texture of her hose and slip. A week, indeed. A lifetime had passed in seven days. Perhaps her feelings weren't real. Maybe she'd only been swept along by the moment, an air-filled balloon accidentally caught up and borne aloft in a gusting wind. But then if that were true, why had her balloon world blown apart instead of gently falling back to earth when she had read Mangas's note?

Suddenly she knew that trying to deny her love, trying to pretend it hadn't been real, would bring her no comfort. There would be no easy way back from the place Mangas had taken her, the place she now knew she had so rightfully feared to go.

Time passed unnoticed as Lenore minutely re-lived the previous day, uselessly searching each action, each conversation for a nuance of meaning she might have missed. When at last she raised her head from her knees and realized the sun had nearly gone down, she still couldn't understand what had led Mangas to write that damnable note.

Letting the paper slip from her fingers to the deeply carpeted floor, she rose stiffly and walked to the kitchen. The aspirin she swallowed gave little immediate relief to her throbbing temples, which ached even worse when she wandered back through the apartment and switched on a lamp to fight off the encroaching darkness. On her way to the bathroom, she solemnly noted that her apartment had never seemed so lonely. Never had she known such an empty feeling when walking through the rooms. Mangas had done so much more than simply steal her heart. He had altered her life so drastically that despite all her efforts, it would never be the same.

And this hellish upheaval is supposed to be better than never having loved at all! She wanted to scream her rage, her frustration, her pain at her reflection in the bathroom mirror. Wetting a washcloth to put over her face, she began to laugh. The more she remembered how hard she had fought against becoming involved with Mangas, and how tenaciously he had pursued her, the louder and more desperate her laughter became.

Only when the memories brought a sharp stab of pain that made her stomach knot in protest did the laughter transform into hiccuped sobs. The tears she had denied finally fell, forming deep brown circles on her cinnamon-colored silk blouse.

When finally the tears were spent, Lenore sank once again into the corner of the sofa, the cool washcloth pressed to her swollen eyes. She knew that even though her life had been forever changed, in time she would get over Mangas Taylor. He would eventually fade to a bittersweet memory, as easy to deal with as any other. Now she need only get through this time of aching loneliness and rejection.

Perhaps she should call Paul. She knew he would stay with her, taking the edge off her sorrow, a loving companion through the worst days. And she also knew that if she asked him not to, he wouldn't prod her for answers.

No, she ruefully acknowledged. He wouldn't question her because he wouldn't need to. He had intuitively guessed the reason for her happiness; he would most certainly guess the reason for her sorrow. She was lucky to have a confidant like Paul. So many of her other friends had become little more than acquaintances. Although it was painful to acknowledge, she had to admit there was no one to blame but herself. Her work had come first for too many years. Friends needed nurturing, and nurturing took the time she had single-mindedly lavished on her job. Did everyone have to lay such huge sacrifices on the alter of success, she wondered. Or had she merely succumbed to a particularly destructive and insidious type of tunnel vision?

Almost without realizing what she planned to do, Lenore reached for the phone. Before dialing she glanced at the clock. Allowing for the hour difference, it was ten-thirty in California. She hesitated when she realized that a phone ringing so late would bring instant worry to her mother. But the need to hear her warm familiar voice overrode everything else, and Lenore proceeded to dial. It had been months since she'd talked to her parents, but it was her mother's comforting familiarity that she craved as desperately as she had when she'd first left home for college.

Her mother. The most loving and giving person Lenore had ever known. Her inspiration. . . and the wellspring of her deepest fears. A brilliant woman who should have been a doctor healing people, instead of a nurse following the orders of men who stood in her mental shadow. But parents who thought it unseemly for a woman to practice medicine and a husband and family who needed the income her job provided had kept her from realizing her potential until she was too old to go back to school.

As a young girl, Lenore had often wondered

how many people had died or would die because her mother had never become a doctor. When she was a teenager in the throes of becoming a woman herself, she had lain in bed at night and vowed she would never let happen to her what had happened to her mother.

How easily she had abandoned her resolve to keep her life uncomplicated and therefore free of attachment when Mangas Taylor had come into her life. In so short a space of time, she had become emotionally dependent on a man.

Impatiently she listened to the long-distance clicks as the connection went through. One, two, three rings. *Oh, please let them be home,* she prayed. Just as she was about to hang up after the seventh ring, she heard a breathless, "Hello."

Taken aback by the unexpected timbre of the voice, Lenore hesitatingly asked, "Who is that?"

"Lenore?"

"Mark? Oh, Mark, how wonderful that you're home." She heard his low chuckle.

"I'm not sure about how wonderful it is. I'm here recuperating from a broken leg."

"I didn't know...."

"Don't sound so crushed. It was a simple break and is healing beautifully. The only problem I've had is finding something long enough to slip down the cast to scratch the back of my calf."

Lenore laughed. How good it felt. They talked as easily as if they'd seen each other the day before instead of two years earlier. Lenore learned he was house sitting for their parents, who had taken off on their annual trip to Hawaii a week early. Almost in the same breath, he gave her the news that their favorite childhood drive-in movie was being torn down to make room for a shopping center. After another half hour of shared information and promises to get together soon, they were about to say goodbye when Lenore asked the question she had vowed she wouldn't ask the minute she had discovered Mark on the other end of the line. She was surprised at how smoothly it came out, as though the answer were of no consequence. "I understand you know Mangas Taylor."

There was an infinitesimal pause before Mark answered. Lenore knew she hadn't fooled him. "Yes, I've met him several times. Why do you ask?"

"What's he like?"

"Tall, good-looking, kinda quiet...." And for the second time, "Why?"

"Dammit, Mark," she grumbled, "you'll never change. Can't you just answer a question for me without having to know my motives for asking it?"

"All right, all right." He laughed. "Let's see...Mangas Taylor.... He's probably one of the most interesting people I've ever met.

Quickly analyzing my feeling, I'd have to say it's probably because he's such a good listener. You don't find many of that type around anymore, especially in the circles where I run. He has the ability to make you feel special when he's talking to you, kinda like, of all the people in the room, you're the most fasinating. He seems to get along with everyone, yet somehow I suspect he's a loner in reality. Most certainly not someone a woman with any sense would willingly become involved with.''

"Why not?"

"He's known as a 'love 'em and leave 'em' man. Judging from what I've seen, he deserves the reputation. I can't ever remember him being with the same woman twice." He chuckled. "Not that he's about to run out of willing companions, mind you. It's positively disgusting the way they line up when he's around."

Lenore fought to keep her voice light. "Sounds as if you could be a little jealous."

"Me? Never!" His voice lost its teasing quality. "You're not thinking about . . . ."

"Me? Never! Just idle curiosity, that's all. I met the gentleman in question at a social function about a week ago, and he mentioned having met you."

"Well, just in case you've been entertaining the idea that he might be someone you could be interested in, get rid of it. Even if he didn't have the loyalty of an alley cat, he's still not your type."

"I don't know what all the fuss is about, Mark. You know I have better sense than to get involved with someone like Mangas Taylor."

"Aw, Lenore... you didn't."

She sighed wearily, tired of the pretense. "We're all entitled to do one really dumb thing in our lifetime. I've just used up my option a little early."

"Want to tell me what happened?"

"No.... What I really want is to find a dark cave to hide out in for a while and then forget all about it."

"Are you sure?"

"Mark, you've already helped me more than you could possibly know. The rest will take time."

"I could—"

"You already have. Now hobble off to bed, and give my love to mom and dad when they get back from Hawaii."

"You want me to punch Taylor in the nose the next time I see him?"

Lenore couldn't help but smile at the image his words evoked. "And what would you do if I said yes?"

"Ever hear of hit and run?"

She laughed. "Mark, I love you. Now say good-night and go to bed."

Before he would hang up he made her promise to call him in a few days. She did, assuring

him she wouldn't even remember who Mangas
Taylor was by the end of the week.

The lie hung heavily in the air as she placed
the phone back on its stand. If only it was true.
If only she could get Mangas Taylor to disappear from her mind as easily as he had bulldozed his way in.

BY THE TIME THE WEEKEND WAS OVER, Lenore
knew the only antidote for the ache that accompanied her every thought or action was her
old panacea, work. She plunged into complet-
ing the San Juan Saving and Loan project with
a tenacity that excluded everything else. The
work that she brought home with her let her
crawl into bed each night too exhausted to lie
awake and think of Mangas—but not too tired
to keep him from her dreams. Once asleep,
she was again at his mercy. Nightly she re-
lived their week together, knowing again the
joy that had been hers. By day she knew only
the loss.

On Monday of the fourth week, the phone
rang as Lenore was getting ready for work. Before she had finished saying hello, a bubbly
feminine voice interrupted her.

"Hi, Lenore, this is Samantha. I won't keep
you long. I know you're getting ready for work,
but I just heard that the apartment I wanted was
free, after all, and I promised myself the minute
I found some place to live I could call you. So

that's what I'm doing." She laughed. "Can you tell I'm a little excited?"

Lenore sat down on the edge of her bed, an unfamiliar smile of pleasure on her lips. She didn't even try to make sense out of Samantha's ramblings, knowing an explanation would come along eventually. It was a family joke that her younger cousin had been born in high gear and would probably someday give the undertaker a run for his money. Lenore's aunt had been totally gray before she turned forty, something Samantha had taken complete credit for, saying it had not only made her mother look distinguished but also twice as beautiful.

Switching the phone to the other ear, Lenore held the receiver with her shoulder while she attached her opal earring. "Samantha, I can't think of anyone I would rather hear from on a gloomy morning. I tried calling you back time and time again, but you're never home. How are you?"

"Couldn't possibly be better." Coyly she added, "Meet me for lunch, and I'll tell you all about how I really am."

"You're here? In Colorado Springs? No wonder I could never get you."

"Well, you needn't sound so surprised. Colorado Springs is not the end of the earth, you know."

"No, but it's not exactly like a drive up the peninsula to San Francisco, either. As a matter of fact—'' Lenore laughed ''—you're the first relative from California who's dropped in for lunch in ever so long. Is Bob with you?''

Samantha's voice took on a hollow quality. ''He's not with me, but he'll undoubtedly be one of the topics of conversation over lunch. If you can make it, that is.''

''Name the place. I've worked through enough lunches lately that I can take the entire afternoon off. And there's nothing I would rather do than spend it with you.'' After discussing several possibilities, they decided to meet at a place where Lenore knew the staff wouldn't mind if they lingered over coffee.

THE MORNING PASSED more quickly than usual, only a phone call from Adrian interrupting the smooth flow of work. He asked if she would accompany him to a political dinner he had been coerced into attending, telling her he also had a favor he wanted to ask. Before she had a chance to remind him she only considered him a friend and thought it better that they didn't date, he assured her there would be no strings attached to her acceptance.

Lenore started to refuse, anyway, but the thought of spending another Friday night with only painful memories for company made her decide almost anything would be preferable. Although she had already turned him down twice during the two preceding weeks, and despite her earlier resolve not to see him at all, she was begrudgingly grateful for the distraction she knew he would bring. Besides that, her curiosity was piqued over the favor he had so mysteriously mentioned. When finally, after an obviously long hesitation, she agreed to accompany him, his stammered answer made her realize he hadn't expected her to say yes.

Afraid that she would forget their "date" by the time the weekend arrived, she flipped through her desk calendar and wrote a note to remind herself. The last thing she wanted was a repeat of her panicked performance nearly a month ago, when she had momentarily forgotten they were to meet. The memory made her wince. She needed only to close her eyes, and the entire episode played before her like a scene from a movie. A horror movie that ended with Mangas saying goodbye and walking away from her forever. Somehow, since that evening, Adrian and Mangas had become subtly intertwined in her mind, although she recognized the tie as irrational. Perhaps that was another reason she had told Adrian she would go to dinner with him, hoping that somehow she would discover a clue to understanding what had happened to make Mangas leave her.

Dammit! Lenore threw her pencil down on the desk. Why did every thought lead to Mangas Taylor? When would she begin to exorcise his ghost? He was gone. There had been nothing in his note to indicate any possibility he would be back. But, then, even if he was to come back, would she want to have anything to do with him again? Maybe there was a streak of masochism in her. She glanced at her watch. Lunch with Samantha was going to be a godsend. If anyone could pull her out of herself and her perverse insistence on allowing thoughts of Mangas to control her life, it was her indomitable cousin.

Lenore grabbed her jacket and headed for the door, pausing only long enough to gather the work she wanted to take with her. Within twenty minutes she was walking through the double doors of Bartlett's Restaurant. Sitting at the choicest table in the room, the only one that had a totally unobstructed view of Pikes Peak, was Samantha Baxter.

As she crossed the room Lenore smiled to herself. How nice to know some things never changed. It seemed her cousin would always be able to wave a magic wand and things would come to her. Spotting Lenore coming toward her, Samantha jumped up and came to meet her. Her shimmering cap of blond curls bounced gaily as she greeted her cousin enthusiastically. After clasping Lenore in a bear hug, she held her away and looked at her critically. "Have you given up eating?" she scolded.

Lenore laughed. "It's good to see you, too."

"Seriously, are you all right?"

"I've been working a little too much lately,

that's all. When I do that, I forget to eat. I'll put it all back on as soon as things slow down. *You* look marvelous." Lenore almost added something about married life obviously being agreeable, but then remembered Samantha's mysterious reference to Bob and thought better of it.

"Thanks. What you see before you is the result of months of strenuous effort. I'm certainly glad you noticed. It would have been real tough for me to find a way to casually work my diet-and-exercise regimen into the conversation, but I wasn't about to let you get away without noticing."

Lenore hugged her again. "I'm so glad to see you haven't changed."

After the waiter had checked with them for the second time, they laughingly stopped talking long enough to look at the menu before resuming their conversation. Lenore glanced out the window at the view of the magnificent mountain that so dominated Colorado Springs. She stared at it a long moment before she turned back to Samantha. "Did I hear you correctly this morning when you said you'd found an apartment?"

"That's just part of my news...but let me start at the beginning." She folded her hands in front of her, resting them on the white linen tablecloth before she took a deep breath and began. "Bob and I are divorced."

A tiny gasp involuntarily escaped Lenore's

lips. Samantha and Bob had seemed such a perfect couple. She would have bet they had a marriage that was sure to succeed.

"I know what you're thinking," Samantha said. "Everyone was shocked when we told them. Mom and dad even insisted we see a counselor. They were devastated when I told them the divorce was entirely my fault, that I was the one who wanted out. They couldn't seem to understand I'd changed, that I'd grown and Bob hadn't. He was still the fine, loyal, loving man I'd married—and he was still someone who insisted a wife's place was in the home, no matter how tough the economic times, no matter how desperately bored she had become, and no matter that there would never be children to fill the home.

"Leaving was the hardest thing I've ever done, even though I knew that if I stayed, I would die inside inches at a time. I tried staying in Salinas after the divorce but finally knew I had to leave when it became obvious that everyone, including Bob, was waiting for me to 'come to my senses.' They all thought he and I would eventually get back together."

"That must be why mom never wrote anything about it," Lenore said. "She probably figured she would wait until everything was back to normal and then tell me."

"And I never said anything, because somehow it just didn't seem the appropriate message to include with a Christmas or birthday card. Anyway, when I finally decided I had to leave, I remembered how you'd gone on and on about Colorado Springs the last time you were home. It seemed as good a place as any to make a fresh start. So here I am.''

"How long have you been here?''

Samantha smiled sheepishly. ''Three weeks,'' she mumbled.

''Three weeks! Why didn't you call me before now?''

''I promised myself I would do it on my own, that I wouldn't contact you until I'd found a job and a place to live. I knew you would have insisted on putting me up, and I was afraid I would get so comfortable I wouldn't want to move out. For all my shouts of 'give me independence,' I have to confess there are moments when I feel sheer panic.''

Smiling, Lenore reached out to cover Samantha's hand with her own. ''I know the feeling well.''

Lunch was served, and they continued to catch up on the news covering the years they'd been apart. When they arrived back at the present, Samantha told Lenore between bites of her gigantic club sandwich that she'd found a job with an insurance company, where the pay was mediocre but the co-workers fantastic.

Later, after they'd made eager plans to spend the weekend together, they waved goodbye to each other in the parking lot. Lenore watched as Samantha drove away in a bright red compact car, immeasurably grateful her favorite cousin had come back into her life, and at just the right time. As they had been good for each other when they were children, so they would be again. They would bask in the pleasure of each other's company and share the special healing power of laughter.

Lenore's smile of triumph made her feel as radiant as she looked. She walked the short distance to her car, but as she stepped from the curb, a flash of motion caught her eye. She glanced up to see a man coming out of the restaurant. Before sunglasses covered them, she saw a pair of deep blue eyes look in her direction. She caught her breath in surprise. Although nothing else about the man even faintly resembled Mangas, his eyes were the same mountain-lake blue. She was plunged back into the abyss of emptiness she had left such a short time ago.

Quickly glancing away to hide the well of tears accompanying the sharp stab of painful memories, she jabbed her key into her car-door lock. Once inside the shelter, she folded her arms across the steering wheel and laid her head on them. "Damn you, Mangas Taylor," she choked. "Damn you to hell."

CHAPTER NINE

MANGAS THREW HIS HALF-EATEN SANDWICH on the desk, making Barbara Arden jump in surprise. At her scowl, he defended his actions. "It tastes like cardboard."

"The cafeteria sandwiches have always tasted like cardboard—that never stopped you from eating them before. Besides, if you had eaten it at lunchtime instead of now, it probably wouldn't be so dried out."

Mangas glared at her. "And what's that supposed to mean?"

Letting out a breath of air in an exaggerated sigh, she tossed the clipboard she'd been holding on to the desk, leaned back in her chair and looked directly at Mangas. "It simply means that up until today, every time I've seen you eat a cafeteria sandwich you've eaten it with as much attention as you give anything else you eat—which is little or none. How come all of a sudden something that has always been unpalatable has become more so?" She didn't wait for him to answer. "Frankly, I can't understand you lately. For weeks now you've been acting like a different person, like someone who's carrying the world on his shoulders. Are you getting merger pressure you haven't told any of us about? If you are, I think I have a right to know."

Mangas ran his hand along the back of his neck. "No," he finally admitted. "It isn't the merger that's been on my mind lately. Actually, we're getting along even better that way than I had dared to hope. I'm still convinced we're going to win that one...or die trying." A mirthless laugh punctuated the afterthought.

He walked back around the desk and sat down. He had avoided being with Barbara, had actually gone out of his way to keep from seeing her for almost a month. He knew it wasn't fair. There was no way she could know that just catching a glimpse of her as they passed each other in a hallway brought incredibly painful memories that usually kept him from getting any work done for the rest of the day. Since his return from Colorado Springs, Barbara had become a link to Lenore for him. An excruciating link. A constant reminder of someone he desperately wanted to forget.

Barbara leaned forward. "Then what is it, Mangas? It's obvious something's bothering you. Not only do the circles around your eyes get darker every time I see you—you're even grumpier than usual when something doesn't go just right. In short, you're not the same man I used to stay up with all night in a drafty old warehouse. You used to be fun to be around at least once in a while.''

Of all his friends and associates, Barbara Arden probably knew him better than anyone else. Partially because they had known each other so long and had gone through so much together, and partially because she was who she was, a person who cared deeply about her friends. Mangas had always maintained she had missed her calling, saying she would have made an outstanding saleswoman. She had, in fact, done some selling in the early stages of Apache's growth when they had all worn multiple hats, but had claimed she hated it and would never do it again. And never had.

Short and stocky with mellowed red hair and freckles, she had a disarming smile. Mangas had seen her work out engineering problems that others had claimed impossible as if they were just a little tougher than homework assignments in Computer 1A. He gave her much of the credit for Apache's eventual success and the largest piece of the employee profit-sharing program.

''There's an old saying,'' she said softly as she watched him toy with a pencil, absently running it through his fingers in a repetitive motion, tapping first one end and then the other on top of the massive oak desk. ''Trouble shared is trouble halved.''

"So you think I should dump whatever it is that's bothering me on your shoulders, huh?"

"Something like that." She smiled encouragingly. "Just remember. I'm tougher than I look."

The understatement brought a responding smile. "Barbara, you're tougher than *I* look."

"So...."

Mangas swiveled his chair to the side and stared out the wall of windows directly across from him. With infinite patience Barbara waited. Finally, after several minutes had passed, he began. "Do you remember going to school with a woman named Lenore Randolph?"

"Of course. Even though I was two years ahead of her, we were good friends all through school. Regrettably, we haven't kept in touch, but I still think of her as one of my favorite people."

"I met her when I was in Colorado Springs." Long painful seconds passed in silence.

"And?"

He slowly went on, his voice a hushed monotone. "And fell in love with her."

Another gusty sigh came from Barbara. "I would never have guessed what it was that was bothering you, Mangas. I'm sorry. I should have been more sensitive. I suppose this means she's already married?"

"No."

"Then I don't understand."

"She's involved with someone I once knew."

"I'm surprised you let that stop you— No, I think a better word is stunned. I'm stunned you let anything stop you. He must be a hell of a friend."

"You *don't* understand, Barbara. This particular person and I go back a long way. Without boring you with the details, there is a deep mutual hatred between us that hasn't lessened in the decade since we last saw each other. If anything, the feeling has grown."

"Friendship I think I could grasp, but I can't even begin to comprehend why you would let hatred overpower love." Her voice expressed naive dismay.

Mangas winced. "It's a little more complicated than that. It involves behavior and motives on my part that I'm not too proud of."

Barbara fidgeted in her chair, finally kicking off her shoes and tucking her feet beneath her. "I want you to realize I don't really believe what I'm going to ask you, Mangas. But it's something I have to know before we go any further." She cleared her throat. "It doesn't bother you that this other person knew Lenore...." She frowned. "Hell, why mince words? It doesn't bother you that she has slept with him, does it?"

"My immediate impulse is to deny such a thing is even possible, but that's a lie. If I now sincerely believed Lenore and...and this man were intimate, it would bother the hell out of me. But I'm convinced they're not now and that they never were. Even if they had been long-time lovers, it wouldn't change how I feel about her.''

"Then once again, I have to say I don't understand.''

"That's it. I don't understand, either. All I know anymore are feelings. Feelings and the knowledge that what drove me away from her has become so insignificant since then that I've cursed myself every day for being a fool.''

"So why don't you go back?'' Her voice rose in exasperation.

"Partially because of the way I left. Partially because every morning I expect to get up and discover my feelings are as transitory as I've tried to convince myself they are. And partially because I'm afraid of the depth of my love for her—afraid of what a powerful pervasive force it is. I've just about convinced myself it's better to end it now.''

"You can't honestly believe you'll eventually stop loving her as you might stop liking a brand of coffee, can you? Well, let me guarantee you that you won't. Not if you really love her as deeply as you think you do.'' Anger crept into her voice. "If you're ever lucky enough that the loss finally does become a dull ache, then you'll only shed tears for what might have been.''

Mangas swung his chair back around to stare

critically at Barbara, trying to fathom the deeper meaning behind her emotional outburst. He found her eyes sparkling with unshed tears.

"I once loved someone that way," she said quietly in answer to the unspoken question in Mangas's eyes. "You don't have to tell me about black hours of loneliness. But I wasn't given a choice, as you have been. The man I loved died in a war I had protested against and called him a fool for going to fight. I never had a chance to tell him how sorry I was or how much I cared for him or anything, ever again."

A single tear slid down her cheek. "I don't want you to think I don't love Peter. He is and has been more than I had dared to hope for. But it's not the same kind of love I once had, and never could be. I knew I could only survive that kind of loss, that kind of pain once in my life, so I chose warm and comfortable the second time around. I haven't ever regretted it, but every once in a while I feel a lingering trace of that love I once knew, and its loss still hurts terribly."

"Death. . . ."

"Only prevented me from doing something to change things. It didn't make the loss more painful, nor did it eventually make it easier to bear, because I knew he wasn't alive somewhere, that I couldn't have him regardless. It only made the loss irrevocable. . . unlike yours."

They were interrupted by the buzz of the intercom. Mangas reached over to depress the switch.

"Yes?"

"You wanted me to remind you not to keep Ms Arden past five o'clock, Mr. Taylor."

"Thank you." He was looking at Barbara as he spoke, and saw her eyebrows rise in question. "I don't want you to have any reason to quit. Apache needs you now more than ever." He stood up and walked around the desk. "Now go home and give that baby of yours a kiss for me."

"You're not getting rid of me that easily. Peter is a fantastic father. He and the baby will get along fine without me for a few hours." Mangas leaned against the corner of the desk, his long legs stretched out in front of him. "I think I've talked about this as much as I want to. Certainly a hell of a lot more than I planned to. Why don't we call it a night?"

Barbara's stare was unflinching as she nestled deeper into the chair. "Maybe you hadn't planned on telling me what was going on with you, but you did. By doing so you made me a part of it, and I'm not going to leave until we've at least come to a logical conclusion to the conversation."

Folding his arms across his chest just as stubbornly, Mangas stared back at the entrenched mound of humanity sitting in front of him. She would leave if he insisted. But if she did, he would be sending away the one person he could talk to about Lenore. And perhaps talking was the catharsis he needed. Perhaps talking would help put Lenore in proper perspective. Despite what Barbara had said, he didn't believe the memory of his brief affair would haunt him forever. He only needed a little more time. Just a little more.

Suddenly he knew the last thing he wanted to do right now was talk about Lenore while each breath he took felt labored with the pain of remembering her. "And what, in your opinion, would be a logical conclusion to this conversation?"

"I haven't made up my mind yet."

"Oh, I see," he grumbled. "Am I supposed to send out for dinner?"

Undaunted by his change in mood, she smirked mischievously. "Sounds good to me."

"Listen, Barbara, I have a meeting tonight, and—"

"If you'll recall, so do I. And don't try to feed me any garbage about needing time to prepare for it. I happen to know you're only there to observe." She picked a piece of lint off her navy blue skirt. Swiftly, in a softened voice and without any warning, she attacked. "Tell me, does Lenore still wear her hair short and curly like mine?"

"Dammit, Barbara," he raged, "what are you trying to prove?"

"That you're lying to yourself. Go ahead. Try to convince me that my innocuous little question about a friend I haven't seen in years didn't hit you like a sledgehammer. It's written all over your face, Mangas. That stoic expression of yours tells me more than I need to know."

Glaring at her, he moved back around the desk. "Since when is my private life any concern of yours?"

"Aha! Your ultimate insult. You always try to hide behind an outdated coat of rusty armor. Do you really think you're going to drive me away by telling me it's none of my business? When did that ever stop me before? Besides, if you had sincerely felt that way, you would never have told me about Lenore in the first place. Now stop behaving like someone who's been condemned to live his life in solitary confinement and open up a little."

Long minutes passed with only the occasional sounds of people leaving the plant and heading for home interrupting the silence. Once again, staring out the bank of windows across from him as though he were lost in another world, Mangas finally spoke. "She wears her hair long now, in soft waves that brush her shoulders when she turns her head."

"Does she still seem like a coiled spring ready to take off at any minute?"

A tender private smile of remembrance

brought pain to his eyes. "The first time I saw her I thought of the newborn colts I used to care for when I worked on a ranch. The world was so magical to them. It held such promise, and they embraced it with such innocence."

"Is she successful?"

"Very close to being. Her talent is often diffused, since her work is forced through committee judgement and she's allowed herself to be convinced she needs that type of thing to survive. But her star is beginning to shine on its own—much to the chagrin of the men who head the company she works for. The contractors and their subs who have worked with her on various jobs give her a great deal of respect." He smiled. "Less than half the ones I talked to even bothered to preface their statements with, 'For a woman.'"

"It sounds as if you were checking up on her. Why?"

"The reasons sound so stupid and hollow now." He turned to glance at her. "And I don't care how much you badger me. I won't tell you what they were."

She laughed. "You sound a little like my five-year-old nephew, who told his mother through chocolate-covered lips that she could hang him up by his thumbs and make him walk a plank, but he still wouldn't be able to tell her how a bite had been taken out of the cake she'd baked for company."

"Thanks." He laughed in return. "That certainly puts everything in proportion. But I'm not sure whether you're trying to tell me that my behavior or my motives are childish."

"Since you haven't told me enough about your motives for me to know, I reserve judgement. As for the behavior, I don't think children are capable of causing themselves such prolonged pain. They are usually more selfish and quicker to find a way out of their misery."

"If there were a way out, Barbara," he murmured, "I would welcome it with all my heart." He paused, then went on as though she weren't there. "Sometimes, in the blackness of the night, when I try to look forward to a life without Lenore, it seems like no life at all...."

CHAPTER TEN

LENORE MADE ONE MORE QUICK TRIP through the bathroom cabinet to make sure she hadn't forgotten any of the paraphernalia she would need to keep herself presentable during her week and a half in Aspen. Knowing there were plenty of stores where she could pick up anything she might leave behind didn't help. Somehow logic never gave her the peace of mind careful packing did.

The thought of spending time away from Colorado Springs and the constant reminders of Mangas had developed more and more appeal as the time to leave drew nearer. She had discovered that the "favor" Adrian had mentioned weeks ago involved having her stay at his home in Aspen while she worked with the contractor on the condominiums. The trip turned out to have a special unanticipated appeal. When Adrian had first approached her with the idea, she had almost refused him. Then he had mentioned he was going to be in Europe the entire time she was to be in Aspen, and she had reconsidered. What had finally convinced her that it

was indeed only a favor he was asking—not
something she would one day find out had other
implications—was her realization that he had
approached the other architect on the project
with the same proposition.

A week and a half in country spectacular
enough to make anyone's problems seem insignificant, with only a few hours each morning
devoted to work and the rest of the day free to
spend exploring mountainsides, was just the
medicine she needed to heal her soul. She could
hardly wait to get started. The pain of Mangas's
leaving hadn't eased with time, as it was supposed to. Two months should have been long
enough to bring her some relief from the dull
ache she carried everywhere with her.

She closed the cabinet drawer and returned to
the bedroom. As she tucked a sweater she had
decided not to take back into the closet, a soft
knock on the front door distracted her.

Darn! The last thing she wanted right now
was a visit from her long-winded next-door
neighbor—the only one who ever ignored the
bell. For a second she considered pretending she
hadn't heard the summons. Then she relented,
knowing if the neighbor caught up with her later
on her way to the car, the explanation would
take twice as much time.

Prepared to launch into a rapid-fire mono-
logue as to why she couldn't visit, Lenore was
speechless when she opened the door and dis-

covered. . . Mangas on the step. He looked terrible. His once superb healthiness had been
replaced by a sickly pallor. His cheeks were deep
hollows sharply outlined by his jaw and cheekbones. A blue black stubble of beard made his
eyes seem even more haunted, as though he was
burning with fever.

"I'm sorry, Lenore," he said slowly. "I tried,
but I couldn't stay away."

A band suddenly tightened around her chest.
She struggled to take a breath. "I don't want
you here," she at last managed to say. *Oh, God,
help me,* she silently pleaded. *Help me to be
strong enough to turn him away.* An inner voice
commanded her to run. But her feet refused to
move. Her mind demanded she scream her rage
at the unbelievable pain he had inflicted on her
again by merely appearing at her door. But the
words refused to form. Incredibly, she realized
she also wanted to reach out and brush the wave
of hair back from his forehead, to try to ease the
weariness from his face with the touch of her
fingertips. But her arms were like lead weights
at her sides.

"Please," he said softly, his voice filled with
weariness, "let me come in and talk to you."
And softer yet, "Let me try to tell you how
much I love you."

How could he speak such words to her? How
could he reject her so brutally, and then expect her
to welcome him back so he could finish the job?

No! She wouldn't let him back into her life. She couldn't. Rebuilding her emotional balance was just too devastating a task.

"No," she finally breathed. "I think you probably said everything you had to say in your letter. You were right—we're not good for each other. It would be a mistake for us to. . . ." As if it were happening in slow motion, she saw him reach for her. There was plenty of time for her to escape, to step away from him or to simply turn aside. But her body didn't move. While her mind cried out that she didn't want him to touch her, her arms denied the words, creeping around his neck, as with a deep shuddering sigh he brought her to him and held her.

"No!" she sobbed over and over against the front of his shirt. "I don't want you back in my life. I want to forget you. I want to forget we ever met."

Gently Mangas picked her up and carried her into the living room, nudging the door shut with his foot. She had lost weight, he sadly noticed. Where she had been so beautifully rounded before she was now angular. Would he ever be able to make up for what he had done to her? Were there words enough to tell her how sorry he was? He had never before spoken aloud the things he knew he must tell her if she were to understand him and why he had abandoned her, even though he loved her. Could he now?

A compelling love story of mystery and intrigue... conflicts and jealousies... and a forbidden love that threatens to shatter the lives of all involved with the aristocratic Lopez family.

⌐Mail this card today for your FREE gifts.

TAKE THIS BOOK
AND TOTE BAG FREE!

Mail to: **SUPERROMANCE**
2504 W. Southern Avenue, Tempe, Arizona 85282

YES, please send me FREE and without any obligation, my SUPERROMANCE novel, *Love Beyond Desire*. If you do not hear from me after I have examined my FREE book, please send me the 4 new SUPERROMANCE books every month as soon as they come off the press. I understand that I will be billed only $2.50 per book (total $10.00). There are no shipping and handling or any other hidden charges. There is no minimum number of books that I have to purchase. In fact, I may cancel this arrangement at any time. *Love Beyond Desire* **and the** tote bag **are mine to keep as** FREE **gifts even if I do not buy any additional books.**

134 CIS KAKV

Name	(Please Print)

Address	Apt. No.

City

State	Zip

Signature   (If under 18, parent or guardian must sign.)

This offer is limited to one order per household and not valid to present subscribers. We reserve the right to exercise discretion in granting membership. If price changes are necessary you will be notified. Offer expires December 31, 1984.

PRINTED IN U.S.A.

SUPERROMANCE ™

EXTRA BONUS
MAIL YOUR ORDER
TODAY AND GET A
FREE TOTE BAG
FROM SUPERROMANCE.

◄ Mail this card today for your FREE gifts.

Mangas sat down in the same corner of the sofa where Lenore had sat two months earlier after reading his letter. Almost immediately she tried to move off his lap. He tightened his grip around her waist. "Stay with me," he pleaded. "I need to be able to touch you, to feel you beside me, while I talk to you."

"That's exactly what I don't want you to do," Lenore said as she defiantly shifted away from him and stood up. She paced the short distance between the sofa and the fireplace.

"I don't know how or why it happened," she went on, "but I would be an idiot to deny that for a brief moment, a long time ago, there was something between us." A brittle laugh seemed to mock her words. "Thank God it was only physical. I pity the woman who ever lets herself get emotionally involved with you, Mangas Taylor. Unless, of course, she's the type who enjoys thoughtless self-centered men. But just in case you haven't noticed, I'm most definitely not that type. The one attraction you held for me is gone. We have nothing in common anymore."

Her chin rose slightly as she planted her hands on her hips. "Now get out of here," she said, trying to hide the tiny tremble in her lower lip. "Everything we have to say to each other has been said."

"We have a lifetime of words left to say to each other, Lenore," he said, his voice gentle but as unyielding as hers had been. Leaning forward, his elbows on his knees, he rubbed his burning eyes. "It's new to me," he began. "Although it's become a thought as familiar as the feeling it produces, I'm afraid I'm still going to sound a little awkward saying it aloud...." He glanced up to see her staring at him intently, a look of puzzlement on her face as she waited for his next words. "I love you," he finally, simply stated.

Sudden unbidden tears made her eyes sparkle. "Damn you," she gasped.

"I love you," he repeated softly. "I know now that it's something I'll never stop saying or feeling, Lenore." He held out his hand to her.

"Damn you...." Her voice had become a hoarse whisper. Almost as if she had no other choice, her hand stole over to his. Slowly he took it, closing his fingers around hers in a touch so loving, it made her catch her breath. He stood up and moved to her side, reaching out with his free hand to tuck a strand of hair behind her ear.

"You're wrong, Lenore. It wasn't just something physical between us. If for some reason we could never make love to each other again, I know I would still feel the same toward you as I do now. I won't deny what we shared two months ago gave me a pleasure I have never had with anyone else, but the feelings I have for you go so very much deeper than that."

She felt herself swaying toward him as the words she had ached to hear drew her like a magnet. Then, remembering the pain he was also capable of inflicting, she forcefully resisted the pull.

"Oh?" she demanded. "And when did you first discover this wondrous feeling? As you wrote your tender parting message? Perhaps as you tucked it in the doorframe?" Pulling her hand from his, she bit her now obviously trembling lip and turned to walk away.

Mangas grasped her shoulder, forcing her to look at him. She stopped struggling when she saw how his eyes pleaded with her to listen. "Actually it was the night before I wrote the note," he admitted with obvious pain.

She caught her breath in surprise. "That's what you meant when you said we affected each other in ways that weren't good for either of us?" Her eyes grew wide with disbelief. "What could you possibly have thought that loving me would do to you? Did you think me a Circe? A Medusa?"

"Did I think you an evil enchantress? My God, yes! What else could explain the way I felt? But that wasn't what drove me away. What made me leave was knowing how loving you would change my life forever."

She was dumbfounded. How strange that she hadn't guessed he'd been driven by the same fears that had driven her. "And now? Are you telling me something has made you change your mind?'' she hesitantly asked as she looked into the deep blue of his eyes, seeking her answer there as much as in the words he would use.

''Now I know that no matter what I do, no matter how strongly I try to deny it, my life is incomplete without you. You made me see there had always been something absent. It took some time to realize that I might strive to convince myself that what was missing wasn't important...but I would never succeed.'' His hand touched her cheek. ''Even though you've never been inside my home, the past two months the rooms somehow seemed empty without you there. I found myself reaching for you in a bed you had never shared with me.'' He smiled gently. ''In the evening, I would stand on the redwood deck that goes around the back of the house and watch the sunset behind the Santa Cruz mountains, then turn to go in and be surprised you weren't there to accompany me.''

The pain and hurt melted from her heart, taking with them the anger she had used to deny them. But what refused to leave was the fear of being hurt, should she allow herself to believe him.

As if reading her thoughts, he moved his fingertip to her lips to stop her from speaking. ''Shh,'' he whispered. ''You don't have to tell me—I know. Trust is something that, once destroyed, has to be reearned. That's why I've come. I will spend as much time as it takes to regain your faith, so that when you give me your love it will be without reservation.

"But one thing you must believe first. What I offer you, I have never given to another person. No one knows who I am or where I come from. My background is simply something I've never been able to share. Even now, as much as I love you, sharing it with you will be hard for me, and I will probably do it poorly...." He stopped and looked to her for understanding. Yet before she could answer him, he went on. "Even though it will be hard for me, I have to tell you. It's the only way I know of to make you a true part of me. But not now.... If I tell you tonight it won't be the way I want to tell you. My mind is like a sieve.... Only my love for you is big enough for me to grasp and hold." His eyes burned expressively. "My life would be empty without you." Lenore reached up to touch his face. "I'm rambling, aren't I?" he murmured with a smile.

She ran the tips of her fingers over the coarse stubble on his chin, then lightly traced the tiny lines at the corners of his eyes. Her own eyes sparkled with unshed tears as her hands went to the back of his head to pull him to her. She answered him in the best way she knew.

For an instant, the kiss they shared was softly hesitant, as if both of them were unsure of their welcome. Then, when Mangas felt Lenore's lips part beneath his, a deep moan, eloquent in its implications, vibrated his chest. He crushed her to him, imprinting his desperate need in the way he held her. Finally forcing himself to break the kiss and to be content with holding her, Mangas buried his face in her hair.

Breathing deeply of the poignantly remembered fragrance of sweet herbs, he swayed as he was struck by the memory of her hair tickling him as they made love. His stomach knotted with the force of his desire. Knowing he couldn't fight that desire with Lenore in his arms, he held her away from him. "I think we'd better find something else to do. My resistence is all but gone."

"Mangas...." The way she said his name, it became a verbal caress that washed through him like a warm wave. "I would not say no...."

He let his hand slide down her arm. "I know. And if I didn't feel our future depended on what happens between us now, I would make love to you until you were numb from pleasure and begged me to stop." His fingers touched her wrist, then clasped hers. "I want you more than I thought it was possible to want anyone. But more important than anything else right now is building something between us that will last forever. If that means waiting, I'll wait." He brought her hand to his lips and kissed the palm.

"I wish I could tell you that you were wrong," she whispered. "But as much as my body cries out for you to make love to me, part of me is holding back."

They looked into each other's eyes; understanding passed between them. They would start again, at the beginning, and their love would become indestructible. Tremulously she reached up to touch his face, and for the first time felt the fever of his fatigue. She shook her head in admonishment, smiling sadly. "Come over here. Sit down and tell me why you came courting looking so terrible."

When they were once more settled on the sofa, this time with Lenore lying comfortably across Mangas's lap, he answered her. "I took off from work early yesterday... I was halfway there when the thought of facing an empty house became unbearable.... Here I am."

"You left yesterday? You drove fourteen hundred miles without stopping?"

He smiled. "It took me two months to make up my mind to come, but once I finally did, I didn't want anything to delay me."

"Did you at least stop to eat?"

"I wasn't hungry."

Lenore stared at him. More eloquently than words, his actions told her how desperately he'd missed her. She leaned her head against his shoulder. "Even though you look like hell and it was a terribly stupid thing to do, I'm so very glad you didn't stop. If you had, I wouldn't have been here when you arrived." The thought made her feel rather ill. "Another ten minutes and I would have been gone."

He pulled her closer. "Things like this could have me believing in fate." He lightly kissed the top of her head. "And where would I have had to go to find you?"

"Aspen. Ever been there?"

A small private smile gently curved his mouth. "No, my love, I've never been to Aspen. I'm afraid it was a little rich for my blood when I lived in Colorado. It was on the bottom of my list of 'must sees.'"

"And now?"

"It seems it has suddenly acquired a compelling charm. Why is it we're going, if I might ask?"

"A group of condominiums I designed are under construction, and I have some work to do with the contractor. That will only take a few hours each morning. I'll have the rest of the day free."

"Sounds promising...."

Lenore sat up so she could look at him. "Can you come? Do you have the time?"

He stared at her for what seemed an eternity before answering. "I told you I would take the time. There is nothing in my life as important as you are."

They loaded Lenore's luggage into her car,

which was larger, deciding to wait until they reached Aspen to go shopping for Mangas. She drove the winding roads to the resort, while Mangas valiantly but futilely tried to stay awake to keep her company. Gritting her teeth as usual, she traveled the narrow steep climb over Independence Pass, and as usual, mentally kicked herself for not taking the longer but less-daring northern route. The blackness of early morning greeted them when they finally reached Adrian's house. Mangas came instantly awake when she turned off the softly clacking engine of her Mercedes diesel.

He quickly looked around to get his bearings before glancing back to her. "I'm sorry, Lenore. I didn't mean to pass out. I'll make it up to you."

"That's all right. Anyone who drives almost halfway across a continent to see me can do no wrong." She smiled warmly, murmuring, "I'm putty in his hands."

The deep clefts she remembered so well appeared in his cheeks as a rakish smile lit his face. "Putty is most definitely not the word I would use."

Sudden warmth coursed through her, accompanied by memories that made her shiver. "I certainly hope this celibacy you've chosen for us to adopt is going to be a short-lived thing."

He leaned over and kissed her with obviously

restrained passion. "If you only knew how impossible you make it for me when you say things like that."

Reaching for him to renew and deepen their kiss, Lenore said, "Remember, this wasn't my idea—at least not solely."

"Are you trying to tell me now that you don't agree?"

"When I feel like I do right now, I haven't a rational bone in my body. All I know for sure is how much I want you to make love to me."

He cradled her chin in his hand, gently. "When the time is right."

A quick kiss on the end of her nose let Lenore know Mangas's moment of vulnerability had passed, that he was in complete control again. Letting out a pent-up sigh of frustration, she left the car and headed for the house. Lights cleverly hidden in the shrubs lining the walkway made the short climb easy even in the blackness of night. Adrian obviously had a caretaker, she noted absently. Not only were the plants trimmed—the driveway and walks had been freshly swept. How had she got the impression it had been months since anyone had been here?

The key slid easily into the lock. The heavy door opened with only a light nudge. Quickly she went to the closet and punched the series of numbers Adrian had given her to shut off the alarm. Mangas followed her into the hallway, a suitcase in each hand. "Nice," he commented as he looked around the impeccably decorated living room. "Is this a company house?"

"You've got to be kidding. When old M., L. & M. sends someone up here, the lowly employee stays in an econo motel." She walked through the deeply carpeted sunken living room, indicating Mangas should follow her. "This place belongs to a friend of mine, who also happens to own the condominiums I'll be working on. When he found out I was headed this way, he asked me to stay here as a favor. Some favor, huh? He wanted to make sure everything is still working all right before the snows set in. He doesn't get a chance to come here very often anymore, so he grabs anyone he finds is headed this way." Turning to make sure he was still following her, Lenore was startled to see a scowl on Mangas's face. She shook her head in disbelief. "If you're thinking what I think you're thinking...well, don't."

The scowl turned to a look of puzzlement. "What did you say?"

Embarrassed, Lenore realized she'd misinterpreted Mangas's expression. He had obviously been lost in a world of his own. "Never mind. It isn't worth repeating." She stopped and leaned against the oak railing of the staircase. "We have a slight problem. There's only one bedroom."

Mangas glanced up the stairs. They led to an open loft. "And I suppose that's it?"

She nodded.

He turned and looked more closely at the living room, his eyes coming to rest on the huge U-shaped sectional sofa that sat in front of the floor-to-ceiling, brick-and-stone fireplace. "The couch looks comfortable enough."

"Mangas, I . . . ."

He smiled at her obvious discomfort. "Stop worrying. Believe me, I've slept in worse places." Passing her on the stairway, he softly added, "I'll tell you about them sometime."

They found enough extra linen in an upstairs closet to convert the sofa into a moderately comfortable bed. When they were finished, Mangas walked Lenore to the stairs, where he took her into his arms. Standing on the first step, she was nearly as tall as him and could almost gaze directly into his eyes. She was startled by what she saw. Beyond the fatigue and obvious love radiating like a force field from him to settle over her, she thought she could also detect a glimmer of fear. As though reading her thoughts, he softly said, "I find I don't want to go to sleep. I'm afraid I'll wake up and discover this has been nothing but a cruel dream."

They were words of love—words that told her how much he'd missed her and how pervasively she had haunted his dreams. "Touch me, Mangas," she whispered. "See that I'm real."

With infinite tenderness he kissed her. "This is so new to me, this sharing of myself. Forgive me if I stumble."

Her fingers caressed the hair at the nape of his neck. "It isn't a path I'm familiar with, either." Their lips met again. "You know, Mangas, you don't have to sleep down here," she murmured against his mouth. "The bed upstairs is large enough that we could share it without ever touching each other."

"You give me credit for a lot of control I don't possess."

She was unable to deny his words as he possessively took her mouth, ending the teasing little kisses she had been giving him with a deep hungering one of his own. With a groan of frustration he pulled her arms from around his neck. "We should both go to bed, I think," he murmured indistinctly.

She opened her mouth as if to say something, but hesitated. The words were left unspoken. She had started to tell him she loved him but decided to wait for another time. Despite the few hours he had slept in the car, he looked exhausted, and she knew he wouldn't let her tell him something so important to them both, and then simply walk away. There would be time later—a lifetime. She blew him a kiss, turned and went up the stairs.

Mangas watched her leave and cursed himself for being a fool, for letting her go. When finally she disappeared, he went back to the sofa and began removing his clothes. Fatigue slowed his motions but failed to dull his mind. Although he attempted to bury them, Lenore's words echoed perversely in his thoughts. "This place belongs to a friend of mine...he asked me to stay here."

If only Mangas had been able to doubt who the friend happened to be. But the gleaming gold initials on the matched bar glasses had taken care of that, stripping away all possibility that the house belonged to anyone other than Adrian Winchester III. Would Adrian forever be a wedge between himself and Lenore, he raged. Would it ever be possible to truly dismiss the man from his life, as he so desperately wanted to do?

Mangas turned out the lights and settled his long frame onto the makeshift bed. It had taken every bit of his strength to stay in this house, not demand that they go somewhere, anywhere else. Forcing himself to lie calmly on his back, he tucked his arms beneath his head and stared at the ceiling. Lenore's softly faint shadow moved sensuously across the exposed beams as she readied herself for bed. His eyes followed her with poignant memories of the afternoon they had spent making love. When her arms went over her head to pull off her blouse, he caught his breath with the remembered beauty of her full breasts. His hands ached to touch their roundness, his mouth longed to caress the taut nipples, his mind cried out to once again hear her soft moans of pleasure, pleasure he had brought to her.

His jaw clenched with icy determination. He would not let Adrian destroy what he'd waited a lifetime to know. He must find a way to forget all that had happened before. All the bitterness and pain must be left behind. Yet how could he exorcise this demon that had lain sleeping in his heart for so many years—a demon that had awakened with such a black and demanding vengeance that he knew, if he wasn't excruciatingly careful, would destroy a love as powerful as the one he felt for Lenore.

Tomorrow they would begin to rebuild their relationship. He would find a way to say the words he'd never spoken to another person. He would give himself to Lenore, knowing there was no other way. Trusting would make the loving whole, whole and indestructible.

She leisurely finished getting ready for bed, as if she somehow knew Mangas watched and she wanted him to know what he had denied them both.

A deep burning need knotted his stomach as he watched, a need made worse by knowing she would eagerly welcome him if he but climbed the stairway separating them. With a groan of denial he turned away from the image, covering his eyes with his arm. Perhaps tomorrow would be the day that was right for them.

CHAPTER ELEVEN

LENORE AWOKE FROM A DEEP SLEEP to the smell of cooking bacon. She lay in bed for a moment, staring at the ceiling, trying to figure out not only where she was but also what was going on around her. The night before came back in a warm wave of happiness that washed over her, soul cleansing.

Without stopping to comb her hair, she pulled on her robe and bounded down the stairs. Rounding the corner to the kitchen, she pulled up abruptly at the sight that greeted her. Clothed in a pair of tan walking shorts and navy blue T-shirt, Mangas looked fresh scrubbed and incredibly handsome. "You're really here," she blurted out.

He looked up from the eggs he'd been cracking into a bowl and smiled. "That's supposed to be my line, remember?"

She smiled, too. "I remember." Noticing the still-unpacked bags of groceries on the table, she automatically looked down at her arm, where her watch usually was. "What time is it?" But before he could answer she added, "How long have you been up?"

"It's a little before nine, I've been up a couple of hours, and before you ask, I found an all-night grocery that happened to carry a remarkably snappy selection of clothing."

Suddenly aware of her disheveled appearance, she tried to comb her hair into some kind of order with her fingers. Wiping his hands on a towel, Mangas walked over to where she stood. Staring at her, he laced his own hands in the golden brown tangle of her hair, then gently clasped the back of her head and drew her against him. His tender kiss made her forget her stomach had been demanding nourishment only moments before. Now all she could think about was the more immediate hunger he had aroused. She settled herself into the inviting plains of his body, smiling in triumph at his instantaneous response. His hands slipped down the curves of her back to cup her buttocks and press her more intimately against him.

When, with a final quick kiss, he released her and returned to the stove to check the sizzling bacon, she planted her hands on her hips and glared at him. "Just how long is this going to go on?" she demanded, frustration underlying her quick anger.

He feigned such a perfect look of innocence that she almost laughed despite herself. "Well?" she finally managed to add in the most exasperated tone she could muster. Before he turned to pour the bacon grease from the pan,

Lenore caught the look of seriousness that flashed across his face. Instead of going on with the meal preparation, he returned the pan to the stove and walked back to her. Leaning comfortably against the doorframe, he reached out and caught a tendril of her hair, letting it curl softly around his finger as he talked.

"I'm sorry if it seems like I've been playing games with you, but in spite of every vow I've made myself take, every good intention I tell myself I have, I can't keep away from you. The importance I've placed on becoming friends before we again become lovers dims every time I'm near you. I've almost convinced myself that because the sexual part of our relationship is so damn good, the other is certainly sure to follow—almost—" he chuckled "—but not quite." Softly he added, "More than anything I've ever wanted before, Lenore, I want to hear you tell me you love me. . . ."

Immediately she tried to tell him just how very much she already loved him, but he stopped her before she could utter a sound.

"But not until you truly know me. Not until you know everything about me will I be able to accept those words from you."

"Don't you know nothing could possibly change how I feel about you?"

He held her. "Oh, my beautiful naive Lenore. How I wish I could believe that."

Suddenly she realized there were no words she

could use that would convince him. She would have to wait for him to tell her what it was that haunted him so terribly. Then and only then could she proclaim her love and know he would be able to believe her.

She followed him back to the stove, where she stood behind him and wrapped her arms around his waist. "I hope you don't think that means I'm going to keep my distance." She could feel him quietly chuckle. Peeking past his shoulder, she nudged her chin against his arm. "I have the weekend free. Any suggestions?"

"There is everything you would ever want to take on a picnic in those paper bags on the table."

"Not everything," she said, a teasing lilt to her voice.

He laughed. "How do you *always* get two steps ahead of me?"

"It's my lascivious mind."

"Recently acquired, by any chance?"

"Possibly."

"Lenore...."

"Mmm...?"

"Would you mind removing your beautiful body from my backside before I burn your eggs?"

She stood on tiptoe and traced a moist line down his neck with the tip of her tongue. "Not at all," she whispered sweetly. "Burnt eggs

don't appeal to me." She nipped his shoulder.
"But then, neither do testy chefs."

AFTER BREAKFAST, Mangas did the dishes while
Lenore showered and dressed. They were in the
car and on their way to their picnic before the
sun had solidly claimed the day. When they
reached town and Main Street, where they
would have to decide whether they wanted to go
east or west, Lenore pointed left. She had decided Mangas should see some of the country they
had covered last night while he slept.

Almost an hour into their trip, a group of
abandoned cabins provided all the encouragement they needed to leave the car and go exploring. When they discovered a narrow, softly
gurgling stream, Mangas tested the water and
found it barely above freezing. He wedged the
bottle of wine he'd brought for their lunch between two of the stream's flat rocks and placed
their picnic supplies beside an accommodating
aspen. By the time they returned from their
hike, the shadows were beginning to fall in the
opposite direction and they were ravenous from
their wanderings. They ate the salami, cheese
and crackers Mangas had packed, saving the
grapes to enjoy with the wine as they lay back to
let the sun warm them.

Feeling comfortably full and lazy, Lenore
plucked a piece of lush green grass to chew on
and propped herself up on her elbows to stare at

Mangas. He had his back pressed against the stump of a pine tree that had been felled, possibly by lightning, several years earlier. She rolled over to him and laid her head in his lap, closing her eyes against the brilliant sun. "How could you possibly have gone to Winchester College and never taken the time to cross a couple of mountains to Aspen?" she asked conversationally.

"How did you know I went to Winchester?"

At the guarded tone in his voice, she shielded her eyes from the sun with her hand and looked up at him. "Simple deduction, my dear Taylor. Why else would you be at that horrible function where we met?"

"Yes," he said slowly. "Why else, indeed?"

"Well?" she prodded, not sensing his reluctance to go on.

"The first year I was at the college, I worked as a janitor during the night and sat in on any classes where I could find a willing professor during the day." His voice was a carefully controlled monotone. "When...when one of the school officials discovered what I was doing, he arranged a working scholarship for me so I would eventually be able to get a degree for all my efforts. After I became a registered student, I took the maximum number of units the school would allow per semester. Between studying and the janitorial work, there was little opportunity or any real desire to visit a place like Aspen."

"Your parents couldn't help out with any of your expenses?" It was a natural question, coming from someone who had grown up within the cocoon of a loving family.

"Perhaps if I had known who they were, I might have asked them.... But we never met." This was said as tonelessly, as dispassionately as the rest. "As far as I know, I'm the only living member of my family. My roots go back to the doorstep of St. Mel's Church in Taos, New Mexico." There was a long pause before he went on. When he spoke again it sounded as though he had drifted to another time, another place.

"I've been told I was found wrapped in a hand-woven Indian blanket with a piece of paper pinned to it. The note said the boy inside was Mangas Colorados Taylor. It asked that the person who found him take good care of him, because someday he would become as great a leader as his namesake."

Lenore was afraid to move, almost afraid to breath for fear it would shatter the fragile moment between them. Finally she quietly said the only thing she could. "What a sad thing for your mother to have to do."

"Perhaps...." He reached up and absently rubbed the back of his neck. "I've never been able to conclude whether it was sad or just an easy way out for her."

Lenore blanched.

"There have been a hundred times when I've thought it would make a difference if I could just decide one way or another, that it might make the path I walk easier. . . ."

He waited so long to speak again that Lenore grew afraid that he wouldn't go on. At last he did, but she had to strain to hear him. "When I was very young and constantly being shifted from one foster home to another, I used to pretend she was searching for me and would one day find me. She wouldn't show up on the day I had chosen—almost always I picked a holiday—so I would make up the most incredible stories about why she hadn't come."

His hand found and caressed Lenore's hair. She could feel him trying to reach out to her, but she could also sense how quickly he would pull back if she stumbled in her attempts to reach him. He had led her into a world she couldn't understand: abandonment, a childhood of broken dreams, foster homes... and, she suddenly realized, how much more difficult it must have been because he was so obviously part Indian. The prejudice he would have suffered growing up in the Southwest must have been crushing for a child all alone.

"But then all of that's past history," he went on. "None of it really matters anymore; it's all so far behind me."

Lenore tried to blink away the tears that stung

her eyes. "Are you trying to convince me it doesn't matter, or yourself?"

He stared at her as his hand caressed her cheek. In a whisper he said, "You're far too wise for me, Lenore. You easily see through the barriers that have always kept everyone else away."

As he touched her, she knew a terrible panic. Silently she pleaded for him to stop telling her about himself. Her heart ached too much at the thought of the lonely little boy he had been—of the lonely man he had become.

His hand moved to wipe away the tears that had formed at the corners of her eyes despite her attempts to keep them in check. With a quiet sob, she turned to her side so that she faced away from him. She couldn't let him see her cry—she knew it wasn't tears he wanted from her.

When he spoke again his voice had developed an icy edge. "I hope what you're feeling isn't pity."

The force and tone of his words made her shudder. It was as if the chilled water running beside them had suddenly overflowed the banks, engulfing. She sat up, pulling her legs to her chest and resting her forehead on her knees. "Pity isn't something I could ever feel where you're concerned," she said evenly. "If I had to put a label on what I'm feeling at this very minute, it would probably be fear. I've never known anyone as strong as you are, or as powerful. To overcome that kind of child-hood...to succeed in a business where so many others have failed.... Do you ever lose, Mangas?"

Suddenly he knew a fear of his own. A fear that he would never be able to share himself with anyone. He had let Lenore into a corner of himself where he had never permitted another person to go. Then the minute she got too close, he had reacted as he had with everyone else. For an instant he had been ready to crush her had she shown him too much compassion, too much understanding.

And with the inner knowledge of the type of man he was, he knew how easily she would be crushed. To him she seemed as vulnerable as a butterfly that had lived its entire life in a world of sunshine and flowers. She had never known the black storms that had marked his life. There was no shelter for someone like Lenore against the fury he could unleash, the fury he had so ef-fectively learned to use in self-protection. He closed his eyes against the image his thoughts had conjured up. He would rather die than hurt her. Rather live without her than watch her be destroyed because of the man he was.

He heard a movement and looked up to see Lenore gazing at him, a burning desire to under-stand what had just happened between them shining in her eyes.

As he gazed back at her, a deep conviction filled him. No, he would not give her up again. He could not. She was his one chance to finally know the world he had been a stranger to his entire lifetime. His one chance to become a person able to reach out to another. He wanted her; he ached for her. More than any of the other forces that had ever driven him, he longed to have her beside him always.

Wordlessly he reached for her, and she came to him and clung, burying her face in the curve of his shoulder. Neither of them moved nor noted the passage of time. It wasn't until a whispered breeze blew around them, causing the heart-shaped aspen leaves to tremble and brush a hurried kiss across Mangas's face, that he realized there were twin streams of moisture running down his cheeks. His own tears. He was astonished. Never in his memory had he ever cried.

Before he could wipe them away, Lenore roused herself and saw what he was doing. Capturing his hand, he brought hers to his mouth and gently kissed it. She moved so that she brought her leg over his and straddled him. How desperately she wanted to tell him she loved him. How effortlessly, how naturally the words formed in her mind. But not yet. As he had asked, she would wait until he was ready to hear them. Then she would never stop telling him. Holding his face with her hands, she kissed away the lingering traces of his tears.

He held her with infinite care; his hands barely brushed her back. Slowly his touch increased its pressure as her kisses lengthened and her breath began to come in short gasps. When she could stand the denial no longer and at last sought his mouth, he pulled her to him with a yearning that told her his defenses had been stripped. His emotions were naked before her.

He explored her mouth—tasting, touching, caressing in a way that made her loins ache with the need to have more of him. His hands moved to her hips to pull her nearer, to press her closer against the fire that burned in his own loins. From her hips, his hands moved to her thighs, gently stroking the highly sensitive flesh. With stunning ease his fingers slipped beneath the silky elastic band of her shorts. She gasped at the quick stab of pleasure his touch sent through her. Catching his hand, she stilled him.

"Don't do this to me if you intend to stop."

He studied her, looking for his answer in her eyes. "Do you really want me to make love to you here?" he asked huskily.

"Yes!" she breathed. "I want to make love with you here; I want to make love with you now."

"Lenore, if we do this now, it won't be the

way it should be for you, the way I want it to be.
I no longer have the power or the control—''

''It's about time—'' she interrupted him. Her
words were cut off when he covered her mouth
with his, and she understood what feelings she
had unleashed in him.

His kiss fiercely demanded that she respond
in kind. His hands lost their earlier hesitation,
roaming over her with a passion that swept
away her awareness of anything else. She welcomed the pent-up feelings he had waited to
lavish on her, welcomed *him* once they had removed their clothing and he was pressing her
into the softness of the blanket, covering her
body with his own.

It was nothing like the time they had come
together before. Their need was driving. There
was no pause for caresses or whispered words.
When Mangas would have slowed to be sure Lenore followed, she urged him on. Desiring him
as he desired her, with an intensity that erased
all timorousness, she kneaded and stroked him,
glorying in his answering sighs and moans of
pleasure.

When she was taken to the point where her
world consisted only of a breathless anticipation, she cried out Mangas's name. He stopped
and looked at her, pausing, too, on the brink,
while slowly, tenderly he kissed her, delaying
the final moment of pleasure for them both until the tension became explosive. Lenore reached

for him, running her hands down the tapered length of his waist before slipping onto the hills of his buttocks. Purposely she began to move her hips. The seductive, insistent rhythm elicited a deep moan of pleasure from Mangas. He moved inside her and intimately touched her, and this time he did not stop. He took her all the way, joining her in the loving culmination.

In the last moment of their lovemaking as they lay together gently caressing, breathing the sighs of fulfillment, a torturous thought accompanied the heart-swelling physical satisfaction for Mangas. Again, with blinding clarity, he saw that should he ever have to face life without Lenore, he would become a shell.

In knowing her, in loving her, he had changed his life irrevocably. By giving her the part of himself he had never shared with anyone else, he could never go back to the way he had been before he met her. He had not only opened himself to her with his revelations; he had been forced to relive his past in order to take her there.

Eventually he would tell her the rest. He would tell her how, when he turned eleven, he ran away from the last foster home he had been placed in, settling on an Apache reservation to try to understand who he was. How on his sixteenth birthday he was forced to accept that he didn't belong in the Apache world any more

than he had belonged out of it. It was then that
he began living within himself, never, except for
the doomed period with Jacquelyn Winchester,
allowing himself to believe there was any other
way.

Telling Lenore about the Winchesters and
how his own relationship with Adrian had led
him to her would be the hardest. Adrian, his
parents. . .and Jacquelyn. It had taken Mangas
years to understand why he had deluded himself
over Jacquelyn. In his young mind loneliness
had been a force more powerful than any other.
It had diminished in importance as he grew
older, losing its cutting edge. . .until Lenore.
But it hadn't been loneliness that had led him to
her, or even a desire for revenge, really. It had
been an instinctive need for love—that previous-
ly foreign currency in his life that he now
wanted to spend lavishly.

Shivering with the coolness of the afternoon,
Lenore cuddled closer to Mangas. He held her
for a moment longer, then playfully kissed the
tip of her nose. "Time to get dressed. As much
as I like trying, I can't quite keep all your lovely
body warm. The last thing I want is for you to
get sick."

"Like your women to be strong and healthy,
huh?"

"Especially when I have plans for them
later." He emphasized his words with a deep
lingering kiss. "Besides, if you're going to take

me to dinner tonight, I have to get to a store and buy some clothes.''

"I thought you took care of that this morning." She smiled as she sat up, winking at him over her shoulder. "And how did *I* wind up taking *you* to dinner?"

"Whenever I prepare breakfast and lunch, dinner's on you."

She laughed. "I guess that's fair."

"And while the grocery store's clothing selection was more than one would expect to find tucked between the oranges and canned hams, a few of the finer things were lacking—like slacks and ties."

"All right, all right. You've convinced me. I'll get dressed."

"You had better be quick about it," he growled in answer. "I'm beginning to change my mind."

"You had your chance, fella. Now you can just forget it." She jumped away from him when he reached for her, and it was another ten minutes before they began to get dressed.

THEY ARRIVED BACK IN ASPEN in time for Mangas to pick up enough clothing for the week. After putting the packages in the car, they went into Crowell's for ice-cream cones—double chocolate fudge for Lenore and strawberries and cream for Mangas. His arm resting across her shoulders, they walked the three blocks to the Aspen Music Festival ticket office and bought tickets for the coming Tuesday-night concert, the Friday-night ballet, as well as the Saturday performance of the play, *Cat on a Hot Tin Roof*. Leaving the office, Mangas looked over to Lenore and winked. "Want to bet we never use any of these?" he said in a seductive voice, handing the tickets to her.

Lenore could feel her face turning red. She glanced surreptitiously at him as they walked. "Is that a promise?" she asked coyly.

His delighted laugh made her smile. "Do you want it to be?"

As if talking to herself, she shook her head and answered. "I can't believe you're the same man who only this morning flatly refused to make love to me, even though I wantonly threw myself at him."

"This afternoon you effectively demonstrated the error of my ways. No one has ever accused me of being a slow learner."

She slipped her hand into his. "Oh, I'm so glad to hear that."

WHEN THEY RETURNED to the house, Mangas announced he was going to go running while Lenore took her shower. Anticipating that he would be gone for at least a half hour, she decided to take a bath instead. Adding a generous scoop of her bubble bath to the huge claw-foot tub, she filled it completely with hot water before easing herself in.

She scrunched down in the fragrant foam until it reached her chin, closing her eyes and letting the events of the past twenty-four hours float through her thoughts like large puffy white clouds in a summer sky. She smiled at the memory of the oath she had sworn a hundred times in the two months she and Mangas had been apart: under no circumstances would she ever let him back into her life. How easily she had capitulated. How desperately she had wanted to.

For them to fall in love was insanity. His life was in California, hers in Colorado. They had so much to decide, so many things to work out if their affair was to go on after Aspen. Even the thought that it might not brought a sadness that made her catch her breath. It was unthinkable that anything would come between them again. This time, their love would be strong enough. Wouldn't it? Surely her convictions were stronger than those of others who had loved before her, and yet lost that love. Had Samantha and Bob started their lives together with the same sureness?

What would her family say, she wondered, not to mention Paul Shaughnessy, Samantha, Mark. After her conversation with him the day Mangas left.... She grimaced. She would have to spend a great deal of time reassuring her brother that Mangas wasn't the man he appeared to be.

Marriage. What would she say if he asked her? A face-splitting grin marked her answer. She would say—yes! But then maybe she wouldn't wait for him to ask. Perhaps she would ask him. Without hesitation, she knew he would like that. He would take delight in such an obvious and demonstrative proclamation of her love.

A heaviness intruded on her thoughts as she remembered what Mangas had told her earlier that day about himself. How different it would be for any children they might have. Not only would they have two doting parents, they would be at the center of a far-reaching and loving family of grandparents, aunts, uncles. . . .

Startled out of her reverie by the sound of the door closing downstairs, Lenore realized she'd been daydreaming far longer than she'd intended. She wasn't even washed yet. Mangas called out to her, and she bit her lip, reluctant to admit she was still in the tub. Finally, when he called her again, she answered, "I'm taking a bath."

He bounded up the stairs to the door. "Do you mind if I come in and shower while you're finishing?" She glanced at the glass-enclosed shower stall across the room, realized she couldn't remember sharing a bathroom with anyone since college. Suddenly the idea sounded marvelous. "No, I don't mind at all."

Since she hadn't seen him leave, she was unprepared for the way he looked when he came in. Dressed only in nylon shorts and running shoes, he was once again the athlete she had admired while standing on the bridge at Winchester College. Only this time he was close enough for her to reach out and touch him. His presence was overpowering. It seemed impossible for any man to be so beautifully proportioned. The tawny color of his skin, the light sheen of perspiration emphasized the leanly muscled contours of his arms and thighs. His waist and hips seemed impossibly narrow in comparison to his shoulders, but Lenore knew that was only an illusion. How easily her arms held him, how comfortable she felt beside him because of her own height.

Groping in the shower to turn on the faucets, Mangas glanced over to Lenore while he waited for the water to get hot. "Want to tell me why you have that silly grin on your face?"

"I was just remembering the first time I saw you."

"You mean when you stood on the bridge and watched me run laps?"

Her mouth dropped open. "You saw me?"

"Why else do you think I left the trail and came down to run on the track?"

Lenore slipped deeper into the few remaining bubbles. "Will I never be able to have any secrets from you?"

"Never," he laughed as he stepped from his shoes and shorts into the shower.

Unwilling to immediately rouse herself enough to pick up the soap or washcloth, Lenore observed at her leisure as Mangas showered. Even in the confines of the tiled enclosure, he moved with an easy natural grace.

She snapped out of her reverie when she realized he had just shut off the water. Quickly reaching for her washcloth, she grabbed the soap and began to work up a rich lather. She was busily rinsing herself when Mangas came to stand beside her, wearing only a smile on his face and a towel wrapped around his waist.

"I promise I'll be ready in a minute," she vowed.

He knelt down so he was level with her. "I seriously doubt that," he said, his voice a deep caress. His finger traced the thin line of bubles covering her breasts like a shimmering gossamer gown.

"No, really. . . I can get ready incredibly fast when I set my mind to it."

"Or linger enticingly long, perhaps?" His finger dipped below the water and made a slow circle around the acutely sensitive areola.

Determined to resist his teasing, still she fought an almost overwhelming urge to move so that his wandering hand would come in contact with her nipple. "Now why would I want to do that?" she innocently asked.

His hand fleetingly brushed the tingling flesh that would have had him linger, then moved on to fan out lightly but possessively across her stomach. "Shall I show you?" he asked softly.

When his hand moved lower, she caught her breath, unable to hide the tension building inside her any longer. "I thought you said you wanted me to take you out to dinner," she gasped.

Before his mouth closed over hers, she heard him murmur, "Food for the body can be taken care of later...."

As if in answer to his comment, a low growl came from Lenore's stomach. Mangas broke the kiss and looked at her, his eyebrow humorously arched in question. "Can you do that at will?"

She laughed. "Ignore it." She whispered, "I have a demanding body, always insisting it be fed—" her hand came down to caress his waist, gently tugging at the tightly wrapped towel "— but certain appetites take precedence."

"This time it's going to be your stomach that wins out." He brushed a kiss across her forehead. "The next time we make love, beautiful Lenore, I don't want anything to interfere— not the weather, not work and most definitely not a hunger for food. I want us to spend an entire uninterrupted night together. I want you to know such sensual joy that you will forever crave my touch—such satisfaction that you will luxuriate in it. I want to touch and to kiss and to caress every inch of you. I want you to become as addicted to me as I have become to you.''

''And you think after telling me that, I'm going to calmly get dressed and go out to *dinner* with you?''

''As I said before, one appetite at a time, my love.'' He gently touched her lips with his own in a restrained kiss that was full of promise. ''Now show me how quickly you can get ready,'' he coaxed.

Torn between satisfying the need that consumed her and waiting for the night Mangas had promised, Lenore finally sighed her acceptance. Hastily she finished her bath and carefully fixed her hair and makeup, then went into the bedroom to inspect her wardrobe.

She chose to wear what she felt was the most beautiful dress she had ever owned. Smiling, she remembered wondering at the urge that had made her pack it. Could she have subconsciously been hoping Mangas would appear?

She ran her hand over the electric-blue crepe de chine creation with its gracefully flowing sleeves, low neckline and softly full skirt. It was a designer original she had spent a small fortune on last month. Foolishly, she had thought an obscenely self-indulgent act would make her forget Mangas, if only for a little while. Somehow it seemed fitting that she should wear it for him now.

After putting it on and checking herself one last time in the closet's full-length mirror, she stepped into her heels and slowly descended the staircase.

Mangas put aside the magazine he was reading, staring at her as she came into the room. A sense of unreality permeated him. Could this really be happening? After finally accepting that he would never have what others took for granted, Lenore had come into his life. If only he could tell her how much she meant to him, how her existence had filled him with joy. Would the depth of his feeling frighten her?

As she came up to him, he stood and welcomed her into his arms. Holding her tenderly, he pressed his lips to her temple. "You're the most beautiful woman I've ever known. Watching you come down the stairs took my breath away."

"I'm really not beautiful, but I love knowing you think I am."

"You can't sincerely believe that."

"My legs are too long...."

"I wouldn't have them any other way. They fit perfectly around my waist when I make love to you...."

"My eyes are too big...."

"Your eyes are the mirror to your inner spirit. They reflect who you are so completely. And the person I see through them is someone I've fallen deeply in love with."

So faintly he had to strain to hear, she said, "My mouth...."

"Was made to fit mine." He brushed his lips against hers. Gently he teased the corners, captured first her lower, then her upper lip between his own. The kiss deepened as his playful strokes ignited something stronger. He delved into the sweetness past her teeth, feeling her rising desire for him.

"I'm sorry," he said breathlessly as he broke the kiss. "I promised you we would go to dinner, and I'm having trouble making it to the door."

She smiled. "Dessert should always follow the meal." Slipping her arm through his, she walked with him out of the house.

CHAPTER TWELVE

THEY WENT to a tiny French restaurant at the foot of Aspen's main ski lift. The evening was warm and fragrant with the special lushness of summer that seems to come more dramatically to the Rocky Mountains than anywhere else. Wanting to enjoy the out-of-doors as well as the street musicians, Mangas requested a table on the terrace. The soft tones of superbly played chamber music surrounded them as they studied their menus.

"I assume the instrumentalists are from the music school?" Mangas asked conversationally.

"Probably," Lenore answered absently, not looking up from her menu. "I understand the school draws over eight hundred students every summer, and that almost all of them are as gifted as these people seem to be." Reaching a decision about what she would have for dinner, she laid the light green folder on the table. "The school's faculty and guest conductors read like a list of who's who in the music world. People come all the way up here from every corner of Colorado just to attend a single concert.''

The waiter arrived to take their order. Mangas and Lenore smiled at each other in private pleasure when they discovered they had chosen the same meal, steak in filo cooked medium well.

''And would *mademoiselle* or *monsieur* care for an appetizer?'' the waiter asked.

''Would you like to share an order of escargot?'' she asked.

He wondered what she would say if he went into greater detail about when he had first run away from the foster homes to live in the hills above the reservation. He had been terrified of being found and sent back, so in desperation had eaten too many creatures similar to escargot to ever think of consuming them again, no matter how elegantly prepared. ''Perhaps another time,'' he answered simply.

The waiter nodded and left with their order, promising to return quickly with their wine.

Lenore reached across the table to take Mangas's hand. She was suddenly as anxious to know as much about him as she could. She wanted to become a part of him—as he was now, as he had been before. ''Did you ever discover anything about the Indian leader you were named after?'' she gently inquired, trying to lead him back to the conversation they had started that afternoon.

Mangas looked down at their interlocked hands. If only the telling was easier, or unnecessary, he thought. "Mangas Colorados was a chief of the Chiricahua Apaches," he began. "In some of the books I've read he was also called Red Sleeve. Supposedly he was very tall, almost as tall as I am, and he was a noted war chief." His thumb moved slowly over the back of her hand as he spoke. "But then, the Chiricahua people were especially noted for their height and for their fierceness against the white man. Something they paid dearly for in the end. Today not a single reservation bears their name. Except for old movies, they are essentially a forgotten people."

"Do you think you're one of them? That perhaps that's why your mother used the name of one of their chiefs?"

His name had been a silver thread to the only past he had ever allowed himself to consider. Never spoken aloud to anyone, the dream was something so private, he had trouble answering Lenore's simple question. "I've considered it." There was a long pause before he slowly continued. "At least the name Mangas Colorados was a lot easier to trace than Taylor."

Lenore didn't know what to say to help him, so she just listened.

"When I left the reservation—" He looked up to see the surprise in her eyes and remembered he hadn't yet said anything to her about the years he'd spent with the Indians. "I'll tell you about it another time," he promised. "Anyway, when I left the reservation I went back to Taos to see if I could find anyone who had the last name of Taylor. There were many... too many. I don't know what I expected, but it never happened. I would search until I found someone who was exceptionally tall or who had blue eyes like mine, and I would follow them for a while. I'm sure I frightened a few of them in the process—a gangly, shabby-looking teenager with overly long hair haunting their footsteps—I can imagine what they thought.

"Since I didn't know what it was I was really looking for, it isn't very surprising I always came away disappointed."

The waiter appeared with their wine. When Mangas had sampled the Chardonnay and indicated his approval, the waiter finished pouring, then discreetly disappeared.

"I understand you weren't the principal's favorite child when you were in school," Mangas said, turning the conversation away from himself.

Lenore laughed. "Oh, you're wrong. I was his very favorite child—to send home. I was always in deep water for some infraction of the rules. How did you find out about that?"

"My secret," he said mysteriously.

She thought a minute. "Barbara! You've been talking to Barbara Arden. What else did she tell you? Not all of my dark past, I hope."

"Not enough. I never tire of hearing things about you."

Her eyes smiled at him over the rim of her glass as she raised it to him. "What a lovely thing to say."

He acknowledged her salute. "How did this terror of the Salinas Valley grow into such a respected and solid member of the business world?"

"In fifty words or less?"

"Take a hundred if you need them," he offered magnanimously.

"I'm still fighting. I've just learned to be more civilized about it. I learned there are ways to get what you want without being belligerent or too confrontational. I also learned to accept what I couldn't change." She laughed. "You have no idea what an accomplishment *that* was. My life became so much easier when I finally stopped trying to turn everyone in our community into card-carrying feminists. Now I can actually keep my temper as well as keep my mouth shut at family gatherings— when one of my ancient uncles starts proclaiming the world would be all right if women would just get back into the kitchen where they belong."

Mangas's eyebrows rose in skepticism, causing Lenore to laugh again.

"Well, *almost* keep my mouth shut. At least I don't get into screaming matches anymore. And my mother doesn't have to listen to as many lectures on what she did wrong when I was growing up." Wistfully she added, "At least I don't think she does. It's been so long since I've been back that I really don't know what's going on at home anymore."

"Well, let me fill you in. We lost a few beaches to storms last year, but they're coming back," he teased. "The real estate keeps shifting. Somedays, coming home to see whether I'm still living on a hilltop or have slipped into the valley below is just about the only excitement I get." Suddenly serious, he went on, "You're welcome to come home with me. . . ."

While he had made the invitation once before, casually over their first dinner, it was the first time since they'd gotten together again that either had hinted at anything beyond Aspen. Before she could answer, the waiter appeared with their French onion soup. He placed it before her, and Lenore inhaled deeply, her eyes closed in appreciative expectation. Delicately taking a spoonful of the hot liquid into her mouth, she discovered the taste lived up to its promise. "Do you suppose they would sell us some of this to take home for lunch tomorrow?" she asked between bites, their earlier conversation forgotten.

"I can't imagine anyone refusing you anything."

"Oh, how I wish that were true.... However, it seems to me that at times you do a pretty good job."

"Not true. Name it. Whatever it is, it's yours."

"Now?" she asked in a sexy whisper.

Mangas laughed aloud. The happy sound brought Lenore a flush of pleasure. "I fell right into that one. I always seem to forget the devil that lurks behind those angel eyes."

"That could be dangerous," she warned, a tiny seductive smile curving her mouth.

He studied her for a moment. "Do you know you have damn near destroyed any chance I had to make it through dinner without wanting to strip that erotic piece of material from your creamy body and make wild passionate love to you?"

Her eyes grew wide in horror. "You would really do that kind of thing—here?" she gasped. Not waiting for his reply, she dropped her outraged pose and became openly inviting. "Although now that I've had a moment to consider it, the idea does have some possibilities."

Mangas's eyes narrowed as he stared at her. Slowly he started to get up.

Lenore reached over to stop him. "I give up," she laughingly conceded. "This one goes to you." When he was seated again she took another sip of wine. "Just how far would you have

gone?" she asked, curious to find out whether
or not it had been necessary to yield quite so
easily.

The sparkle in his eyes sent a shiver down her
spine. "That's something you'll have to be content never knowing." His voice was husky with
meaning.

Determined not to be outdone, Lenore met
his gaze, her eyes conveying an unmistakable
message of her own. "Just in case the occasion
should ever arise," she said softly, "please be
careful with the dress. It cost me a small fortune."

Mangas shook his head in defeat. She was
more than a match for him—more of a woman, more of a friend, more of a companion
than he had hoped to ever find. He felt such
happiness he feared it could never continue.
People just weren't this lucky. It was as if a
soothsayer had suddenly appeared in the
darkest recesses of his mind and begun to chant
a prophecy of doom.

Lenore reached over to touch his hand.
"What's wrong?" she asked, concerned at the
change she saw in him.

"It's always been difficult for me to accept
what others seem to take for granted. I guess
you might say I'm always waiting for the other
shoe to drop."

Relieved it wasn't anything serious, Lenore
squeezed his hand. "Sometimes I just don't

know about you, Mangas Taylor. First you overwhelm me with flattery, then you liken me to an old shoe. But I'm tired of talking about me. I want to get back to you."

He glanced at his watch. "You have exactly two hours. Then the time for talking is over."

"You have the most delicious way of saying things."

"You're on the clock," he warned.

"Okay, okay. Tell me who taught you to play the piano."

"You mean play *at* the piano, don't you?"

Lenore clicked her tongue, chastising him. "Modesty doesn't become you."

He settled back in his chair, a deep eloquent sigh signaling his reluctant acceptance of the interrogation. "When I was around eight or nine, I stayed in one foster home for almost a year. It was the longest I ever stayed in any of them— mostly it was a matter of months, sometimes weeks. Anyway, the woman who ran the home, Mrs. Irene Caldicott, also taught piano. As long as I sat quietly, she would let me listen in on all the lessons. On evenings when her head didn't ache too badly, she let me use the piano to practice. Eventually the thought of having a piano of my own became a private symbol of success. It was the first thing I bought when I finally had a semipermanent place to live.

"I still have it . . . an old, secondhand upright

with a crazed varnish finish that I found advertised in the paper. Despite assurances to the contrary, I'm afraid to have it refinished in case it will affect the tone. It's unbelievably ugly, but the sounds it makes are beautful.'' *Was this really him, babbling on and on about an old piano no one else knew or would even care that he owned?*

"Do you ever play for people, or are you always as secretive as you were at the college?''

"I can't think of anyone else who even knows I play.''

"Why? You must know you're as good as most professionals. And I know you go to parties.''

"It's just something I've never felt like sharing with anyone. Besides,'' he added, a smile in his eyes, "I think your assessment of my ability is slightly prejudiced.''

She guessed that no matter what she said, he would consider her blinded by her feelings for him, so she didn't bother to argue. "Why is it I feel there isn't much you've ever shared with anyone?''

"There's never been anyone until you. . . .''

Was this the right time to tell him how much she loved him, she wondered. Was it the moment to tell him her heart was swollen with loving him, and that the feeling grew deeper and richer with every new thing she learned? No. He wouldn't want to hear something like that while they were dining in a restaurant. It shouldn't appear to be thrown into the conversation between courses of a meal, as if it were merely something else to say.

They declined dessert but lingered over espresso as Mangas answered Lenore's probing questions about Apache Computers. Excitement shone from his eyes as he relayed the struggle he and his small group of employees had gone through in the beginning.

"The big companies didn't want to become involved in small personal computers because they didn't want to compete with themselves." He shrugged expressively. "The field was wide open, and I walked in. Now, of course, they're rushing to catch up, and in the process knocking off all the small businesses created while they sat back twiddling their thumbs. So it's a matter of either absorbing someone who happens to be in their way, or putting a rope around the competitor's neck and pulling it tighter and tighter. Subtle sabotage, costly irritations—such as slowing down or cutting off suppliers or distributors, are effective. A company like Apache is painfully vulnerable. If the smallest component isn't shipped in time, the dominos fall for miles. If the best distributor in an area, or the one who is used to handling us, signs with someone else, we're stuck with finding a new way to get our product to market."

"And this is what's happening to you now?"

When he gave her a how-did-you-know-that look, Lenore explained, "A friend—as a matter of fact the architect you met on the roof, Paul Shaughnessy—told me about an article he'd read relating to your company."

"At the moment we're still at the stage of 'amiably' discussing the possibility of merger, which really means I sell, they take over, and either I get the hell out and into something else, or I accept a figurehead position in the newly formed conglomerate. I expect negotiations to break down anytime now, when they finally realize I'm just buying time to make Apache's position stronger for the battle that's coming."

"How will you fight them?"

"The only way possible. Apache has to grow big enough that we can offer deals as sweet, not only to the customers but to the dealers, even if it means operating at a loss for a while. It will put us on a fine edge. We'll either stay upright or fall on our faces."

"And since Apache is privately owned," she surmised, "that translates into Mangas Taylor could lose everything."

"It's a possibility, but not one I'm dwelling on."

Lenore felt drained of questions. She was stunned by just this glimmer of understanding of what was happening to Mangas and Apache Computers. She wanted to help, and the realization that there was nothing she could do was a gnawing frustration. Slowly she shook her head. "You've given me too much to think about—believe it or not, I've run out of questions."

"Then let's walk down to where the musicians are playing and express our appreciation."

"That's a marvelous idea."

They talked as they strolled hand in hand down the center of the street, which had been closed to traffic and brick-lined to make a pedestrian thoroughfare.

For the first time in her life Lenore told someone about her mother. Mangas listened to her impassioned speech about the tragic waste of her mother's talent, asking a question when he felt she needed one to go on, but otherwise listening quietly and carefully to what she said. Realizing how much she was unconsciously revealing of herself, he at last fully understood why she had fought coming to him so fiercely in the beginning.

Lost in sharing yet another part of herself, Lenore hardly noticed the buildings they passed, their facades, a crazy mixture of Victorian and early Western, the lanterns and shrubs with benches around them reminiscent of an earlier slower time, the musicians on the corners. The combined impression was rustically charming, encouraging Aspen's many other visitors to linger after their evening meals.

Mangas easily found their particular musicians. After listening to them a while longer, he added his contribution, dropping the neatly folded bills into a decrepit-looking cello case.

Farther down the street, they were drawn to the haunting refrains of a softly strummed guitar. A young woman, dressed in a peasant blouse and skirt, sat on a high wooden stool, playing as though lost in a world of her own. The song was obviously one of love—love shared, love celebrated. As they listened she looked up from her guitar and smiled at them. Suddenly it was as if she played only for them, understanding how appropriate it was to do so.

When she finished and the applause had died down, Lenore and Mangas thanked her before moving through the crowd back to the quieter section of the street. They stopped a few minutes later to look into a shop's display case. Catching Lenore's gaze in the reflection of the window, Mangas murmured to her image, ''I can hardly move anymore with wanting you.''

Her hand came up to touch the cool glass where his face shone back to her. ''I thought I was the only one,'' she breathed. ''You seemed to be in such control.''

''Only an illusion, my love. Only an illusion. . . .''

ALTHOUGH IT TOOK less than fifteen minutes, the ride home seemed agonizingly long. When their hands touched over the console, it was as if an electric current passed between them. There were no words spoken; none were needed. All they could possibly say to each other was expressed in their eyes, in the loving glances they exchanged.

After they arrived back at the house and parked the car, Mangas walked with Lenore to the door. His arm lay lightly across her shoulders in a casual yet familiar way. They were quietly preparing for, anxiously awaiting the evening's real beginning. Each ordinary movement that led them toward that beginning felt as though it was being conducted in slow motion. Finally the door was unlocked and closed and Lenore was at the closet disengaging the alarm. She turned back to the hallway and began to reach for the light. Mangas's hand stopped hers.

"Not one minute longer—not one second—will I wait to feel your body against mine," he vowed, his voice deep with his need for her. He pulled her to him, his arms enfolding her and repeating the message in the strength of his embrace. "Will I ever get enough of you?"

"Never. I am a drug you must forever take or you will—" Her words were lost as Mangas claimed her mouth with his own.

"I believe you," he murmured as he pressed his lips to her throat. "I believe you are an addiction. One that I will never be able to overcome. My only hope...my only relief will be living my life with you beside me.''

It was as if they both realized at the same time the implications of what he had said. For long moments they stared at each other in the moon-lit hallway. Finally Mangas broke the silence. "It was wrong for me to say that now. I know we have to first become friends, that we have to let some time pass. That will be the real judge of whether or not we should be together. But the words were out before I realized what I was say-ing. I am so full of loving you I can think of nothing else.''

Tenderly he touched her cheek, then her chin to bring her lips to his for a kiss. "Loving is new to me. I'm not sure of the rules or the proper etiquette. Forgive me any faux pas,'' he murmured. "Be patient with my desire to en-close you in my world and never let you leave.'' He kissed her again, the pressure infi-nitesimally stronger, the wanting a minute less restrained. "Teach me how I should love you, Lenore. Teach me so I can make your life what you have made mine. I want to bring you such joy. I want you to feel such happiness. I want you....''

"And *I* want you to stop talking and kiss me again,'' she said, pressing herself against him.

The crooked smile she had learned to love took on a rakish quality. "Is that all you want? Will a kiss satisfy your every desire?''

Her hand stole to his thigh. "Will it yours?" She felt the back of her dress opening and the sound of her zipper as the teeth released their grip.

"A kiss would be like a thimbleful of water thrown on a burning building. Don't you have anything else to offer?" He eased the dress from her shoulders and bent his head to nuzzle the exposed skin.

Her breath came more quickly, more shallowly. "What did you have in mind?" With persistent tugs, she freed his belt from its loops. Pulling his shirt from his pants, she began to press the buttons through their holes.

"For me or for you?" He caught her dress at her waist with one hand, unhooking her bra with the other.

She looked up at him and smiled. "Both."

Before answering, he deliberately draped her dress and bra over the love seat beside them, adding his jacket and shirt to the small collection of clothing. Moving over to sit on the arm of the white velvet sofa, he drew her with him and stood her between his outstretched legs. "At this particular moment, what I had in mind for you was something like this...."

Leaning forward, he took one of Lenore's already tingling nipples gently between his teeth, caressing the captured flesh with his tongue and evoking a pleasure that was close to pain. She looked down at his head, now cradled between her breasts, and became acutely aware of his hair softly brushing her skin. A feeling of such tenderness passed through her that she caught her breath in surprise. Laying her cheek against the top of his head, she entwined her fingers in his hair and held him closer. "And what was it you imagined for yourself?"

It seemed a long time before he answered. "Perhaps it was this...." He hesitantly reached up to take her hand in his, directing her until she intimately touched him.

"I want to learn how to please you, Mangas," she whispered. "I want to know how to give you the incredible pleasure you give me."

Slowly he shook his head in wonder, holding her face between his hands. "How could you possibly think you don't?"

Wordlessly they agreed it was time; wordlessly Mangas led Lenore up the stairs. He finished undressing her beside the bed. When her pale blue half-slip, her stockings and panties were discarded he stood back from her and purposely stared. "Your legs are a perfect length," he began deliberately. "Your eyes are filled with such welcome, such trust, such beauty that they give me grave doubts whether or not I'm good enough for you. And your mouth...to look at it as it is now, warmed from my kisses and slightly open as if asking for more, is seductive beyond words."

They stretched out languorously on the silken

sheets. "Shall I tell you about your breasts? Or how excited I get when I put my arms around you and know I'm holding a woman, one who is so beautifully rounded where I am flat...so nicely concave where I am rounded." His hand settled at her waist, massaging. "Perhaps if I told you about the softness of your inner thighs and how extraordinarily erotic they feel when pressed against my hips...."

She turned on her side to face him. "And shall I tell you how you affected me as I watched you run? What a lustful creature you created before we had even met?" The tip of her finger traced the outline of his mouth. "Would you like to hear how you move me now when you smile that crazy lopsided smile of yours? Or touch my hand? Or whisper my name?"

"Lenore...Lenore...Lenore," he murmured against her finger.

Her leg slid across his, and he reached down to pull it higher so that her thigh rested against his hip. Placing his hand lovingly on her hip, he began showering tender kisses on her eyelids, her nose, her chin. As he kissed her, his hand trailed to her waist, where he stroked the silken skin with the touch of a butterfly's wing. Without pressure, without demands, he overwhelmed her senses. Soon her body was exquisitely sensitized and responsive to his every contact. With infinite care he stroked her, massaging from her waist to her navel...then lower to the inviting warmth of her inner thighs. Soft sighs began to punctuate her breathing as Mangas spoke words of love against the fragrant hollow at the base of her throat.

And then, as if a gently rolling sea had suddenly turned stormy, Lenore felt a surge of desire sweep through her. She grew impatient with Mangas's lingering lovemaking. Her breasts became taut for his touch. A twisting want burned in her loins.

Still he kissed and touched, his hands coming into contact with nothing more intimate than the indentation at the top of her thighs as if unaware of the growing need that threatened to consume her. Instinctively she began to move against him, pressing her hips closer to his, her body more firmly against his seeking hand, finally reaching out to touch him. Her hand roamed across the plain of his stomach, and she felt as well as heard his sharp intake of breath. As she moved lower, the tender kisses he brushed on her mouth lengthened and deepened. When at last she again savored the feel of him, she realized he could hold back from her no longer.

Eagerly he took her mouth, imploring that she give as well as receive. His hand moved to her breast, cupping the firm flesh while rolling the erect nipple between his thumb and finger. The storm they had created washed over them.

They were lost in their world of sensation, devoured by waves of desire, knowing only the hunger that ruled them.

"Now, Mangas," she whispered huskily. "Love me now."

But still he waited, playing her until she was unbelievably taut with anticipation, with wanting him. Then, when she was sure she could take no more, he entered her.

Their union was as before, an instant of flaming passion tempered by loving actions. Lenore had begun to learn the little things that heightened Mangas's pleasure, and in doing them had discovered a joy beyond words. She was able to bring him such happiness.

And then, as if they were long-time and practiced lovers, they traveled the final path of their lovemaking together, ending in a pulsating culmination of ecstasy before drifting slowly back to the reality of their physical world.

Mangas stretched out beside her, drawing her into the shelter of his arms. Resting her head on his shoulder, her leg languidly lying across his, Lenore felt a contentment ripple through her like tiny waves from a pebble dropped in a pond.

Mangas's voice broke the silence. "You frighten me, Lenore."

Startled, she raised her head to look at him. The dim light accentuated his strong features, making her think once again of the haunting porcelain statue she'd seen in the lobby of the Broadmoor. "Why would you be afraid of me?"

"I reach a point where I think you mean as much to me as you possibly could—and I turn around to discover you've captured yet another part of my heart. Your importance has grown until I wonder how I would go on without you if something should ever happen to us."

She pressed her lips to his shoulder. The words were different, but the thought was the same one he had expressed to her before. Why, she wondered, was he so afraid of losing her? It hadn't been her who had left. And then a picture of a lonely little boy who had grown up seemingly abandoned by the world came to her mind.

"Have no fear, my darling. You'll never have to find out how you would get along without me," she easily promised. "It would take an earthquake to separate us. And this isn't earthquake country."

Responding to her lighter mood, he slid his hand underneath her chin and raised her face to meet his seeking mouth. "If you think a mere rumbling and yawning of the earth would keep me from you, you don't know how strong willed and determined I can be. No, my love. It would take a force stronger than nature to keep me from you."

Determined to completely destroy his pensiveness, she playfully ran her fingers across his ribs. "That sounds so 'Me Tarzan, you Jane,'" she teased. His appreciative laughter let her know she had succeeded.

"Well, I guess if I have the name," he growled, "I might as well play the game." Aggressively he turned her over and began to rain kisses over her face. Their lips met; she responded with an eagerness that made him pull back and stare down at her. "Just what did you have in mind, my wanton little witch?"

"As I recall, you promised me a night filled with sensual delight.... Surely you haven't forgotten."

Flat against the length of her, he grasped her hands and held them over her head. "You issue the most provocative challenges."

Her eyes widened in mock horror, while a smile tugged at the corners of her mouth. "Why, I would never want to toss down a gauntlet you wouldn't eagerly pick up."

With tender moist kisses, he began to trace a line down her throat. "A promise *is* a promise...."

His huskily spoken words sent a shiver of anticipation through her. "I think I remember something about 'every inch of my body.' Does that sound familiar to you?"

"Vaguely," he answered as he took her earlobe between his teeth. "Can you give me a few more details?"

Suddenly, as her words created graphic mental images of Mangas's promises, a hot flush of embarrassment brought an uncomfortable warmth to her neck and face. She was still too new and inexperienced in the gentle game of lovemaking—still too shy about her own body in front of him not to feel that perhaps she had gone too far. Intimately touching her with his hands was one thing. With his lips. . . . As if he could see in the dark, Mangas reacted to her sudden unease with a hearty laugh.

"So the lady went a little too far."

Instantly her chin rose a defiant notch. "As I recall, there was something about touching or stroking. . . or—" she swallowed to try to dislodge the lump in her throat "—or kissing."

"Ah, yes. Now I remember." With a fluid movement he turned her to her stomach and began to massage her shoulders. His large strong hands glided over her body with the ease of silk rubbing against satin. Muscles she hadn't realized existed responded to his touch, tensing, then deliciously relaxing.

Leaving her torso, he moved to her feet, kneading and squeezing until she felt the effects of too many years of high-heeled shoes disappear as if drawn out by a magic ointment. Next he moved to her calves, then to her knees, then to her thighs. With long sure strokes he pressed familiarly, closer to the burning core he had re-kindled with his exploring fingers.

Mangas finished massaging her with his hands. Again he returned to the now-familiar territory, remapping the contours of her body with his more sensitive lips. By the time he had rolled her over and started to gently knead her arms, Lenore was beginning to think she could take no more. When his hands went to her waist and started their journey upward, she was sure of it.

"Mangas," she breathed as she reached up to touch him, to bring him to her.

A wicked smile and gentle turning away of her hand were her only answer. Involuntarily she began to move against the pressure of his hands. A deep breath escaped as a pent-up sigh when he possessively cupped her breasts and began to caress them in slow circular motions, the friction hardening her nipples. Mangas took first one and then the other into his mouth, where his tongue did what his hands had done before. She moaned softly in reaction to the intense pleasure. Imperceptibly at first, her hips began to move, seeking a release from the building ache that grew more powerful with each passing moment.

"Mangas," she breathed again, her voice filled with wanting.

His mouth moved to the valley between her breasts, down to the smaller valley at the center of her stomach. With greater intensity, her hips picked up a timeless rhythm in answer to his own growing need. His hands, his mouth teased, yielded, demanded. A soft cry of welcome greeted him when finally he joined her and they once again traveled their now-familiar path of passionate release.

Afterward, when they lay wrapped in each other's arms, Lenore snuggled contentedly closer to kiss Mangas's cheek. "You are rapidly turning me into a sensual creature who lives only for your touch."

He opened one eye and peered at her. "Does that mean you're ready for me again?"

She laughed happily. "Give me a few more minutes to come down from the last sweep through the clouds."

"Mmm. . . what a beautiful image. I will forever picture us that way when I think of making love to you."

"The image is nothing compared to the beautiful experience."

He smiled. "Yes, it was, wasn't it."

Their conversation now drifted in shared thoughts, all inconsequential, all terribly important to lovers. The pauses grew into comfortable silences. Suddenly remembering she hadn't yet spoken the words aloud that she had wanted to all day, Lenore lightly kissed his chest from where she lay nestled in his arms. "I love you, Mangas Colorados Taylor," she said softly.

When he failed to answer, she raised her head to look at him to see why. His face reflected contentment and happiness even while he was lost to sleep. Lenore smiled, feeling a deep contentment of her own. There would be years and years ahead for her to tell him of her love. Gently she again pressed her lips to his chest. She would begin to tell him in the morning. What possible difference could a few hours make?

CHAPTER THIRTEEN

THE MORNING DAWNED full of sunshine and promise. Lenore stretched lazily beside an already awake Mangas, curling back into his side when she was finished. He kissed the top of her head.

"Good morning," he said. "You slept well, I trust."

"Like a hibernating bear. And you?"

"Like a log. It amazes me how well. I haven't shared a bed so comfortably with someone since I was eleven years old."

She ran her hand teasingly over his stomach. "Am I an improvement?"

He thought for a minute. "Seems to me my old partner didn't snore. Other than that—ouch!"

She had found just enough extra skin at his waist to grasp between her thumb and finger in a hard pinch. "I don't snore!"

"I'm not complaining," he said, trying to pacify her.

"I don't snore," she insisted, refusing to yield ground.

His answer was cut off by the chime of the doorbell. They looked at each other in question. Lenore shrugged. "I can't imagine who it might be."

Mangas went to the closet for his robe. As he was walking past the bed on his way to the door, Lenore laughingly stopped him. "We forgot to remove the tags."

He pulled them from his sleeve and tucked them in his pocket. Before starting down the stairs he turned and looked at her. "Don't go away."

"Fat chance."

Mangas was still smiling when he opened the front door—when his world was destroyed as completely as an egg in the hands of a one-year-old child. Standing on the other side of the threshold was Adrian Winchester. Wordlessly they stared at each other as surprise rapidly gave way to rekindled hatred.

"You. . ." Adrian sputtered. "What are *you* doing here?"

All the old feelings Mangas had thought had diminished since knowing Lenore rose to the surface in a swell of hostility that made his hands unconsciously clench into fists in the soft velour pockets of his robe. "Hello, Adrian," he said evenly, his tone contradicting his emotions.

"You bastard!" Adrian breathed. His face had started to turn a motley red. A lifetime of training in socially acceptable behavior failed him as he stood on the doorstep and unceremoniously shouted. "What in hell are you doing in my house?"

"I was in the neighborhood," Mangas answered softly.

Suddenly Adrian's eyes darted into the open doorway. While he stared into the space behind Mangas, his expression changed dramatically from puzzlement, to recognition, to fury. Mangas turned to see what had attracted his attention and discovered Lenore descending the stairs, her golden brown hair in tumbled disarray from sleep, a yawn distracting her from what was happening at the front door.

Mangas tried to step outside and close the door behind him, but Adrian hit the door with his hand and knocked it out of his grasp. "Leave her out of this," Mangas warned, his voice low and threatening.

But Adrian was like a man possessed. He either didn't hear or chose to ignore Mangas's words.

From somewhere close behind him, Mangas heard Lenore's startled gasp. "Adrian! What are you doing here? You're supposed to be in Europe."

Adrian's eyes swept the living room, lingering meaningfully on the carelessly discarded clothing lying across the back of the love seat. "You bitch!" he spat. "It's obvious to *me* what you're doing here. How long have you and this half-breed been playing brave and squaw? How long?'' he screamed.

Words of protest and anger flew into Lenore's mind but were lost before she could say them. Mangas had grabbed the front of Adrian's jacket and was shoving him back across the threshold.

"Get out of here, Winchester." Adrian looked back at the man who towered over him, fear stamping his features. And then as he stared, his expression changed from fear to one of stunned understanding. He looked like he had suddenly solved a vexing problem.

"You," he gasped. "It was you." Adrian staggered backward as though he'd been struck. "You're the bastard who gave Bingham the check." His eyes darted to Lenore. "And you were the one who timed it. You've been in on it together from the beginning. You let me think the college would be mine. You made sure I spent a small fortune on it and then snatched it away. You tried to make me look like a fool...."

"Adrian," Lenore began, then realized the futility of trying to talk to him as he was now. Again the words died before they were spoken.

He ignored her pleading voice and continued to back down the steps as he spoke, even in his anger shrinking from Mangas's menacing presence. Now standing on the sidewalk, he glared at them before he turned to walk away. Abruptly he turned back. "You're fired, Lenore!" he shouted in final spiteful triumph. "Go back to Colorado Springs. I don't want to see you near my condominiums." That time when he turned, he left.

Mangas shut the door and went to Lenore. "Let's get out of here," he said wearily. "I think I've put you through enough humiliation today without having to face him again should he decide to come back."

"Wait a minute." She moved away from his outstretched arm. "Do you understand what just happened?"

"Yes," he reluctantly admitted. "I wish to hell I didn't."

"Then tell me." Her voice had risen to a higher than normal pitch. It was the only thing that betrayed the frantic turmoil raging inside of her. "I certainly think I have a right to know."

"Not now," he answered more abruptly than he'd intended. "We'll discuss it in the car."

Unable to contain the emotions that tore through her any longer, Lenore reached out to grasp Mangas's sleeve as he tried to move past her. "The hell we will!" she shouted. "I've just lost control of one of the best projects I've ever handled, been called a bitch by a man who once called me a friend and been accused of things I can't even comprehend. And you tell me *you* understand everything that's happened. Well, why don't I?''

With a terrible sense of dread, Mangas admitted to himself that he had waited too long. An inner voice had warned him all along that his relationship with Adrian should have been the first thing he confessed to Lenore. But dammit, how could he have? He had feared she would turn away if she knew the truth, that once she discovered how he'd planned to use her, she would refuse to ever see him again. ''Lenore,'' he pleaded. ''Everything you say is right. You do deserve to know, but now isn't the best time to discuss it.''

Unshed tears of frustration and rage made her eyes sparkle. A flash of understanding made her catch her breath in surprise. ''You don't want to tell me because you're afraid of what I'll do if I find out.''

The truth of her words cut through him like a finely honed knife. His hands hung at his sides, open and empty in defeat as he softly conceded, ''You're right.''

''Mangas, what is it?'' she pleaded. ''Please tell me. It can't possibly be as bad as you think.''

It was futile to postpone what had to come. ''The reason I watched you at the college, the reason I pursued you afterward, was because I thought you were sleeping with Adrian. Cuckolding him seemed the ultimate revenge. I was using you, Lenore. For my own corrupt reasons, I was using you.''

She blinked. Her expression went blank, as if he had spoken to her in a foreign language. Then, as the words echoed through her mind and came to rest in unalterable form, a pain started to radiate through her chest. The pain took her breath away. Inanely she wondered if it were really possible for a heart to break. She looked at Mangas and could see her suffering reflected in his eyes as he witnessed her struggle. ''Why,'' she was finally able to whisper past the lump in her throat.

''I can't answer that anymore. None of the old reasons make any sense.''

But he must answer. Her heart cried out for an answer—something, anything, that would make the pain go away. ''What happened that made you hate *him* so much that you would do this to *me*?''

He started to reach for her but was unable to bring himself to touch her. He wanted to wipe away the tears streaming down her cheeks, but his hand refused to come in contact with her face. He wanted to take her in his arms, but his mind refused to let him. He would do anything, pay any price if only he could erase the hurt he saw in her eyes.

''The man at Winchester College I told you about yesterday, the one who sponsored me and arranged for the scholarship that saw me through school, was Adrian's father.'' He began slowly, desperately wishing he could have told her this at another time, another place. ''He was a quiet man who preferred the academic life to the industrial one he'd inherited. As soon as Adrian was old enough, his father turned everything over to him.

''Mr. Winchester also had another child, Jacquelyn. She was very much like her father and would come up to the college to get away from her mother and Adrian whenever she could.'' Mangas stopped talking, reaching up to rub the back of his neck. He was wrestling with the words and the memories they evoked. Another minute passed before he went on.

Although she seethed with frustration at the delay in the telling, Lenore waited silently for him to continue.

''Anyway—'' he shook his head resignedly, his hand falling back to his side ''—to make a long story short, we fell in love. Blissfully, stupidly, we made plans to get married. Even though they were extremely long-range plans, the minute Adrian found out about them he went into a rage. He came to where I was working at the time and meticulously outlined why I was an improper match for his sister, even going so far as to describe any children we might have as mongrels.''

Lenore blanched. She had heard Adrian make

offhand bigoted remarks in casual conversation and knew that Mangas was probably making less of an ugly scene.

"At the time, none of it bothered me too badly. I had had previous run-ins with Adrian at the school, and I knew his type so well that I had developed a thick skin. It wasn't until I arrived home that night and found Jacquelyn's letter that it began to sink in: she and I were not alike. She had listened to Adrian. He had convinced her that with my background, we would never be socially acceptable as a married couple in her beloved Southwest. She even parroted his sentiment that our children would be condemned to a life of misery. I believed at the time that Adrian had forced her to write the letter, if I could only see her, talk to her, everything would be all right." How hurt he must have been—how emotionlessly he told the story.

"I started hitchhiking to their house in Colorado Springs, and was arrested for vagrancy just outside the college gate. The sheriff of the small town—a town that owed so much to the college's continued support—held me just long enough for Jacquelyn to be packed off to Europe.

"It was during this time that I discovered the real reason why Adrian's and Jacquelyn's father chose to stay at Winchester College instead of in Colorado Springs. He was not only a quiet unassuming man; he was totally dominated and intimidated by his wife and Adrian. He lent me a sympathetic ear, but advised me not to even consider fighting them. He said there was no way I could win, that I should forget Jacquelyn and get on with my life. He even dropped hints I chose to ignore, suggesting Jacquelyn wasn't pining for me as I was for her. It took me several more miserable months before I really understood what he was trying to tell me." Mangas began to pace the short space between the stairs and the love seat, where Lenore had curled up into a tight ball as she listened.

"Since there was no way I could follow Jacquelyn to Europe, I decided I could wait until she came back to Colorado. My seasonal job ended and I suddenly discovered, thanks to the far-reaching Winchester influence, that I was virtually unemployable. The only places willing to hire me paid minimum wages."

A bitter smile, so different from the one she had come to love, slashed his mouth. "Adrian would show up periodically to watch me wash dishes and to remind me how foolish I had been to—as he put it—try to crawl out of the gutter and improve my social position on the backs of the Winchesters. He was one cocky bastard back then—not a great deal older than me, but so sure of his position and so confident I wouldn't do anything as stupid as trying to retaliate. So he methodically made my life hell."

Mangas paused. His own mocking laugh interrupted his revelations. Lenore felt the coldness of his laugh, bone deep as she had felt the icy water of the stream they had made love beside only the day before.

"In the strongest tradition of romantic literature, I hung on and waited for Jacquelyn to come back—that is, I hung on until Adrian pulled the perfect coup de grace. I was working the midnight to 8:00 A.M. shift, and he arrived with the morning papers. Without saying a word, he strolled across the room to where I was busing dishes and threw a section of the newspaper in front of me. Staring back at me was a picture of Jacquelyn and her new husband, smiling. The caption said they had recently returned from Europe.

"I left Colorado the next day and didn't see it again until the week I met you."

Lenore got up from the love seat and walked over to the stairs as if in a trance. She started to climb but found herself unable to expend the energy. She felt as if she'd been attacked by a giant bird of prey. All that remained was a desperate sense of self-protection that wouldn't allow her to think of Mangas or the pain he had suffered because of Adrian. She could only take so much. She was filled with the agony of Mangas's betrayal.

With growing intensity, as if coming out of a fog, she demanded, "And even after all of this time, you still hate him so much you wanted revenge against him? The years haven't dulled your anger even a little?'' How desperately she wanted to understand. ''When you discovered you still wanted revenge, wasn't taking the college land from him enough? I'm assuming Adrian was right . . . you are the mysterious benefactor?''

''Yes.''

''Wasn't that enough?'' She didn't trust her voice above a hoarse whisper. Tears she tried to keep from falling burned her eyes ''Did you have to use me, too?''

''It was. . . .'' He let out a sigh. There was no defense. ''No,'' he said as softly. ''I didn't have to use you. I had no right to use you.''

''Adrian was right,'' she concluded, losing her fight with the tears. ''You are a bastard. To cold-bloodedly use me, to actually plan to use me as you would a pawn on a chessboard—''

''Lenore, don't—''

''Don't what? Be hurt? Be angry? Don't what, Mangas?''

''Don't close the door between us.''

''How can I close something that was never really open?'' She pushed away the arms he had reached out to her and ran up the stairs

THE RIDE BACK to Colorado Springs was torture for both of them. Mangas drove, while Lenore stared unseeingly out the window. The silence became an ugly barrier between them that neither was able to surmount. When they arrived at Lenore's apartment and were parked in her carport, she immediately reached for the door handle. Mangas grabbed for her arm to stop her from leaving.

"We have to talk."

"What more is there to say?"

"I don't care what words we use. We have to find a way to settle what has come between us."

"There aren't enough words for that."

"Lenore, please...."

"All right," she said wearily. Somewhere in her heart she felt a flutter of hope that Mangas would say something that would make the hurt disappear, something that would let them go back to the way they'd been. Ruthlessly she shoved the hope aside. She would not play the fool again. Twice was enough; three times was unthinkable.

Mangas followed her into the apartment, setting the luggage beside the door. Lenore walked across the living room to open the drapes. When she turned back to look at him, her expression was guarded, her eyes cold. "Say what you have to say, Mangas. Then leave."

"I can't believe you would let go of what we have so easily."

"What we have?" she asked, her voice heavy with sarcasm. "Let's just go over what it is we have." She ticked the points off on her fingers.

"We have a relationship built on lies and deceit. We have a friendship founded on half-truths. We have a love affair based on fiction." Despite her promise to herself to remain calm, her voice began to rise. "We have as much in common as one of your computers and an abacus."

"And love?" he asked wistfully.

She turned to gaze out the window, hoping he hadn't seen the pain she knew had flashed through her eyes. "You can't love someone you're afraid of."

More than anything else she had said, these words brought a heaviness to his heart and an insidious eating away of his hope. "Why are you afraid of me?"

"Since we met I've been trying to convince myself that you're really no different from anyone else I've ever known. But it isn't so. I've tried to imagine what it would be like to go through what you did as a child . . . and then going on to find a way through college the way you did. And then . . . what happened with Adrian and Jacquelyn.

"How did you climb out of that hole and immediately start to build Apache Computers as if nothing had happened? I guess what I'm trying to say is, you've never needed anyone, Mangas, and I'm not like that. If I allowed myself to love you—" she spoke the lie as easily as the rest "—I would need you like I needed air to breath. Yet you wouldn't need me. That would eventually destroy me. I can't let that happen.'' She continued to stare out the window at her tiny patio, knowing if she turned to face Mangas he would see the lie she'd spoken. In hiding her own reaction, she missed seeing the effect of the blow she had struck him.

How could she be so wrong about him, he wondered. The love he had ached to give to someone as a child, the companionship he had denied himself all his life lest he become too vulnerable—both of these he had lavished on her. There was no way for him to protect himself this time. He had eagerly opened his heart to her, and it would not close. He would need her; he would suffer her loss, every moment of his life. ''I had hoped there would be time for us to come to know each other as friends, and that it would lead to a love that would last our lifetime. But I guess too much has happened. . . .''

''Yes,'' she murmured. ''We can't go back, and I don't want to go on.''

His shoulders slumped in defeat. ''Every instinct tells me to stay and fight but—I can't. You're wrong about me, Lenore, but I have to recognize that there are no words I can use to convince you of it. Tomorrow when you think of me, wonder also if it's possible that tied up in your fear of me isn't a little fear of yourself. Perhaps the real reason you left home and never went back was because you were afraid of what and who *you* are. From the discussions we've had, it seems to me that you feel everything and everyone in your background taught you women were supposed to be subservient to men. Are you so warped by that idea that you have made yourself believe that to love any man is to risk becoming nothing but his reflection?

"Is it possible you can't allow yourself to become involved in a relationship, because you're afraid you're not strong enough to keep your own identity? Or could it be you're afraid that somewhere deep inside you lurks a woman just like your mother? Is it possible you can't accept the idea that even if your mother could change her life, she wouldn't want to? I don't think your fear centers so much on how strong I am, as on how weak you think you might be."

She turned to glare at him, her anger bubbling to the surface like an unwatched pot. "I thought your degree was in engineering. I didn't know you also specialized in psychiatry."

"Sarcasm isn't—" His words were cut off by the ringing of the telephone.

Lenore answered, listened a moment, then handed the receiver to Mangas. She walked over to the fireplace and waited for him to finish.

Despite all that had gone before, she had to fight an urge to go to him and put her arms around him when she glanced back and saw how totally vanquished he looked. He stood and listened for a long time, making only an occasional short comment that made no sense to

Hanging up the receiver, he turned to her. "I have to leave. I want you to know I would stay as long as I had to if there were any hope for us."

"Do you want me to drive you to the airport?" How civilized she was behaving, even as her world disintegrated.

A sad smile twisted his mouth. "I brought my car, remember? I'll leave it at the airport and send someone out to drive it back."

"I hope everything's all right." She hadn't meant to say that. It sounded like such a polite and proper and appropriate thing to say—without meaning, without caring.

Rather than answer with something as inane, Mangas turned and walked to the door. Then, as if he'd forgotten something, he turned and looked at her. For long moments he stared, emblazing an image in his mind that he knew would come back to haunt him, yet unable to stop himself. "Someday," he said softly, "when you can look back on this, Lenore, look back and know how very much I loved you."

"And I you..." she breathed. But he was gone before the words had formed on her lips.

CHAPTER FOURTEEN

As LENORE READIED HERSELF for work the next morning, she preempted the constantly resurfacing thoughts of Mangas with ideas for upcoming projects at work. She would use work as an antidote to the emptiness he had left behind. She'd done it once before. Only this time, she realized with a wrench, she wouldn't delude herself that he would return. Perhaps it would be easier that way. But her tears told her how wrong she was.

When she arrived at work, her secretary silently watched her pass, then immediately followed her into the inner office. "The senior Mason wants to see you the minute you come in," she said in a hushed voice.

Lenore groaned. Obviously Adrian had wasted no time filing his complaint. "Thank you, Jackie," she replied without enthusiasm. "Tell him I'm on my way, would you?" She put her briefcase beside her desk and dropped her purse in a file drawer before starting down the hallway to the opulent west-side offices.

David Mason's secretary indicated she

should go right in, something Lenore could never remember doing in all her years with the firm. She smiled at the irony of being given first-class treatment for something she was sure was causing waves. She had always been made to cool her heels in the outer office when it had come time for recognition of a job well done.

When the always-proper David Mason failed to rise as she entered the room, she knew she was in bigger than usual trouble.

"Ms Randolph, I cannot begin to express my disappointment in you," he began without preamble.

"Good morning, Mr. Mason." If she was going to take a flailing, she wanted it to be under the best possible circumstances. Firing back at him as she truly wanted to was not the approach that would win her any medals for contrite behavior. She had learned a long time ago that a good offense was not a good defense with this man. It was better to act humble, with a generous helping of repentance thrown in for good measure. That way, the ordeal was over in half the time. Defend yourself, and you could be in the confines of the inner sanctum all day.

"No, Ms Randolph, it is not a good morning. Never in the history of Mason, Langly and Mason has one of our employees brought such shame and evidence of misconduct to our firm."

"I beg your pardon?"

"Please don't act coy. As one of the liberated crossovers in our society, you don't have the feminine grace necessary to bring it off."

"Crossovers?" she inanely repeated, too stunned to say anything else.

"Mr. Winchester has informed me of your nefarious involvement in the fiasco at the college and the disgusting display of moral turpitude he discovered in Aspen."

Ignoring her earlier resolve, Lenore said, "I was in no way involved in anything that took place at the college." She spoke as carefully as possible, trying to control her rapidly shortening temper. "And what I do on my own time, as long as it's legal and does not involve this firm, is no one's business but my own."

"You are wrong, Ms Randolph. Everything you do, on or off this job, is the company's business."

Forcefully she bit back an angry retort. "May I go now?"

"Yes, indeed. And you may keep going. You are fired."

Lenore caught her breath. "You're firing me because Adrian Winchester came whining to you that I slept with a man while I was in Aspen?" she asked incredulously. "Did it ever occur to you that the reason he might be so upset is because he had his own plans for me? Or would that be all right with Mason, Langly and

Mason? I suppose it would have been proper for me to sleep with anyone I wanted to as long as he's a good client.''

"You're losing control, Ms Randolph."

"You're damn right I'm losing control, Mr. Mason. I've given this company some of the best designs it's turned out in years, without ever once demanding full recognition. I've played all this company's corporate games by all their stuffy rules—''

"Now you're rambling, Ms Randolph. Nothing you say will ever convince me to change my mind. It was only under the most extreme pressure that I agreed to let you work for us in the first place, when the others insisted we had to have a woman in the ranks to prove we are a progressive company. Well, let me tell you what a sweet victory it is for me to be proven right in the end. You have no business in this field, and I consider it my privilege—no, make that my pleasure—to tell you so.''

Lenore straightened her spine so that she was looking down at him from her greatest possible height. Slowly she enunciated her words. "I want you to be sure to remember my name... *David*. The day is going to come when it returns to haunt you." She swiveled on her heel and left.

By the time she reached her office again, she was trembling. Passing her secretary without acknowledging the "what's up," expression on the other woman's face, Lenore entered the office and closed the door behind her. She leaned heavily against the beautifully grained oak, looking across the room to the window she had gazed out of so often. A hiccuped sob escaped despite her determination to keep it inside.

Being fired hurt so much worse than she could ever have imagined.

She had devoted her entire career to this company, thinking her efforts were not only welcome but appreciated, by those in charge, at least. How could she have been so blind?

Come on, Lenore, she ruthlessly chided herself. *Where's your backbone? Remember it was you who wanted to be the feminist pathfinder in a male-dominated company—no one pushed you into it. You have no right to be shocked that this happened. It's happened to hundreds of women before you and will happen to hundreds again.*

Besides, she tried to reason, what was she really leaving behind? How many real friends had she made? Her talent and her drive were portable quantities. Even though most of her work had come out with the firm's name stamped on it, she had begun to make a name for herself in the small architectural world of Colorado Springs. Surely landing a job with another firm wouldn't be hard.

Despite her efforts at justification, despite

her determination not to let what had happened destroy her, the half hour it took to gather her belongings was almost more than she could bear. Even her old reliable propensity for using anger to get her through difficult situations failed to work its magic. She considered and quickly discarded the possibility of taking the firm to court. She knew she would eventually win a sex-discrimination case in any courtroom in which it was tried, but to do so would be to drag her relationship with Mangas before the public. The press would have a field day with him, the tabloids would make his life hell. She couldn't sacrifice him to prove a point, or even to defend her principles. She would give up her dream before she would hurt him like that. Not to mention the pain she herself would endure at this invasion of privacy.

Her hand was on the door ready to twist the knob for the last time, when she purposefully bent down and laid her belongings on the floor. Staring at the room she had many times regarded as her first home, she forced what had happened that morning from her mind. For just a moment she wanted to remember the good times, the personal triumphs when a client was especially pleased, or when, after a particularly long battle, a fresh design would race from her mind so fast she would have to struggle to get it down on paper. Integrally involved with the good memories of the room were the times she had spent here with Paul Shaughnessy. She would miss him terribly—the quick consultations, the shared problems, the commiserating smile when everything seemed to go wrong, the brief hug of congratulations when they went right. They would remain friends, but the day-to-day sharing would be over.

Enough, she admonished herself. Maudlin thoughts weren't going to make it any easier to walk those thirty yards to the elevators. Thank God it was Monday and early, she thought as she gathered up her belongings again. The gossip mill wouldn't be in full swing for another hour yet, giving her time to make her exit with as little fuss as possible.

She should at least take the time to stop, say something to Jackie, thank her one last time for being a secretary ten notches above the job description. But she knew if she did, the tears burning the back of her throat would force their way out no matter how hard she tried to prevent them. She was determined to leave with dignity if it killed her.

But she almost didn't make it when she came through the door and saw Jackie openly crying. "I see the gossips are working earlier than usual this morning," Lenore said with a sigh, walking over to the desk. "I was going to call you later... maybe ask you to go to lunch with me.... It's a little hard for me to express my gratitude right now...."

"I understand, Ms Randolph," she said behind her crumpled tissue.

"I left some things in the office for you—that watercolor of the Black Canyon of Gunnison and the Smithsonian reproduction of the Mayan figure. I know you've admired them several times. It's a poor way to thank you for all you've done—"

"I can't imagine working for anyone else." Fresh tears glistened in her secretary's eyes.

"Don't do that, Jackie," Lenore gently scolded. "It's hard enough for me to leave already."

They said goodbye, and Lenore started down the hallway. Her footsteps slowed when she passed the turn she would normally take to Paul's partitioned office. Quickly she picked up speed, deciding she had put herself through enough already. Even though she desperately wanted to talk to someone, and she knew Paul would be the perfect someone, as he always was, she couldn't bring herself to stay in the building one minute longer. She would call him later, and they would get together somewhere and share a bottle of wine while decrying the injustices of life. She blanched when she realized it wasn't really Paul she needed to get together with. It wasn't Paul she wanted to make her feel better about what was ahead.

Arriving home and walking into her empty apartment drove her even deeper into the realm of unreality that had surrounded her since yesterday morning in Aspen. It was such a simple thing to do, to come home, yet she found she was lost in the familiar territory. To be there in the middle of the day on a Monday totally disoriented her. Everything seemed out of kilter. She kept waiting for the tears to come, but her eyes remained dry. All she felt was a chilled numbness. After wandering around the apartment for some time like an animal trapped in a maze, she spotted her suitcases in the corner where Mangas had left them. At least unpacking would give her something to do, she thought absently as she carted them into her room.

Unsnapping the lid, she clasped her hand over her mouth in horror when she saw what was lying across the top of the contents. She had forgotten they'd been forced to pack Mangas's clothes with hers, since he didn't have a suitcase with him. This physical evidence of the man she loved was more painful than she would have believed possible.

At last the tears came.

THE REST OF THAT WEEK and all the next were spent job hunting. It wasn't until she'd gone through six extensive and enthusiastic interviews, then later been coolly or awkwardly told no openings were available, that she finally accepted that David Mason was killing any chance

she had to find another job in Colorado
Springs. And if she couldn't find work where
people knew her, what would it be like if she
moved to a town where she was a stranger?
While she hadn't run out of firms to apply to,
none of the remaining ones were involved in the
kind of work she wanted to do.

Standing in the kitchen fixing a chicken salad
for dinner, Lenore listlessly chopped the celery
as she considered her options. At least she
wasn't hurting financially. Living for so long
with her job as her single purpose in life had left
her with litle time or opportunity to spend
money on anything. Most of each paycheck had
been banked, and while the interest she'd earned
had been dismal because she hadn't shopped
around for a better investment, at least the principal was still there.

She heard footsteps on the sidewalk, and
looked out the window to see Paul Shaughnessy
coming her way, carrying a plain brown bag.
Wiping her hands on a towel, she went to the
door to greet him. "You're just in time for dinner." Her smile was her first genuine one since
she'd seen him last.

"Put on your glad rags. I'm taking you out."

"Are you sure you want to? I'm making
Chinese chicken salad, and there's plenty."

"Stay as you are," he said without hesitation.
"You've convinced me we can celebrate just as
well here as at some dumb restaurant."

"I could use something to celebrate. Come in and tell me about it."

He stepped past her into the kitchen, where with an elegant flourish he pulled a bottle of Dom Perignon from the bag.

"Wow!" Lenore commented appreciatively. "Whatever it is we're celebrating, it must really be something special."

"You'll not get a hint until we have our glasses raised in a toast."

Lenore went to the cupboard and pulled out two slim champagne glasses. Shaking her head over his slower performance with the cork, she clicked her tongue and teased, "What's keeping you?"

"Patience."

His excitement had begun to infect Lenore, and she found she was growing anxious to hear his news. With a loud exasperated sigh, she said, "Do you want me to do that?"

"What?" he exclaimed in horror. "You would take over this last bastion of male supremacy?"

"Supremacy?" She laughed.

"Ah, but just because you *might* happen to get the cork from the bottle quicker than I does not mean you could do it with as much style. Let us keep our priorities straight here. There are some things only a man can do properly. We—"
He was interrupted by a tiny explosion as the bottle finally relinquished its hold on the cork.

Solemnly he poured the bubbling liquid into the awaiting glasses, took one from Lenore and touched it to hers. "To Shaughnessy and Randolph...." Unable to contain himself any longer, he shattered his rigid composure with a mischievous wink. "Or if you really want to get pigheaded about it, Randolph and Shaughnessy."

Lenore stared at him, slowly lowering the glass in her hand. "What are you talking about?" she asked in a hushed whisper, suddenly afraid of the answer.

"As of this afternoon, I'm unemployed. And since my dream has always been to have someone really terrific as a boss... I chose me—and you, of course. But I figure you'll be too busy doing all the things you do so well that you won't have time to look in on me, so I'll have to look in on myself, so to speak."

"Paul, what have you done?" She already knew what his answer would be, but she still had to ask.

"I quit," he answered simply.

Her shoulders slumped; her facade crumbled. She set her glass on the counter and thought a moment before quietly saying, "How did you know?" She had carefully avoided telling him how her interviews were going, glossing over the truth the few times he did persist with questions. Yet somehow he had seen through her.

He shrugged. Suddenly serious himself, he

leaned pensively against the cabinet beside her. "It wasn't too hard to figure out what was happening. With your talent, you should have been fighting off prospective employers by now. When you weren't, I guessed it was either Winchester or Mason doing a hachet job on you. There's just no way you could fight them both in this city."

"If you know that, then what makes you think we could succeed on our own?"

"Unlike you, Lenore, I was never happy at M., L. & M. Going out on my own has been a dream I've harbored since graduating, but I had sense enough to know I wasn't ready for solo flight. Sometimes decisions are taken out of our hands. I can't say I'm sorry. In truth, I'm damned excited." A little sheepishly he added, "Your misery is a dream come true for me. But I didn't just let my enthusiasm overrun me. I've given the idea a lot of thought and decided we could survive on the small stuff until everything blows over. Between us we have lots of contacts who aren't big enough to give a damn about Winchester or Mason, who will see us through the rough times. They won't make us rich or famous, but then we won't starve, either. Once we've worked our way back into the inner circles—" his voice softened menacingly "—we'll run those sons of bitches at Mason, Langly and Mason out of business."

Lenore smiled, his enthusiasm making her

believe it could happen. "It sounds like we're getting ready for a gunfight at the O. K. Corral."

"Hmm.... I like the sound of that, partner." He picked up her glass and handed it to her. "Let's drink to it."

THE NEXT MORNING Lenore discovered she could awaken with a headache from one too many glasses of expensive champagne as easily as from too many cheap ones. She and Paul had stayed up late into the night, discussing plans and hopes for the new firm, each taking turns playing devil's advocate and trying to find reasons why it might not succeed. In the span of a few hours they had learned more about each other—both their dreams and their fears—than they'd learned over the entire life of their friendship. They had ended the evening with a firm handshake, a warm hug and high hopes for their future together...and, after a flip of a coin, they had decided to name their new firm Randolph and Shaughnessy. Still, Paul had got in the last word, conceding it was fair, after all, that the business's *oldest* partner should have her name first.

Now, holding her head, Lenore wandered into the kitchen for a glass of water and aspirin before venturing into the unforgivingly bright sunshine to retrieve the paper from the front porch. After fixing a cup of coffee, she propped her pillows against the gleaming brass head-board and crawled back into bed. She soon found that with several sips of coffee and a de-termined effort, she was able to concentrate on the tiny print in the real-estate section of the paper. She had volunteered to search for an of-fice while Paul did the preliminary work neces-sary to get a business license and set up their partnership. They had decided both of them should be present when they made their applica-tion for a loan.

To go into business under current market conditions was insane, improbable and incred-ibly foolhardy, but it was also a lifeline. For the first time in two weeks, Lenore was truly excited. If anything could make her forget Mangas, surely this would, her days and nights would be so filled with activity that her mem-ory of him would surely fade. The pain that now filled her heart would soon be a thing of the past.

Dropping the paper in her lap, she gazed un-seeingly out the window. What foolish games she sometimes tried to play. According to her mother, as a child "let's pretend" had been her favorite. Obviously she had never grown out of it. To think she could so easily forget Mangas Taylor—she was playing the ostrich with its head in the sand. He was stamped on her soul, as impossible to remove as ink from silk. She would never be without dreams of him. The best she could hope for would be a dulling ache, in time. . . .

The phone rang. "Have you found someplace yet?" Paul said in answer to her hello.

"Three or four possibilities. I'm going to call the agencies as soon as my head stops throbbing."

"Well, don't wear yourself out. I've just come into two tickets to the Founder's Charity Ball, which happens to be tonight. It's time for us to start mingling, to let all those possible future clients know that Colorado Springs's newest architectural firm is almost open for business."

They went on to discuss the time and attire before hanging up. Lenore leaned back against the pillow and closed her eyes. It felt so good to have something to do again. Although she had tried to deny it, panic had started to set in when it became obvious her job prospects were diminishing. How marvelous that she and Paul had something to offer each other. She wouldn't want to be considered a charity case.

On top of everything else, she was pleasantly surprised to discover her headache had disappeared. As she hopped out of bed and headed for the shower, the phone rang again. This time it was Samantha.

"How's it going?" her cousin asked cheerfully, checking the status quo as she had every day since Lenore lost her job. It was as much an invitation for Lenore to share her problems, if she were so inclined.

"It's going marvelously."

"You've found a job!"

"Well. . . not exactly. One kind of found me, you might say. Meet me for lunch and I'll tell you all about it."

FALL CREPT INTO LENORE'S DAILY LIFE almost unnoticed as the flurry of activity continued. An office and furniture to fill it were found. A logo was designed using a severely modern *R* and *S* and then hurriedly printed on business cards and stationery. Last they hired a sign painter to display their names tastefully but prominently on their office door. Their business loan, partnership papers and licensing had been processed without a hitch and with unheard-of speed, allowing the partners to make plans to open for business far sooner than they had dared hope.

At last the day arrived, one that left no doubt winter was around the corner. Lenore and Paul met at the outside door of the office at eight-fifteen for a private ceremony commemorating the occasion. The local paper had promised to give them a column or two in the business section, but the staff photographer wasn't due for another hour.

The conference room between their offices was soon filled with the aroma of freshly perked coffee as they prepared their breakfast of orange juice and croissants. When everything was ready and they were seated, Lenore raised her glass of juice and proposed a toast. "To us, Paul. May we succeed in business as well as we have in friendship. You're one hell of a guy, and I owe you more than I can ever repay."

He smiled warmly. "I just know a good set of coattails to hitch a ride on when I see them."

Halfway through their casual meal, Paul grew serious again. "Lenore, I want you to know I've avoided saying anything up until now because I really do know it's none of my business. Also, I keep telling myself that just because we're partners, it doesn't give me the right to pry into your personal life. But obviously neither argument had succeeded, because I'm going to do what I know I shouldn't, anyway. I don't expect you to tell me what happened. I don't think I even want to know—"

"Paul, will you stop beating around the bush and get on with it?"

"Is there anything that can be done to get you and Taylor back together?" When she didn't answer, he went on. "You hide it well most of the time, but there are occasions when I can see the hurt in you as plainly as I can see the loneliness. Maybe I'm interfering because you were never this way before you met him. I thought

things might get better for you, but they
haven't. Don't get me wrong, Lenore. You handle it well, and it's not that I think your personal
problems are going to get in the way of the
firm—it's just that I can hardly stand to see you
so...so...."

Was her depression really that obvious? She
thought she'd been so careful to hide it. Even to
the point of never speaking Mangas's name
aloud. She thought for a long time. "All right,
Paul," she finally said. "I suppose we could
talk about it."

"We don't have to...."

"I know. It isn't that I think you're prying. I
haven't sought your counsel on this because I
know any discussion is futile. It's like building
sand castles on the beach at low tide...the
dreams, the hopes keep getting washed away. I
would rather not waste the energy anymore."
She smiled sadly. "To answer you more directly...no, nothing can be done. What I had with
Mangas Taylor is as finished as what I had with
Mason, Langly and Mason."

"Does he feel the same way?"

"I don't know...." She tossed her half-eaten
croissant back on the napkin. "But it doesn't
matter. Basically, we are such different people it
would be impossible to bridge the gap between
us—it's better not to try."

"That doesn't sound like you."

Her eyebrows rose in question.

"I've never heard you acknowledge anything was impossible. I didn't think the word was in your vocabulary."

"I've learned a lot of new words lately."

"That sounds ominous."

Lenore looked up to see a teasing twinkle in his eyes. "I didn't mean it quite as melodramatically as it sounds." Pensively she broke off a piece of flaky pastry and nibbled at the edges. "Surely in your twenty-seven years you've met someone you were wildly attracted to, whom you later discovered wasn't your type at all."

He nodded. "The only difference was I didn't brood about the breakup as you've been doing. I was damned grateful it didn't go any further. And that I had sense enough to get out when I did."

"Maybe I need more time to reach that point."

"My bet is you never will."

Her hands trembled revealingly. What a terrible possibility to even suggest. As it was now, she only managed to get through each day because she had hope that the next one would be better. "It doesn't make any difference," she reluctantly admitted. "The break is irrevocable."

Paul started to say something, then paused to listen. Tossing his napkin on the table, he stood up. "I think I hear someone at the door."

Lenore glanced at her watch. "It's too early for the photographer." She got up to join him.

"Stay put. I'll get it." He put his hand on her shoulder as he passed.

While she waited for him to return, she swept the crumbs from the glass-top table into her hand with more force than was necessary. Angrily she crumpled her napkin in a tight ball and tossed it toward the shiny brass wastepaper basket, missing the top by inches and watching the paper bounce against the wall. *Damn him,* she silently swore, cursing his memory, cursing the way he constantly invaded her life. She picked up the paper and put it in the container. Would she never be free of him? He had cast a pall over a morning that should have been an unadulterated joy for her.

The sound of rapidly rising voices drew Lenore's attention to the front door.

"I'm sorry," she heard Paul repeat with diminished patience. "We are not interviewing today. Come back tomorrow and we would be happy to accept your application."

Lenore smiled. If the person with Paul believed her application for office manager would go any farther than the receptacle Lenore had been aiming her napkin at a few minutes earlier, that person was highly mistaken. Should Paul ever make a list of pet peeves that drove him crazy, "pushy people" would be at the top.

"If you would just let me see Ms Randolph, everything would be taken care of *right now*." The words were spoken through clenched teeth.

Lenore turned around in her chair to see if she could put a face to the oddly familiar, infuriated voice.

"Ms Randolph is not seeing anyone today. She is indisposed."

Lenore smiled to herself at the old-fashioned expression, which she'd never heard Paul use before. *"Lenore!"* the now recognizable voice shouted. "Will you *please* come out here and rescue me from this idiot!"

Lenore choked back a laugh and headed for the door. The laugh exploded when she saw Paul and Samantha standing toe to toe, like two comic-book characters about to come to blows.

"Thank God," she heard Samantha sigh when she saw her cousin come into the room.

With a deep scowl, Paul turned to look at Lenore. "Do you know this woman?"

"Indeed I do." To Samantha she said, "What are you doing here this early? The open house isn't until ten. Besides, how did you get the time off? I thought this was the busy season for you."

"I figured you might be able to use an extra hand." She glared at Paul, pointedly stepping past him. "So I took the day off. Somehow this jerk got the idea I was job hunting."

Lenore swallowed another laugh that threatened when she saw Paul's open mouthed reaction to Samantha's scathing assessment. "Before things go from bad to worse, Samantha, dear, let me introduce my new partner." Lenore reached out to help the other woman with her coat. "Samantha, this is Paul Shaughnessy, co-owner of Randolph and Shaughnessy. Paul, this is Samantha Baxter, my irrepressible cousin from California." They shook hands with all the enthusiasm and warmth of a cobra and a mongoose.

"Do you plan to treat all your visitors with equal graciousness?" she said sweetly.

"Only those who barge in unexpectedly," Paul said with equal charm.

"I hope you've had that information printed on your business cards. It would be unfortunate if you were to lose any clients because they had the audacity not to call first and you refused them access."

"*Clients* are always welcome."

"And just what made you think I wasn't a client?"

"I've found that people who can afford to hire an architect usually conduct themselves with a titch more class," he hissed.

Lenore listened to the rapid-fire interchange with eyes wide in disbelief. She could have been one of the fixtures in the room for all the attention they were paying her. It was as if someone somewhere had struck a bell and told them to come out fighting—totally uncharacteristic behavior for both of them.

"That's the most boorish thing I've heard anyone say since I came to Colorado Springs." Samantha dug her hands deeper into her waist. She could just as easily have wrapped them around Paul's neck, Lenore surmised.

"Then it must be because, up until now, you've kept your mouth shut and not provoked anyone," he retorted icily.

"What's the matter with you two?" Lenore gasped as she stepped between them, afraid the confrontation was about to become physical. They both looked at her as if she'd clapped her hands and snapped them out of a trance.

Paul spoke first, filling the suddenly awkward silence. "Shall we begin again?" he asked, looking sheepishly at Samantha.

She looked from Paul to Lenore and then back to Paul, a flush of embarrassment coloring her cheeks, making her look years younger than twenty-six. "I guess it's either begin again or choose our weapons."

The laughter dissipated the last of the electricity charging the air around them. "Have you had breakfast?" Lenore asked, taking Samantha's arm and walking with her toward the conference room.

"Yes, but I could easily be talked into adding something to the cold cereal sloshing around in my stomach.'' She glanced over her shoulder and flushed anew when she discovered Paul gazing intently at her. Lenore smiled at the interchange. She had never seen such a bewildered look on Paul's face. But then he had obviously never met anyone like Samantha.

CHAPTER FIFTEEN

WEEKS LATER, when Paul, Samantha and Lenore were all once again sitting in the conference room, this time eating their lunches, they discovered none of them could remember precisely how it had been decided that Samantha would quit her job and become the office manager for Randolph and Shaughnessy.

Sitting next to each other on the leather sofa and sharing a bag of French fries, Paul and Samantha looked as if they had left their volatile beginning behind them and become fast friends. Lenore chuckled to herself at the suggestion. The daily arguments they always managed to get into were the liveliest things that had been happening around the office. While she and Paul had expected things to be slow in the beginning, they had hoped to at least meet their monthly bills with the small work they thought they would bring in right away.

"Give it another month," Paul said, seemingly reading her mind. "Things are bound to pick up soon."

She smiled. "I'm not worried—just bored."

"You've finished the plaza project?"

"Last week—blindfolded, with one hand tied behind my back."

"Damn," he groaned. "And I missed it."

She laughed. "You blinked."

Samantha popped the last of the French fries into her mouth. Licking a crystal of salt from the tip of her finger, she said, "Does this mean things might get busier around here? Are you trying to break it to me gently that there is a chance I may have to postpone one of my afternoon manicures sometime in the future?"

"Never," Paul answered quickly. "Even if the pace becomes fast and furious, the last thing I want is for you to miss out on sharpening your claws."

Samantha examined first one hand, then the other. "They do have a tendency to be a little dull after we've spent a morning together."

Despite his attempt to hide it, Lenore saw a smile at the corners of Paul's mouth.

"Samantha, only two things keep me from firing you," he said. "Most importantly, Lenore would never speak to me again, and on a professional level you do your job better than anyone I've ever known. However, on a personal level, I've never run across anyone who is as completely obnoxious and abrasive as you are."

"Thanks, Paul." Her eyes sparkled mischievously. "But you forgot to add that I work incredibly cheap."

"And that almost makes you lovable."

"Oh, what a sweet thing to say!"

"Listen harder next time. I said 'almost.'"

Samantha smiled in gracious defeat. "Your point. But don't let it go to your head," she warned. "I have to let you win one once in a while. It's the only way to keep the game interesting."

Knowing the battle had only just begun despite Samantha's magnanimous proclamation, Lenore reached for the morning paper, exiting from a conversation she was never really a part of. At least she no longer had to worry about what she would find when she returned to the office after an hour or two absence, she conceded. They had no trouble maintaining a highly professional relationship when clients were in the office, though Lenore had begun to feel she was the caretaker of squabbling siblings when the three of them were alone.

Automatically turning to the business section of the paper, she was immediately drawn to the lower right-hand corner, where the headline announced, "Apache Unveils New Computer for Technology-wary Executive." Her eyes quickly skimmed the article, searching for word of Mangas, even though she knew she wouldn't find any. Publicity wasn't the kind of thing chief executives usually handled. Turning to the inside pages for the article's conclusion, she was stunned at the heaviness of her disappointment. His name appeared nowhere in the piece. Going back to the front page, she carefully read the article, seeking clues to Apache's strength in the corporate battle she knew was being waged.

The article was more than an ordinary announcement of a new product; it unveiled a "revolutionary technological breakthrough." Revealing sentences explained how important this particular computer was to Apache—how the company hoped to broaden its distribution and expand its operations as a result of the increased demand. The spokesman for Apache bluntly stated that the company was essentially riding on the success or failure of its newest product, which had been code-named... "Lenore."

Lenore's heart beat heavily against her chest. Her eyes grew misty; the article became an indistinct blur. She pulled the paper closer and higher to hide the emotions she knew were mirrored on her face. Oh, God. She closed her eyes against the pain. Would he forever have this kind of control over her? Would she forever be reminded of him in everything she did? And most painfully of all, from somewhere in her turmoil, a soft voice taunted—did she really want to be free of him?

On the edge of her consciousness, she could

hear the continuing banter between Paul and Samantha. She bit her lower lip to stifle a cry of anguish. They mustn't know what was happening to her. As unobtrusively as she could manage, she rose from the chair and headed for her office.

The door was barely closed before the tears began to fall. Covering her face with her hands to muffle the sobs, she leaned wearily against the cool oak, seeking whatever support she could find for her wobbly legs.

At her most defenseless now, she could no longer righteously deny how she ached to feel Mangas's arms around her—how in the middle of the night she yearned for his lovemaking, knowing all the while he was the only one who could answer the need that gnawed at her insides, that it was useless to seek relief with anyone else. How she longed for the soft caress of his voice. To see his intimate smile of pleasure.

Worst of all, she knew it was within her power to have all she ached for.

How simple the answer seemed. Walk to the desk. Pick up the phone. Call. What kept her from the task? What demon made her live in this hell?

Not a demon at all. It was her innate intelligence overruling her wayward emotions. It was her strong sense of self-protection that kept her from allowing herself to become vulnerable yet again.

The arguments she'd given Mangas when they had parted were as valid now as they had been then. And none of those arguments had anything to do with her own fears, as he had tried to imply at their parting. She had laid those problems to rest the minute she had accepted loving him. For him to imply she couldn't let herself become involved with him because of a fear that she would lose her identity was grasping at straws—a futile attempt to shift the blame for the destruction of their relationship onto her instead of where it belonged—onto him. Because it had been true once that she desperately fought involvement didn't mean that was still true.

Then why, knowing all she knew, did his loss still hurt so badly? Why couldn't she stop loving him?

LATER THAT EVENING, after Samantha and Paul had left, Lenore stopped on her way out to pick up the newspaper she'd been reading earlier. As she folded it in half, a small article in the real-estate section caught her eye. Apparently a large parcel of land she knew Mangas had been looking at for possible expansion had been sold for an industrial complex. When she couldn't find the name of the buyer, a shiver of apprehension brought goose bumps to her wool-covered arms. For all her reinstituted resolve to work Mangas out of her system, she knew how impossible it would be if he was to return to Colorado. She needed more time.

She tossed the paper into the wastebasket as she passed Samantha's desk, suddenly feeling it had become a harbinger of bad news. A new determination was reflected in her long stride as she went out the door. Obviously Mangas was not going to fade easily from her memory. Putting their brief affair into proper perspective was something she was going to have to work even harder to accomplish—starting tonight. She would call that dark handsome general contractor who had been pursuing her for weeks and tell him that she had discovered she was free this Saturday evening, after all.

As Christmas approached, for some mysterious reason neither Lenore nor Paul could fathom, business began to pick up. The small jobs that had haphazardly found their way to the firm since the opening were suddenly supplemented by bigger projects—some of which were actually challenging. Lenore welcomed the work as the desert welcomes rain. She drew as much of it to her as Paul would tolerate, absorbing the mediocre along with the complex.

The work was a salve for her wounds and her pride. She hadn't realized how she'd missed seeing the spark of pleasure in a client's eyes until she began to see it again. In a moment of quiet candor, when she and Paul took the time to toast their growing success, she admitted she would work for almost nothing rather than give up that special glow she felt when a client first saw and exclaimed over one of her designs.

Not until she again experienced that feeling did she realize how devastating a blow David Mason had struck when he had fired her. Despite her angry denial of the possibility, grave doubts about her talent had started to undermine her confidence.

But—she sighed as she carefully laid her pencil down—not anymore.

She straightened from her cramped position of the past few hours, hunched over her drawing board. Stopping for a minute to listen to the quiet, she saw for the first time that it was snowing. It was already Wednesday, she noted in alarm as her eyes went from the window to the large calendar on the wall. There was little more than a week left for Christmas shopping, something she, too, should have done instead of staying behind in the office while Paul and Samantha took the afternoon off to do theirs. She sighed again and stretched. Not only did she have all her shopping left to do—she hadn't even put up her tree.

A loud knock on the reception-area door made her jump. She suddenly realized it had probably been an earlier knock that had broken her concentration. Sliding off her stool, she hurried to the door, smiling at the undignified impression her stocking feet would make but not feeling she and Paul were so comfortably entrenched that she could afford to miss a client while she took the time to put on her shoes.

When she saw who it was awaiting her on the other side of the glass door, she had to fight an almost overwhelming urge to flee. Desperately she struggled to keep her emotional balance. Her hands trembled as she reached for the lock and opened the door.

Dressed in an expensive camel-hair overcoat, his black hair sprinkled with snow, was Mangas. He stared at her with haunted eyes, his mouth a hard line of weariness. He broke the silence between them with passionless words. "May I come in, Lenore? I would like to discuss a business matter with you."

Realizing she'd been blocking the doorway as if to ward off intrusion, she quickly stepped aside. "Yes, of course," she managed to say casually. Her superficial composure gave her hope that she would be able to survive this meeting, which already threatened to tear her into ragged little pieces. "Would you like me to take your coat?" she asked inanely.

He shrugged out of the garment and handed it to her watching her every movement with the rapt attention of a blind man who had recently regained his sight. "How are you?" he asked automatically, immediately angry that he had so easily and quickly gone beyond the business he had come here to conduct. His hand went to the back of his neck, rubbing aching muscles that had suffered too long without rest. Again he cursed his stupidity for thinking he could come to her, no matter what the reason, and then simply walk away unscathed.

"I'm fine," she answered slowly. "And you?" Their gazes met, as quickly broke away. Each knew she had lied, her eyes betraying the falseness of her words.

Mangas's voice was deep and hesitant when he softly and honestly replied. "While I'm not 'fine,' I'm at least busy. The days seem to pass easier that way."

She shoved her still-trembling hands deeply into the pockets of her slacks. "So I've discovered."

"Then things are going all right for you here?"

"Business was a little shaky at first, but it has started to pick up. At least now I'm confident we're going to do all right."

It was hard for him to say what he wanted to next because of the painful memories the words would evoke—but they had to be said. He had carried the added burden of knowing what had happened to her after they'd parted. "I'm sorry you lost your job because of me. I know how much it meant to—"

"Don't be. I'm not." She leaned against

Samantha's desk, bracing her feet on the yellow file cabinet. "Actually, I've begun to think of my firing as the best possible thing that could have happened to my career."

Eagerly he listened, anxious to hear what she was telling him. He wanted to be healed from the wound he carried, to be free of the damning guilt. As he listened he carefully absorbed the sound and the sight of her, as well as the subtle scent of her perfume, which once in a while drifted over to him as the beckoning aroma of a faraway campfire enticed a weary hiker—sensations he would hold close and remember on the cold trip home.

"You see, I discovered I was what's known in the business world as a 'token' woman." Lenore shrugged lightly. "It was my own fault—there were plenty of clues left lying around. I chose not to see them. I guess my gigantic ego managed to let me believe I really was different. I thought my incredible rise through the ranks, without even the mentor a woman usually needs to ease the way in the business world, was due to my sterling talent." She broke off with a disparaging laugh. "Luckily my ego came through it all fairly well intact, bruised but still strong enough. I'm a damn good architect, and with a few of the right breaks, my name will still someday grace important buildings...."

"You have no idea how pleased I am to hear that."

Lenore looked at him, a question in her eyes.

"I would never hire someone to design a building for me who had the slightest doubt about her ability."

The questioning frown disappeared, a look of dawning understanding taking its place. "So you were the one who bought the land."

"Yes. . . and needless to say, I need the building yesterday."

"And you've chosen me to design it for you. Why?"

"Have you forgotten I know your work?"

She thought a moment. "Ah, yes, I remember now. Lowell Electronics." Before she realized how intimate it would sound, she softly added, "I was terribly pleased by your remarks that evening in the music room. Did I ever tell you?"

"No. . ." he answered uneasily, the memory of that night crashing through his senses with the subtlety of an avalanche—the dress, the closeness they had shared, the kiss. . . .

As Lenore watched him and saw what effect her words had on him, the memory of another thing she had never told him made her swallow painfully. She was forced to look away.

She had never told him she loved him. It seemed so wrong now that she had never said those three simple words—so wrong and so impossible to rectify. Steeling herself, she looked into his eyes. In a moment of deep honesty, she said, "I don't think the arrangement you pro-pose would work, Mangas."

"Because of what we once were to each other?"

She nodded.

His voice changed, grew clipped and cool. "I didn't come here to hire you because I once loved you."

Lenore felt as if he had hit her. She was dev-astated by his use of the past tense.

"I came here because you're the architect I want to design my plant. I also hoped the new-ness of your firm would mean you would have more time to devote to the project. As I said before, time is critical." His voice softened slightly. "If it would make any difference to you, we could conduct our business through a third party." He strode to the closet where she had hung his coat. When the last of the buttons had been closed, he turned to her and stared with cold unyielding eyes. "Yes or no, Le-nore?"

Her heart skipped a beat. She knew he wouldn't wait for an answer. She must decide now. But could she work with him, even through someone else, and still manage to put her life together? Could she turn him away?

"I'll do it," she said at last. "Randolph and Shaughnessy is hardly secure enough to turn down a commission like this because of personal feelings."

"And the third party?" Without realizing he was doing so, Mangas held his breath as he waited for her answer.

"To insist on a go-between would be highly unprofessional and not conducive to producing the best results."

"You're sure?" he asked, his voice once again the caress she remembered so well.

Lenore nodded. "When will you have your specifications ready?"

"I have them with me now."

"Can you come back tomorrow morning? We could go over them then. I have the entire time before lunch free." Her mind raced. She would have to get in touch with Samantha and Paul tonight to avoid any openmouthed scenes in the morning.

He glanced at his watch. "My plane takes off in six hours. I could leave the figures with you, and we could go over them by phone or work on them tonight if you're free."

She wasn't, but she easily could be. "Let me see if I can get in touch with someone I'm supposed to meet for dinner and get out of it. I'll be right back."

Mangas watched her walk down the short hallway to her office, and for the first time he doubted his motives for choosing her as the architect for his new plant. While he didn't question for a moment that she was highly capable or that she would do an excellent job, he now wondered if her qualifications as an architect was his sole reason for choosing her.

During their confrontation he had actually found himself hoping she would tell him no. He hadn't anticipated, after all the time that had passed, that she would still affect him so strongly; just looking at her made it painful for him to breath. Maybe he had simply buried the knowledge of his feelings so deeply that he'd been able to pretend they weren't there.

The next few hours passed more quickly than either would have wished. When it became evident that all possible business during their initial meeting had been conducted, an awkward silence settled between them. Finishing the last of his now lukewarm coffee, Mangas set the cup on the table and glanced up to see Lenore staring at him.

She quickly looked away and began to gather up the notes lying around her like large bits of confetti. "I seem to have everything I need to get started...."

"If we've forgotten anything you can call me." Mangas reached for a piece of paper and began to write. "The first number is a direct line to my office; the second is my home number."

When she took the paper from his outstretched hand, she was careful not to touch him. "I wouldn't bother you at home—whatever I had to call you about could be handled during business hours."

"Yes...of course."

It was only then that she realized how cruel she had sounded in her effort to hide her own feelings. It was foolish, even more than that it was useless, to try to pretend they were just two business associates. She dropped the papers she'd been gathering back on the table, leaned her elbows next to the papers and sighed. "I suppose if this is going to work out we should try to find some way to put what we once were behind us."

Mangas left his chair and started to pace the small room. Finally he stopped in front of her, his hands at his sides, his eyes filled with a sorrow that had accumulated the past few months like autumn leaves on a forest floor.

"Coming here has made me accept what I've been trying to deny," he began. "Now that I've seen you again, I know we can never go back— that what we had is truly over. I think I can live with that now, where I couldn't have before. Even after all that's happened, you've managed to build a new life for yourself—a damn good life from the looks of it." He sat down opposite her and took her hands to his.

"If I were to be brutally honest, I would tell you that some dark part of me had hoped you would fail, that you would need me." A sad smile twisted his mouth. "It was a funny thing for me to wish, when one of the traits I find most attractive in you is your ability to take care of yourself.'' She started to interrupt, but he stopped her.

''No, let me finish. I have to say this now as much for myself as for you. If through all of this we finally become friends... I will ask for no more.'' Her gaze was focused on their locked hands, and he softly demanded, ''Look at me, Lenore.''

With an effort she lifted her eyes to again meet his.

''I want to tell you goodbye...and hello,'' he said hoarsely.

She blinked, trying to keep the tears from her eyes. How desperately she wished they had not been two stars whose joining would mean the cataclysmic destruction of both. Just as the tears she had tried to hide finally slid from her eyes, Mangas gently kissed her lips. The kiss held no promise of another; it poignantly marked the end to what had been.

With a naturalness that had been missing between them until then, Lenore leaned against his shoulder and let him hold her. They stayed like that for long minutes before she at last looked up at him with a tender smile and asked, ''Can I drive you to the airport?''

''I'd like that.''

When they were in Lenore's car, waiting for the diesel to warm up, she asked, ''Have you put up your tree yet?''

Mangas stared at her in confusion.

"Your Christmas tree," she reiterated.

"No...." He answered as if he'd planned to say more but had decided against it.

"Neither have I. As a matter of fact, I haven't even bought it yet. Would you mind if we stopped at one of the lots on the way to the airport?"

His answering smile was filled with warmth and pleasure. "I wouldn't mind at all. My plane doesn't leave for a few hours yet."

They stopped at a canopy-covered lot featuring loudly playing recorded Christmas carols to foster the spirit of the season—and more importantly, the spirit of purchasing.

Some time later, Mangas was holding what seemed like the twentieth tree while she stepped back to inspect it. She caught the amused look in his eyes. "I suppose you're one of those people who just walks in and takes the closest tree to the check-out stand," she teased him.

Holding his hands up in a gesture that proclaimed his innocence, he laughingly replied, "I'm willing to stand here all night and let you examine every tree if that's what it takes to find the perfect one."

"Are you hinting you have a better method?"

"I can't say I do."

"Come on. I'm willing to try anything once. Let's hear it."

"You're doing fine," he protested as he

pulled a tree from the stack beside him and held it out for her inspection. "How's this one?"

"You must know that evasion is the quickest and most powerful way to pique my curiosity," she said, ignoring the woefully lopsided tree. "Come on now—out with it. I want to hear how the illustrious Mangas Taylor chooses his tree every year."

He leaned the scraggly bush against the others. With obvious reluctance he finally answered her. "I don't have the problem, because I've never had a Christmas tree."

"Never?" she gasped, too surprised to worry about the possible effect of her incredulous tone.

"Not since my last foster home."

Such a simple statement, yet it revealed so much. Lenore felt a sudden and profound sadness for the child Mangas had been. She wanted to say and do all the things she would have said and done if they had still been lovers. But she knew how unwelcome her response would be now. She struggled for other words, something she would have said to a friend. "I...I guess—"

"Stop right there," he said sternly. "Don't get maudlin on me over a stupid Christmas tree."

"You're right." She tried to smile. Now was not the time or the place for expressing how she felt. "I do have this tendency to attribute my sentimentality to everyone else. Thanks for setting me straight before I made a complete fool of myself. I'm loath to admit it, but I've been known to get terribly sloppy at this time of year.''

''Well, I would suggest you switch back to your ruthless-determination mode, at least for this evening—I don't relish the prospect of missing my plane and spending the night at the airport.''

''And you said you didn't care if I took all night.'' She gave him a sheepish grin as she walked past him, over to the first tree they'd looked at.

Mangas shook his head and laughed. ''I should have known.''

They parted an hour later, after sharing a cup of coffee at the airport that they laughingly agreed was the worst they'd ever tasted. Waving goodbye one last time, catching a last glimpse of him beyond the embarking passengers, Lenore discovered she felt yet a new and different kind of emptiness as she drove home through the familiar streets.

As Mangas watched below him, the sparkling lights of Colorado Springs disappeared. He closed his eyes and tried to swallow the ache that clutched at his throat like a slowly closing vise. Seeing Lenore again had reopened every wound he had thought healed, reopened the old and created a few new ones. What his mind had conceded his heart refused to even consider. The idea, the prospect of spending the rest of his life without her was almost more than he could endure. *Almost, hell!* his mind ruthlessly railed.

CHAPTER SIXTEEN

"BY THE WAY," Lenore heard Samantha shout to Paul. "I *told* you that sweater wouldn't fit. It's so tight it makes me look like I'm advertising."

Paul's mumbled reply was lost to Lenore as she sifted through her notes for Apache's new plant. Having arrived first and gone straight to work, she hadn't yet taken the time to tell Samantha and Paul about the new commission. She leaned back in her chair and considered the importance of what had happened the previous night. Having the firm's name on such a prestigious project, one that was sure to get heavy newspaper coverage simply because of its importance to the area's economy, was almost guaranteed to bring in new business. More than anything to date, designing Apache's new offices and plant would put Randolph and Shaughnessy on the map.

But at what cost to her emotions, she wondered yet again. Already on the negative side was one very long and sleepless night. A night spent trying to decide if it was really possible to become friends with someone who had once been a lover. Especially an old lover who still made her long for him despite every intelligent argument she used to try to destroy the feeling. She was amazed at how eagerly her body's yearnings would have committed her once more to a mad roller-coaster ride.

In the early-morning hours, when her wanting had been at its worse, she had almost convinced herself that it would be better for her to work him out of her system by rekindling the affair and letting it run its course—except before she could reach for the phone and offer her proposal to Mangas, she had soberly acknowledged that what she felt for him would never run its course. For a few hopeful hours she had allowed herself to fantasize. Then brutal reality had intruded. One by one she had listed her original reasons for ending the affair. Nothing had changed. He was, he always would be the kind of man who overwhelmed and dominated everyone he came in contact with. In time she would become just another victim. His life had been lived by a different set of rules—rules she couldn't fathom let alone abide by.

By the time her alarm announced the beginning of another day, the old doubts and fears were as firmly entrenched as before. The only thing new was her resolve to see as much of Steve Collins as she could. The contractor had turned out to be everything any mother could wish for her daughter—wealthy, charming, attentive. He had grown up in a "normal" environment; she could easily relate to him. He was even tempered, and she sensed that if the idea of "revenge" ever entered his mind, retaliation would take an innocuous form reminiscent of a college fraternity prank.

Of one thing she was sure—she would never become embroiled in high drama with Steve. But then neither would she know the raging passion that had swept her to such dizzy heights with Mangas.

Unable to stand the solitude of her office any longer, she left to share her news with Paul and Samantha. As she walked through the conference room, bits and pieces of the conversation she had overheard earlier that morning came back to her, particularly one phrase: "I told you that sweater wouldn't fit." That could only mean one thing. Paul and Samantha had spent their afternoon off—together. Certainly strange behavior for two people who could hardly speak civilly to each other.

Staring at Samantha who was standing in front of the file cabinet, her hands filled with papers, Lenore leaned against the doorframe, her arms folded across her chest. Her expression was puzzled. "Want to let me in on what's going on between you and Paul?" she asked. When Samantha didn't answer right away, Lenore added, "Well, I'm glad to see you at least have the good grace to blush."

"We—we decided to call a truce," Samantha finally, uncharacteristically stammered.

"And..." Lenore prodded.

"And one thing led to another."

"And...."

"And once she stopped talking long enough for me to get a word in edgewise, I informed her I'd fallen madly in love with her." Paul came up behind Samantha and slipped his arms around her waist. He was grinning like the school bookworm who'd captured the prom queen.

"Well, you've certainly shot down the importance of my big news," Lenore teased. "Nothing could top that."

"Aw, go ahead and tell us, anyway," Paul countered. "We'll be tolerant. We could probably even summon up some enthusiasm, should the information merit such a display."

"How does Randolph and Shaughnessy getting a commission that old M. L. & M. would kill for strike you?" The atmosphere became charged with tense anticipation as Paul and Samantha's smiles were replaced by keen interest.

"Lenore, this isn't the kind of information you prolong for dramatic effect," Paul said shortly.

"Bear with me; the story gets a little complicated. Grab your coffee cups and let's go into the other room. I need a dose of caffeine—I've had a rough night."

After the details were explained, Paul leaned

back in his chair and told Lenore that his delight in the commission was tempered only by his concern for her.

"I'm one sleepless night ahead of you," she told him. "I've given the whole thing a lot of thought and I'm confident everything will work out all right. After all, it isn't as if Mangas is going to be here in town. I hope I'm enough of a professional to be able to handle a few business meetings without falling to pieces."

He looked at her skeptically. "Who are you trying to convince?"

"Dammit, Paul, do you suppose you could drum up a little excitement for the project, even if it's feigned?"

"You've just answered my question," he said evenly.

Lenore merely glared at him.

CHRISTMAS AND NEW YEAR'S PASSED, only evenings spent with Steve Collins separating the days of work one from another. Paul took over most of the in-house assignments, while Lenore concentrated on the Apache project. By late January, after walking the land several times and going over the soil analysis to determine where and how the heaviest buildings should be constructed, she had the preliminary sketches ready for Mangas's approval.

Eager to show him the designs, she felt a sharp stab of disappointment when she called and was told he was out of town. Two days later a messenger arrived with the information that he was to hand-carry the plans back to California, and that if there were any changes to be made, Mr. Taylor would be in touch. Lenore was also told that if she hadn't heard from Mangas in two days, everything could be considered approved and she should proceed with the final design and working drawings.

A cryptic message came by courier the next morning, asking that the warehouse be enlarged ten feet so that it abutted the electrical easement and congratulating her on a job well done.

Lenore's disappointment had turned to anger by the time she reached for the telephone. After the third ring a male voice answered. "Collins's Construction."

"This is Lenore Randolph. May I speak to Steve Collins, please?"

"Sure. Just a minute—I'll get him for you."

Within seconds he was on the line. "Lenore, how wonderful that you called. What can I do for you?"

"I find I can make it tonight, after all—if you haven't found someone to take my place."

"I didn't even try. There's no one who could even come close."

"You're a man after my heart," she teased.

But his answer was far from teasing. "You're right...."

Lenore swallowed the uneasiness his huskily spoken words had aroused. "Eight o'clock?"

she asked, deciding it was best to change the direction of their conversation.

"I'll be there."

Replacing the receiver, she told herself she wasn't really using Steve Collins; he was an eager participant in their outings. Besides, she had been very careful all along to emphasize that she wanted nothing more from their relationship than friendship. While reluctant at first, he had finally agree, even seemed content with the arrangement. Still, a twinge of guilt plagued her.

SHORT-LIVED SNOWSTORMS, crossing the Rocky Mountains to dump their white calling cards on Colorado Springs before moving on to the plains of Kansas, marked the coming of spring. The rapidly melting snows, the seemingly incessant storms were minor inconveniences to Lenore as she went from one meeting to the next with consulting engineers and contractors. She was frantic to have everything ready the minute the weather cleared. The Apache project had become the driving force in her life, inseparable from the man whose company would occupy the buildings.

Should anyone have suggested it, she would have heatedly denied that she was more dedicated to this contract than any other. She rationalized the long hours and sleepless nights as time any independent architect had to spend if she expected to succeed. Her almost paranoid attention to the smallest detail she chalked up as a mark of her professionalism.

On one particularly monochrome day, Paul came into her office to visit for a while before heading home. "Think the snow will ever let up?" he commented as he slid a chair across the room so he could prop his feet on her desk.

"I'm beginning to wonder." She leaned her elbows on the polished wood and rubbed her eyes, grateful to Paul for the unexpected break.

"How's it going?" he asked.

A weary smile failed to reach her eyes. "Everything is coming together—all we need now is a break in the weather."

"I heard they're taking bets down at the bureau on whether or not the storms are ever going to stop."

"Thanks," she laughed. "I really needed to hear that."

"Have you heard anything lately from our mysterious friend?"

"Nothing beyond a few scraps of paper approving what's being done or making little changes here and there."

"I thought he was supposed to keep in touch."

"So did I," she said softly.

Paul tossed the piece of paper he'd been folding into a small square onto the desk. "Enough of this idle chitchat. It's time to move on to my real reason for interrupting you.''

At the change in Paul's voice and manner, Lenore immediately became alert.

''Now that the Apache project has slowed down a little, I'd like to go over the upcoming work load with you and arrange things so that Samantha and I could be gone for a couple of weeks without worrying that the whole thing might cave in on you.''

''Planning a trip?''

''You might say that,'' he grinned. ''I think the proper terminology would be honeymoon.''

The happiness she felt for Paul and Samantha was accompanied by a burgeoning ache of loneliness for what she had once had herself. ''Congratulations...and I mean that, Paul.'' Then why did she feel like crying?

CHAPTER SEVENTEEN

MANGAS MANEUVERED through the airport crowd to the car-rental agency, where he finalized the arrangements that had been made earlier that day in California. While he waited impatiently for his car to be brought to him, he glanced again at his watch. Already several hours behind schedule, he had given up all thought of being able to catch Lenore in her office. His hope now was to find her at home.

What he had to tell her could have been conveyed over the phone—probably should have been, in fact. Certainly telling her in person that she wasn't yet free from the torment or the humiliation knowing him had brought her wasn't something he was looking forward to. But he owed her that much. Hell, who was he trying to kid? He owed her that much and more—more than he could ever repay.

As he drove from the airport into town, he thought about the months that had passed since their last meeting in December. Afterward he could no longer fool himself that a platonic friendship was possible between them. For days afterward he couldn't work, reeling with want-ing her. To have proceeded as he had originally planned would have been folly; he had neither the time nor the inclination to be "just a friend." Instead he had stayed away and waited for time to pass—time that was supposed to purge her from his memory, or at least dim his awareness until the thought of her brought only a winsome smile, not the gut-wrenching ache he felt now.

It didn't bring him any pleasure to realize he loved her as deeply as ever. To know that time and distance had done nothing to heal the hurt or diminish the loss of her didn't bode well for the future. The only thing that had changed over the months was his ability to hide the depth of his feelings from others. Even Barbara Arden had remarked that he seemed to have crested the mountain where Lenore was concerned.

As he at last neared her apartment, his heart began to beat faster in anticipation. When he swung into the driveway and saw her car was parked in its usual spot, his heart started to pound so heavily in his chest that it echoed in his ears.

Walk, he told himself when he left the car. What he really wanted to do was run. Fearing he wasn't in control anymore, he was relieved to hear his leather soles tapping against the cement walkway as if he was simply another unhurried visitor. With seeming nonchalance he reached for the small circle of light that was Lenore's doorbell and pressed with a trembling finger. The resultant chime sounded faintly inside the apartment, letting him know his summons had been delivered.

When after the third chime Lenore failed to appear, Mangas was forced to admit she wasn't home. He went back to his car and started to leave, then realized there was nowhere else he wanted to go. He would wait for her here.

LENORE SMILED AT STEVE COLLINS as he made his way across the crowded banquet room. He was trying to keep the drinks he held in each hand from spilling as he passed through the bumping throngs of revelers. Trying to block out a little of the noise, she propped her elbows on the table and cupped her hands over her ears as she waited for him. Conventions were her least favorite places these days, since, for the past six months, she'd attended every one in the area that had anything to do with the building trades. Next year would be Paul's year to do the conventions. She would take over the quiet social gatherings.

After they had finished their dirnks and listened to the opening speeches, Lenore gently touched Steve's arm. "I think I've overdosed on fun and games. Would you mind if we left early?"

"Not at all. I much prefer having you to myself, anyway.'' He brought her hand to his lips and lightly kissed the creamy skin.

A familiar warning signal went off in Lenore's head. Guiltily she acknowledged that Steve was falling in love with her. She had let it happen, hoping his growing feelings might light a reciprocal fire in her. They hadn't. And now she must tell him she thought they should stop seeing each other. But how? There had been enough pain in her own life this year. She couldn't stand the thought of being the cause of it in another's.

As they drove from the convention center, she studied Steve's profile in the light of passing cars. Why couldn't she love him? Why did she refuse to look at him as anything more than a friend? Softly she sighed, again focusing on the oncoming traffic. She would miss him terribly. Paul and Samantha were so absorbed in each other and their animated plans for the future. They were living in a world of their own. Without their company or Steve's, she would once more face the prospect of living only for her work.

How long, she asked herself. How long would her existence be tainted by the aching hollowness Mangas Taylor had left behind?

MANGAS ANGLED HIS ARM to try to catch enough of the dim light around him to see his watch. A flash of headlights caught the gleaming gold band and round face, outlining them in stark detail. Looking up to see a black Porsche drive past, he caught his breath when he recognized the passenger. A calmness like the aftermath of a fierce storm settled over him as he watched Lenore swing her long legs out of the car. He had made a decision while he waited for her to return.

It had taken a long time, but things that should have been obvious from the beginning had finally filtered through to his consciousness. Lenore's love was the most important thing in his life, and it was the only thing he'd ever let go of without a fight. He couldn't force her to love him, but they *could* at least try to work things out. Then, maybe in time, love would happen. Meanwhile he would find a way to survive being near her without touching her. He could wait—he would wait no matter how long the waiting took.

Mangas started when he saw Lenore trip as she walked around the car. Involuntarily his hands moved to reach for her, subconsciously trying to cross the distance separating them. But it was another man's arms that caught and helped her, closing around her waist in a familiar embrace as she laughed at her clumsiness.

Mangas shifted uneasily, fighting foolish feelings of jealousy as he noted how comfortable Lenore and this man appeared together as they headed toward Lenore's apartment. Without knowing he was doing so, he held his breath as they stood for a moment in the porch light and looked at each other.

Lenore hesitated before opening the door, dreading what she would do next but knowing she had already postponed it too long. Impulsively she reached up and touched Steve's slightly beard-roughened cheek. "Would you mind coming in for a while? I'd like to talk to you about something." She could see wariness in his eyes.

"My first instinct is to say no," he replied softly. "I think I know what's coming, Lenore, and if you don't mind, I would like to ignore it on the chance that it might go away."

"Please, Steve. Don't make this harder than...."

His gaze went from her eyes to her mouth. Then, as if hoping to change her mind, he drew her to him and kissed her. In the meeting of their lips, she sensed the depth of his feelings and felt a profound sadness that she couldn't love him in return. Her arms went around his neck. She clung to him, seeking forgiveness for the sorrow she'd caused. How wrong she had been to try to use his companionship to fill the lonely hours without Mangas.

"Hey," he said softly, as if sensing her grief, "do you suppose we should stop entertaining the neighbors and go inside?"

She tilted her head back and looked into his eyes. "Oh, Steve, if you only knew how I wished...."

"I do know. That's what makes it so hard to let go."

Lenore handed Steve the keys When the door was open, they went inside.

MANGAS WAITED for over an hour before he finally admitted that what *he* wanted for himself and Lenore no longer mattered. She had found what she wanted in someone else.

A strange and perverse sense of peace filled him as he made his way back to the airport. Tonight a door left tantalizingly open in his mind had been gently but firmly closed. What he and Lenore had once shared was at long last truly over. At least for her. For him? Perhaps someday.

He would call her tomorrow and tell her about Adrian. He would also tell her how pleased he was with the work she'd done, how enthusiastic his people in California had been when they'd seen the plans for the new plant. He wouldn't tell her that he had come to Colorado Springs to see her.... He wouldn't tell her he still loved her more than life itself.

STILL, WITH ALL THAT HAD PASSED the night before and his supposed acceptance of losing her, it was almost three o'clock the next day before

Mangas picked up the phone to call Lenore. When she heard the deep timbre of his voice, unbidden tears filled her eyes. Impatiently she wiped them away as she fought to control her trembling hands.

The night before had been difficult for her. After much urging on Steve's part, she had given him an abbreviated version of her meetings and subsequent love affair with Mangas. Only then had his shoulders slumped in defeat. Not long afterward he had kissed her goodbye and left. She had lost a dear friend.

"I've been meaning to call," Mangas said, his tone strangely businesslike yet casual, as if he was a salesman about to make his pitch.

Lenore closed her eyes against her surroundings, fighting to display the same careless attitude in her reply. "I was beginning to wonder if perhaps you were adapting a Howard Hughes attitude toward life."

"You did get my messages about how pleased I was with the work you've done?"

"Yes. Once in a while something of that sort would filter through."

There was a short pause before he asked, "Are you angry about something?"

Too quickly she answered, "No. Why should I be angry?"

"Perhaps because I should have shown more appreciation for the extraordinary work you've done on my behalf."

"I've done nothing for you I wouldn't have done for any other client," she lied.

"And most likely any other client would have been quicker and more frequent in singing your praises."

"This could go on forever," she replied tersely. "Surely you didn't call to indulge in this kind of inane conversation."

Mangas rubbed his forehead, trying to ease the headache that had accompanied him back to California. She wasn't going to make the telling easy. He realized now that he had hoped she might be glad to hear from him after such a long time, but her tone of voice and impatient remarks immediately stilled that notion. "There's something else, Lenore. Something I had hoped I wouldn't have to bother you with. But it looks as if I was wrong."

His voice had changed again, had become the deep caress she remembered from the times they had lain together. She had to struggle to keep from crying out at the memory. "Mangas, would you please come to the point? I have a hell of a lot of work to get done before I can go home."

Please, she wanted to shout at him, *tell me what you have to and then leave me alone. It's all I can do to cope with the shambles you leave behind every time I see you or hear from you. I'm too tired to pretend it doesn't hurt, too lost to pretend I know the way.*

"Adrian is suing Charles Bingham and me," he said shortly.

Lenore gasped. "On what grounds?"

"I think the terms used were 'intentional infliction of emotional distress and interference with prospective advantage.'"

"I don't understand what that means."

"Adrian is claiming I had planned all along to donate enough money to keep the college from closing, but that I purposely waited until the last minute because I wanted him to spend his money, time, prestige— I won't bore you with the finer details; the list goes on for half a page. Anyway, he's claiming he was kept from making huge financial gains by my efforts to humiliate him, and that I'm responsible for that loss. Charles Bingham has been accused of collusion. Actually, I think he was only brought into it because of the vindictive nature of both the case and Adrian."

He paused. Before he continued, Lenore heard him sigh. She thought it was the most weary and desolate sound she had ever heard.

"He doesn't stand a chance of winning—at least not financially."

Lenore's knuckles grew white as she clutched the phone. Hadn't Adrian destroyed enough? Hadn't he, too, been through enough? Yet he was perverse enough to want to drag everything that had happened through a court of law.

"Lenore?" Mangas's concern for her echoed

in the way he spoke her name. "Lenore, are you all right?"

"Yes," she finally answered. And then, "Why?"

"I guess old hatreds die hard."

"So I've learned," she said slowly.

"I've done everything I could to try to keep you out of it...but I'm afraid it wasn't enough."

"How long have you known?"

"A few months."

Lenore's mind raced as she struggled to understand what Mangas had just told her, but imagining the far-reaching consequences of Adrian's actions was, at the moment, beyond her.

"Do you understand what this means?" he asked gently, afraid of her answer, yet needing to prepare her for the pain and humiliation she was sure to be put through by the trial.

"I don't know...I can't think...."

"If the tabloids get involved in it—and I can't imagine why they wouldn't—I'm sure we'll be given their usual treatment. But, then, for you it really won't be the tabloids that will do the most damage. The local papers are sure to carry something like this—the trial is going to be held in Colorado Springs."

Lenore leaned back in her chair. She couldn't remember ever feeling so tired. "There's nothing that can be done to stop him?"

"We've tried everything other than settling out of court, and I'm not sure he would do that. I honestly don't think it's the money he's after." Barely audibly he added, "I'm sorry for the way things have turned out, Lenore. I would have done anything to keep you from going through this."

"Anything short of trying to settle, that is," she countered bitterly, thinking of her own choice not to go to trial when she was fired from her job—largely to protect him.

"That would be like an admission of guilt." The words were spoken evenly and with a quiet dignity.

"Oh, Mangas. . . ." She sighed. "You know I didn't mean that. I really do understand. . . ."

"Yes. . . I know."

Frantically she searched for a way to end their conversation before she broke down. He mustn't know how badly she needed him or how badly she wanted him. "Don't worry about me, Mangas," she said, her voice now taking on a cold and cutting edge to cover the longing. "I've been through much worse." And just as the tears started to fall, she flippantly added, "Keep in touch." Blindly she reached out to put the receiver back in its cradle.

THREE WEEKS LATER the summons arrived, calling her as a hostile witness for the plaintiff.

CHAPTER EIGHTEEN

THE CHINOOK WINDS melted the last of the spring snows and any lingering hesitation to start new construction. With the change in weather, Randolph and Shaughnessy's client list grew like an adolescent boy—in wild and ungainly spurts. Lenore and Paul fell impossibly behind in their work when Lenore insisted, despite their loud objections, that Paul and Samantha keep their honeymoon plans.

After a solid two weeks of fourteen-hour days spent trying to catch up, the partners had a conference and decided it was time to expand the firm by adding a couple of part-time draftsmen from the nearby college.

Lenore was reluctant to give up the extra hours, having used them as a vehicle to get through the days and weeks as she waited for the trial to begin. Uncertain how their current or prospective clients might react to her being involved in the upcoming case, she and Paul had decided to adopt a "wait and see" attitude. While the seemingly Pollyanaish attitude worked most of the time, in moments when exhaustion made her the most vulnerable she would suffer a gnawing guilt. She had inadvertently involved Paul in what was sure to become the season's hottest scandal.

Lenore thought she was mentally prepared for what was to come—until the Wednesday morning she came into the office and saw Mangas's and Adrian's pictures juxtaposed on the front page of the newspaper. As if in a trance, she headed for her office.

"So it's begun," Samantha said, bringing Lenore a cup of coffee.

Still staring at the paper, Lenore said, "Obviously it was foolish of me to hope it would be ignored by the press."

"Maybe they'll leave you out of it."

"That's about as likely as California never having another earthquake. Sin, sex and scandal make too-good copy for any newspaper to leave alone."

Looking at the paper over Lenore's shoulder, Samantha commented, "I thought it took years for something like this to come to trial."

"So did I. But it seems that's only true in areas where the courts are backlogged. Colorado Springs must have a very efficient system. Either that or people aren't as anxious to sue each other here."

"Have you seen Mangas lately?"

"No, not since December. I've talked to him a couple of times, but that's all."

"Have you thought about how it's going to affect you to see him again?"

"For heaven's sake," Lenore snapped. "Why should seeing him again affect me at all?"

There was a long awkward pause before Samantha said, "Because it's obvious you're still in love with him."

Lenore glared at her. "Just because your head is in the clouds, don't assume you can ascribe similar feelings to everyone around you."

Samantha sat on the corner of the desk facing Lenore. "I've never been able to understand how someone of your intelligence could be so dumb. If you honestly think you've managed to convince *anyone* that you're no longer in love with Mangas Taylor, you're living in a fool's paradise. For crying out loud, Lenore, what possible good does denying it do? Wouldn't it be easier to get him out of your system once and for all?"

Lenore took off her jacket and hung it in the closet, then went to her desk. The only indication that she had even heard Samantha's emotional outburst was in her tightly clamped jaw, the resultant twitch in the muscle just in front of her ear. Sitting behind her desk, she gave her cousin a look that warned her, if she dared to continue the discussion, she risked an unleashed fury.

Samantha folded her arms stubbornly across her chest. "For Pete's sake, Lenore, that kind of blustering never worked on me when we were kids. What makes you think it's going to work now?''

"All right, Samantha, you tell me something. What possible good would it do to go around broadcasting that I'm...that I'm...." Unable to finish what she had thought would be so easy to say, she bit her lip until she felt the coppery taste of her own blood on the end of her tongue.

"Go on, say it," Samantha urged. "Maybe that's what it's going to take to finally get you over him. You can't spend your entire life pining after a man who doesn't love you." As Samantha saw the look in Lenore's eyes, a slow-dawning understanding was reflected in her face. "My, God," she gasped. "You mean he *does* still love you?" Before Lenore could answer, Samantha exploded again. *"Then what in the hell is keeping the two of you apart?"*

Lenore started to answer—one of the pat replies she had used for so long, both to try to convince herself as well as others—but it just wouldn't come. Finally she sighed heavily and said, "I just don't know anymore."

Samantha stared for long seconds. "When we were growing up together," she said softly, "I always wished I had a streak of stubbornness like yours. It seemed like there wasn't anyone or anything that ever got the best of you. You would fight the toughest teacher in the school for a grade as vehemently as you would an umpire over a strike call you thought should have been a ball. If a dress fell apart six months after you bought it, you took it back to the store— and always got a new one. After high school, you were the only one of all of us girls in the family who went all out for a career—a *real* career.

"I remember how impressed I was when you decided one day that you would move away from home. And it wasn't just to San Francisco, either, like the rest of us who thought we were such hot stuff—you moved all the way to Colorado Springs. I thought you had it all, Lenore. Never once did I guess that somewhere deep inside you were really a quivering bowl of Jell-O, just like all the rest of us common ordinary folk." Samantha plopped into the chair beside her.

"Now that I think about it," she went on, "I don't envy you at all. You've got it twice as hard as I do, because nobody thinks I'm made out of granite. No one expects me to withstand every storm without help."

Lenore put her elbows on the desk and cupped her chin in her hands. In a rare moment of candor she admitted, "Sometimes I feel like a pair of those jeans they show being stretched between two mules." She stared absently at the wallpaper behind Samantha. The room grew as quiet as a schoolroom on Saturday morning.

Samantha broke the silence when she softly

said, "Why don't you tell me about Mangas Taylor? You never really have, you know."

Where would she begin, Lenore wondered. Should she start by telling Samantha how special she felt when she was with Mangas, or should she begin by telling her how Mangas had tried to use her? How she loved him...or how she feared him?

"He's unlike anyone I've ever known..." she began.

The morning disappeared in a conversation that turned out to be a much-needed catharsis for Lenore. It wasn't until later in the day, when the telephone seemed to never stop ringing in contrast to the tranquil morning that they realized Paul must have stepped in and quietly taken over Samantha's desk so the two of them could spend the time together uninterrupted. While Lenore had reached no real conclusions, the sharing with someone sympathetic brought her a peace that made the ache seem easier. Samantha had offered no words of wisdom or advice. She had just listened as a loving friend is sometimes needed to do.

THE DAY LENORE WAS TO TESTIFY, she prepared for her time in court with deliberate care. She knew Adrian had insisted she be called to try to prove Mangas had had inside information on the ski-resort plans for the college. She also knew Adrian was smart enough to realize there was a chance his accusations weren't true, but that he would think himself the winner no matter which way the testimony went. Even if the judge—the only one to hear the trial, since Adrian had decided to forgo a jury—believed her testimony that she and Mangas had never met before the weekend the college was to be closed, all the details of their subsequent affair were sure to be spelled out in clinical detail. Details every current or potential client she and Paul had, or might hope to have, would have to be blind or deaf to miss.

When she arrived at the courthouse, she discovered the proceedings had been closed to all prospective witnesses at the request of Adrian's attorney. The morning dragged by with unbelievable slowness as she waited to be called. Word finally arrived that a lunch break had been ordered and that she was scheduled to be called as soon as the case resumed.

The sandwich she picked out in the courthouse cafeteria tasted like sawdust, the coffee like poorly made espresso. After the third bite, she gave up the attempt to eat lunch. The rest of the break period she spent wandering around the building, lost in thoughts of the conversation she and Samantha had had the previous day.

At two o'clock she discovered there was going to be a further delay, this time while the judge conferred on another upcoming trial. By two-thirty, when she was finally called by the baliff, she was a nervous wreck.

With deliberation, purposely avoiding any visual contact with either Mangas or Adrian, she walked into the courtroom, keeping her eyes trained on the judge and only once looking over to see the warm encouragement in Charles Bingham's eyes. After being sworn in and after Adrian's attorney, William Monroe, reminded the court she had been called as a hostile witness, the lawyer languidly walked toward her. He was dressed in a soft gray suit that made his full head of silver hair seem to glow in leonine splendor. Trim and healthy looking, he had the lazy nonchalant air of a snake lying on the branch of a tree, seemingly innocently waiting for a bird to return to its nest.

"Ms Randolph, before we get into the heart of this thing," he began conversationally, "let's spend a little time establishing who you are, shall we?" As gently as a doting grandfather might have, William Monroe led Lenore through a series of questions that drew a picture of her as an aggressive, assertive and intelligent young woman who just happened to come from an area in California not too far away from Apache Computers home base.

Then, without warning, he struck. He stopped his casual pacing and swung around to face her. "How long have you and Mangas Taylor been lovers?" he snapped.

Out of the corner of her eye she saw Mangas move forward in his chair, and as quickly, his attorney's hand go to his arm. "Mr. Taylor and I are not lovers," she said evenly, without emotion. For an instant she thought she saw a spark of surprise in the lawyer's eyes, but it was gone with a blink.

"Ah," he said, his voice now a soft caress. "Perhaps a lovers' quarrel has changed the tenses?"

"Is that a question?" she parried.

He smiled, and Lenore felt a shiver of fear chase down her spine. Intuitively she knew this man wasn't someone she would ever call a friend, even under the best of circumstances. "Yes, Ms Randolph, that was a question. But I shall rephrase it for you if you like." He walked forward until he stood directly in front of her. "How long *were* you lovers?"

"Less than four months."

"And those months were?"

"June through September of last year."

He turned from her and walked back to the table. "Let's see," he said, riffling through a small stack of papers. When at last he found the one he'd been seeking, he quickly scanned it and then turned to face her once again. "Wasn't June the month of the meeting at Winchester College, called to turn the land and buildings back to the Winchester family?"

"Yes."

He leaned lightly against the desk, his arms folded. "How did you feel about the college closing?"

"I thought it was a shame."

"Isn't that rather an odd reaction from someone who had been hired as chief architect for the college's redesign?"

"No, I don't think so. It isn't an architect's job to approve of every building's demise before she will design something new to take its place." She heard a soft murmur come from the press area.

"Were you with Mr. Taylor during this particular weekend?"

She swallowed. "Yes... part of it."

"Which part, may I ask? And how long were the two of you together?"

"A couple of hours at the most."

"Where?"

"I met him for the first time in one of the school's music rooms."

"And the second time?" he asked, a hound catching the scent.

"In... my room."

"I was under the impression that on this particular weekend the guests were separated into male and female dorms—that the school has no coed facilities."

"That's correct."

"And yet Mangas Taylor visited you in your room?"

"Yes," she said, her chin raising a defiant notch.

"And yet you would have us believe you had met Mr. Taylor for the first time that weekend?"

"Yes." She glared at him. "And I would *also* have you believe that when Mr. Taylor came to my room it was to talk."

His only answer was a knowing smile that he made sure was seen by the judge and the courtroom spectators. "Let's move on, shall we?" Again he looked at the paper he held. "Would you agree, Ms Randolph, that even in this day and age of confused roles for men and women, a man's pride is an important part of what makes him special and unique among his fellow men?"

Knowing she would be damned no matter how she answered, she replied, "No, Mr. Monroe, I'm not sure I would agree with that." To her, a man was special because of the things he did and the way he did them, rather than because of how he might interpret his own actions, an often false pride that some men would still virtually die to defend. As she had expected, Monroe immediately jumped on her answer.

"Is that why you so blatantly took your lover to Mr. Winchester's house in Aspen?"

"Is what why. . . ?"

"Ms Randolph, we could save a great deal of time if you would refrain from playing word games.'' A trace of irritation destroyed his cool demeanor. ''Did you take Mangas Taylor—your lover—with you to Aspen to stay in Adrian Winchester's home because you were totally insensitive to the damage it would do to Mr. Winchester's pride? Were you really unaware of the humiliation it would cause my client to have a long-standing, bitter enemy making love to a woman he thought he cared deeply about in his very own bedroom?''

Lenore calmly answered. ''At the time I was unaware Mangas and Adrian even knew each other.''

He looked at her with withering skepticism. ''Even if that were true, I would still find it terribly difficult to understand why a woman would take a lover with her to stay in the house of a man who was obviously interested in her. And Adrian Winchester had made his interest in you evident over a span of many months, had he not?''

''I was only staying—''

''Would you please answer the question?''

Lenore forced herself to take a deep breath to stifle her urge to rail at him in her defense. When she once again felt calm enough to suffer his attack, she answered. ''I knew Adrian was interested in me, and I did everything I could to discourage it.''

The lawyer chuckled and glanced at the judge. ''I don't know about Mr. Winchester, Your

Honor, but if a beautiful woman agreed to go with me for a weekend in the mountains, even if the dorms were separate, I would consider that an encouraging sign.''

"My weekend at Winchester College was strictly business. I attended the function at the request of my employer." At the sudden gleam in his eyes, she knew she'd been led into a trap.

"And what about the months afterward, when you not only accepted dates with Mr. Winchester but instigated several yourself?" he asked menacingly. "Is it possible that you had not yet gained all the information that Mr. Taylor required for his nefarious scheme to ruin Adrian Winchester?"

When the courtroom was again quiet, she replied. "I went out with Adrian Winchester once last summer—at his instigation—because he was an old friend and at that time I wasn't seeing anyone else.''

Monroe's eyes bored into hers. "In other words, Mr. Taylor was in California for the moment.''

"He was in California, and I had no reason to believe he would ever come back to Colorado Springs.''

The sly look Monroe gave her coarsened his handsome features. "In other words, you're saying you weren't seeing each other on any kind of regular basis?"

"At the time, we weren't seeing each other at all."

He again stopped his pacing and whirled around to face her. "How did you feel about Mangas Taylor during this time you claim you weren't seeing each other?"

She felt the color drain from her face. Stalling for time as she fought for control, she straightened in the hard wooden chair and glanced at the empty jury box. Without looking in his direction, she could feel the intensity of Mangas's gaze on her. Slowly her eyes went back to William Monroe. There was only one way she could answer. Softly she said, "I loved him."

"And when you were with him in Aspen?"

"I loved him."

"And now?"

As if the words were torn from her, she said, "I love him."

"And you would have this court believe you could date two men who have been the bitterest of enemies—proclaiming to love one of them—and that you wouldn't become involved in your lover's scheme to dishonor and cause grievous monetary harm to the other?"

"I wouldn't—I didn't."

He glared at her. "I'm through with this witness, Your Honor."

The judge looked to the other attorney, who was engaged in an animated consultation with Mangas. When at last the men were finished, the attorney rose and said, "No questions at this time, Your Honor."

As Lenore made her way from the courtroom she heard Mangas's attorney ask, "May counsel approach the bench?"

His thoughts in turmoil, Mangas watched as Lenore left the witness stand and walked down the aisle to the exit. She looked only at the back wall, ignoring the courtroom full of people who watched her pass. Her words echoed in his mind and he eagerly savored their sweet sound.

"I love him," she had said, and the words had been without hesitation, without fear. She had announced for all the world to hear that Lenore Randolph loved Mangas Taylor.

Woven into his delirious joy was a thread of anger. Why in the hell had she never told him?

The sound he had been subconsciously waiting for broke into his thoughts when the judge struck his gavel against its wooden stand and announced there would be a fifteen-minute recess.

With incredible effort Mangas controlled the urge to sprint from the courtroom to catch Lenore, knowing that would reinforce to every reporter who witnessed his behavior that something unusual had just happened.

Each seemingly casual step down the aisle toward the double doors leading to the exit became an exercise in self-discipline.

She loved him! She had loved him all along.

When he reached the hallway, his gaze immediately swung to the elevator and the bank of lighted buttons overhead that indicated which floor the elevator car was on. It had started to move again after stopping on the third floor. His control almost gone, Mangas glanced around him, and reassured that he was being virtually ignored, ran for the stairs. He made it down the four flights to the first floor in time to catch a glimpse of Lenore's heather-colored skirt as she headed for the exit.

If people thought it strange to see a man in an obviously expensive and conservation soft brown, three-piece pin-striped suit running through the lobby of the courthouse as if he'd just heisted the day's receipts, they refrained from saying so or from trying to stop him. One or two glanced his way as he caught up with the woman he'd been chasing and grabbed her by the arm to turn her around to face him. But when the pair simply stood and stared at each other, the observers quickly went back to their business.

Lenore could feel Mangas's hands trembling where they lightly touched her shoulders. His gaze enveloped her with such intense hunger and longing that she felt she had been struck by the force of it. For long moments they stood and looked at each other, neither of them uttering a sound. Suddenly, as if only then aware of their surroundings, Mangas grabbed her hand and quickly scanned the area. After trying several doors, he finally found an empty office, and they went inside. When the door closed behind them with a soft click, he whirled to face her, a terrible scowl on his face. "Why in hell didn't you tell me?" he demanded, his voice ragged with emotion.

She wanted to reach out to him, to gently touch the lines of pain she saw on his face with her fingertips, to ease the sorrow they had both suffered with words that would make everything right for them. But she didn't know the words to use. Knew the pain they had suffered because of each other couldn't be erased with a touch.

How could she answer him, she agonized. None of the things she could think of sounded rational—or even reasonable. Finally, in words barely above a whisper, she answered. "I did tell you, once, but you had fallen asleep and didn't hear me. After that—over the months we've been apart—I couldn't. I was afraid of you... but most of all, I know now I was afraid of me."

His shoulders slumped. How easily in his excitement he had forgotten she had had reason to fear him—still did, in fact. What proof had he ever given her that he wasn't really a bastard? What right did he have to ask her to trust him again? "Did you mean what you said, that you had loved me since the beginning?"

"Yes," she said softly. "You destroyed barriers around my heart I had spent my entire adult life building. I loved you even as I told you I never wanted to see you again. It was such an easy way out for me...I was such a coward. Loving you took commitment, but it also demanded I give you a part of me I had never given to anyone before. I was terrified I might have to live the rest of my life as an empty shell, should you take that part of me and leave. And I was terrified that if you stayed, I would become like my mother. I finally realized the only fallacy of my fears: I really had no choice about the giving. You possessed my heart that evening as I sat beside you on the piano bench. It just took me a long time to acknowledge there was nothing I could do about it.

"And I also took a long hard look at my mother and realized she was happy. She had the strength to get through some really hard times. If she had truly wanted to be a doctor, she would have found a way to do that, too. I know now that my father, who loves her with the same schoolboy intensity as the day they met, would have done whatever necessary to help her. What she did was her choice."

Tentatively he reached out to her, knowing there were words he should say but unable to keep from touching her any longer. When she took his hand, he pulled her to him and crushed her against the length of him. The sweetly remembered scent of her hair and the fragrance of her perfume assailed his senses. The feel of her pressed against him was the living of a dream that had haunted him nightly. A joy swelled his chest, so intense it bordered on pain. She loved him! Every dream, every wish, every hope that had shadowed him had come true. She really loved him.

With Mangas's embrace, Lenore felt the last of the crushing burden she had carried slip away. Her heart, for so long heavy with sadness, was now set free with the rightness of their coming together again. She looked up into his eyes. "There are still so many things we'll have to work out. We're so different, Mangas—I'm not—"

His kiss stilled her words. The force and the promise of his lips quieted her protests. With a tiny cry, she wrapped her arms around his neck and pulled him closer still. Her mouth eagerly parted at his insistence, and she welcomed the deepening of his kiss. Immediately they were lost to everything but their need for each other. A need that, when consummated, would soften the sharp edges of their time apart.

Lenore's hands slipped beneath Mangas's open jacket and across the silkiness she found at the back of his vest. Boldly stroking the tense muscles she could feel beneath the layers of cloth, she was elated when her movements elicited a deep moan of barely contained desire from Mangas.

Realizing how dangerously close they were to succumbing to the passions that coursed through both of them, Mangas broke the kiss and looked down at her. "I only managed to get a fifteen-minute break...." His eyes sparkled with sudden amusement. "I've got to get back— or have a damn good explanation for my absence." His breathing came in quick sighs as his hands continued to caress her. "Where will you be— Where can I meet you later?"

Her hand played with the soft hair at the nape of his neck. "I'll wait for you at my place."

He gazed at her intently, the playful look in his eyes now gone. "We have so much to talk about," he said meaningfully. "Perhaps it would be better if we began our evening in someplace less...."

"I'll fix us something to eat. We can talk there."

"Be forewarned," he said huskily. "I have only one hunger that controls me now—and it isn't for food."

Her eyes shone with the joy of being in his arms. "I don't remember mentioning *when* we would eat...."

A low moan once more escaped his lips as he pulled her to him. Against the softness of her hair he said, "You did that on purpose, didn't you?"

"Me?" she answered innocently. "How could you accuse me of such a thing?"

His hands slipped along her neck; his thumbs softly touched and pressed to her chin, tilting her face up for her lips to meet his kiss. When he looked down at her, he was serious once again. "More than I want anything else, I want us to start out right this time. I'll pick you up at six-thirty, and we'll go *out* to eat. We'll go to someplace quiet—someplace dark and intimate." Reluctantly he released her and walked to the door. Before leaving, he turned and stared at her. "I was a fool to let you walk out of my life. We have so much time to make up."

Her fingers went to her lips. She blew him a kiss as he walked through the door.

CHAPTER NINETEEN

THE FIRST THING LENORE DID when she arrived
home was to call the office. She had to tell Paul
she wouldn't be in tomorrow, and to ask him if
he could take the appointments Samantha
couldn't reschedule. She explained that she
wanted to attend the next day's proceedings now
that she had already testified and could watch
the trial.

After several pointed questions from Paul
about her day in court, she finally admitted she
and Mangas were going to see each other that
evening. Expecting Paul's customary teasing,
she was surprised when she detected a catch in
his voice as he said, "Go for it, Lenore. Grab on
to a little happiness. No one deserves it more
than you do."

Fifteen minutes later, just as she was headed
for the bathroom to take a shower, the phone
rang. It was Paul. This time his voice was full of
a self-satisfied mischievousness. In answer to
her hello, he said, "You have the rest of the
week off. Samantha has canceled everything
from now until next Monday—so enjoy."

"Paul, you are the second best thing that has ever happened to me."

He laughed. "I won't even bother to ask you about the first."

When they said goodbye again, Lenore went back to her shower, still planning to spend all the remaining time before Mangas's arrival in decadent attention to every detail of her appearance, despite the now rapidly passing time. She opened the last of the obscenely expensive miniature perfumed soap bars she had received from Samantha for Christmas and breathed in its lovely floral fragrance as she washed away the day's grime.

Once powdered and perfumed, she pulled the loveliest and sheerest of her lingerie from the dresser, an apricot lace-and-silk teddy and matching half-slip. The teddy she put on; the slip and stockings she laid on the bed before she returned to the bathroom to finish her hair. She didn't have to look in the mirror to know her cheeks were flushed with color. Never before had she spent time deliberately preparing herself for seduction, and while on one hand the feeling was wickedly delicious, it was also a little disconcerting. Obviously, she decided, smiling to herself, it wasn't easy for her to give in to the wanton feeling Mangas inspired in her.

She laughed aloud. Was it really possible, after all that had passed between them—the uninhibited love they had made to each other—

that she was experiencing feelings of shyness?

Turning off her blow dryer, she heard the last note of the doorbell chime. A shiver of panic gripped her as she dashed into the bedroom and glanced at the clock on the nightstand. Either Mangas was unforgivably early, or a neighbor had picked an incredibly poor time to call. She grabbed her robe off the closet hook and ran to the front door, calling out, "I'm coming," in answer to the second ring.

She inwardly groaned after peering through the tiny window in the door. It *was* Mangas. Pulling the belt of her robe a little tighter, she opened the door. "You're early," she accused.

"I know. I could have been even earlier if I hadn't stopped for these." He handed her a long white box wrapped with a huge red bow. "I thought I had better work at getting this courting thing down right."

As she reached for the box, she saw the smile on his face slowly fade. His forehead furrowed in puzzlement, and then recognition made the strong lines of his face stand out in sharp relief. "What's wrong?" she asked.

"That robe. . . ."

Then she knew. Without thinking, she had put on the robe she'd worn since their return from Aspen. It was the robe he had bought to wear there, the one piece of clothing she hadn't sent back to him with the rest. The rich velour wrap had been her private remembrance of a lost love. She had spent countless winter nights wearing it while she sat curled on the sofa in front of her fireplace, staring at the flickering fire. Unconsciously her hand went to her throat, where she pulled the robe tighter together.

"Why are you wearing it?" he finished softly.

A dozen answers offered themselves, but only the truth managed to escape. "It was all I had of you."

Still he stared, his face a reflection of the torment he had suddenly been thrust back into. "Never again, Lenore," he said firmly. "Never again will we let this happen to us."

It was a promise she listened to with all of her heart. Her hand went to his face, and she gently ran her fingers along the strong line of his jaw. "Come inside," she said, "and tell me what happened after I left today."

"Going through it is bad enough. If you don't mind, I would just as soon not talk about it."

She didn't mind at all. There would be plenty of time later. Tonight was just for them.

He followed her into the kitchen, where she took a crystal vase down and arranged the long-stemmed yellow roses in the sparkling glass. She glanced up at him. "Thank you. Yellow roses are my favorite."

His gaze followed her every movement, much as a sailor too long from home watches the approaching shoreline. He noted the aching loveliness of her breasts when she reached over her head to get the vase, and in his mind he remembered their fullness pressed against his chest as they lay together. His eyes went to the graceful curve of her hip, plainly visible in the folds of the too-large robe, and he remembered its smooth feel under his caressing hand.

As if she could read his thoughts, Lenore's motions became those of a woman whose body cried out for a man's touch. When the snugly drawn belt loosened and the front of her robe parted provocatively at her breasts, she made no attempt to tighten the sash.

While on the surface they calmly discussed which restaurant they should call for reservations, an undercurrent as forceful as a riptide began to rush between them. Lenore turned to carry the flowers into the other room and saw Mangas's eyes on the triangle of flesh where the robe had fallen open. A shiver of reciprocal desire passed through her. She nervously ran her tongue across her lips and eased her way past him into the living room. The gesture made Mangas catch his breath.

Once she had the roses placed on the table and had twice readjusted a bud that insisted it should face the opposite direction, she turned to look at Mangas. He was standing at the doorway watching her, his face unreadable.

With his feet spread slightly apart, his hands tucked casually in his pockets, he could have made a fortune for the suit manufacturer if even a modicum of his sexuality could have been marketed with the rather staid product. Lenore mentally sighed as she absorbed the male beauty of him. The soft brown of his suit made his skin seem almost golden. The tension between them made the air seem almost too heavy to breath.

Reaching up to rub the back of his neck, Lenore realized his resolve to give Lenore an evening free from any physical pressure from him was rapidly disintegrating. His idea that he should court her slowly so that they could build a solid base for their love—a base that nothing could destroy—began to diminish in direct proportion to her nearness.

But, a fierce inner voice warned, *we must have something to hold us together this time. Something that will see us through, no matter how terrible the storm that might blow our way.* He knew he would merely exist without her.

More than he wanted to make love to her now, he wanted to have her as his love for all time. "Why don't you finish getting ready while I call the restaurant," he finally said.

Lenore felt like screaming. Would she never understand him? His wanting her was as plain as the crisp blueness of his eyes, yet he was pushing her away. Surely he could tell she, too, wanted to make love to him. Had her years of guarded behavior left her unable to communicate her needs, even to this man who had heard her proclaim her love only hours before?

She started for the bedroom when a sudden surge of frustration made her stop. Dammit, she wasn't going to spend the next several hours trying to choke down a meal, when what she really wanted was to make love to him. She turned to see that Mangas had gone over to the phone.

When he realized she hadn't left, he glanced at her, a question in his eyes.

"I've a pulled muscle in my neck," she artfully blurted out. "Would you mind rubbing it for me?"

Smiling, he came over to stand beside her and turned her so that her back was to him. His hands went to her shoulders, where they began to gently knead the tense muscles that ran up to her neck. "Where does it hurt?" he asked.

She pointed to a spot about halfway between her shoulder and neck. "Here," she said, and untied her robe, dropping the material from her shoulders. She smiled triumphantly when she heard the rhythm of his breathing increase slightly. Carelessly letting the robe drop lower, Lenore reached up to move the straps of her teddy, commenting that they seemed to be in his way.

The moment she had dropped the robe from her shoulders, Mangas became convinced of Lenore's intentions. For an instant he had considered sending her on into the bedroom and going back to his phone calling. Then, with a smile of deep pleasure, he reminded himself that although he had been called many things in his lifetime, "fool" had never been one of them. They would talk, they would say all they had to say to each other...later.

As for now.... He pulled her golden brown hair to the side and pressed his lips to the flesh at the curve of her neck. The contact created an explosion of yearning in him. He clasped her arms and drew her to him so that her back rested against his chest. His hands moved to her breasts to cup the roundness and gently pull her closer to him still. Slowly his mouth moved along her richly scented skin in tiny nipping kisses that ended just below her ear. Taking the lobe between his teeth, he touched the burning flesh with the tip of his tongue. After he had left a moist trail along the most sensitive curves of her ear, he softly murmured, "Don't you think you'd better finish getting ready. We'll never get a table...."

His words snapped her out of the delicious lethargy he had so effortlessly induced. She whirled around to face him. The look of dusky passion in his eyes belied his words, and she knew then he had simply been giving her a measure of her own provocative teasing.

As the memory of the first time they had made love flashed through her mind, a smile tugged at the corners of her mouth. How eagerly she had learned from this man—how boldly she wanted to please him. Her hands now pressed against his thighs, feeling the corded muscles as she followed their length to his hips and then to his waist. Meeting his mouth in a quick kiss she said, "Wait here a minute. I'll be right back."

As she walked toward the kitchen she started to shrug the robe back over her shoulders, then hesitated a moment and let it slip off instead, casually dropping it into the chair as she passed by.

Mangas grinned at the incredibly seductive gesture she had managed to bring off with seeming innocence. He wasn't sure what the piece of clothing she wore—or almost wore—was called, but he was sure he had never seen anything more erotic. The lace that rode high on her hips made her legs look impossibly long and sculptured.

Careful, Mangas, he warned himself. *If she sees how quickly you're losing control, you'll scare the hell out of her. She'll think you're turning into a raving madman.*

When Lenore came back into the room, he noticed one of the straps had again fallen from her shoulder and now exposed a tantalizing section of her breast just above the softly probing nipple. When she saw him looking at the creamy expanse of skin, she smiled.

"I chose this particular garment very carefully. I'm glad you approve." Stopping in front of him, she began unbuttoning his vest. "I hope you don't mind," she added softly, "but I decided your idea about going out for dinner was just plain dumb. The more I thought about it, the more I realized that if we went out, I would simply have to find some way to get through a horrendously frustrating hour and a half, when what I really wanted was right here—right now.'' She nuzzled the spot on his neck just below his ear.

''I took some shrimp out for a salad,'' she murmured. ''If you insist, though, we can go out to eat . . . as long as it's later. . . .''

She had finished with his vest, moving on to his shirt. ''I hope you don't think I'm being too forward or pushy about this,'' she said as her hand slipped beneath his shirt. ''But after spending months with only a dream image of you, there is no way, now that I have you where I want you, that I'm going to let the real thing go for a plateful of food.''

A wonderfully happy laugh was her answer as Mangas bent over and picked her up. ''Lenore Michelle Randolph,'' he growled. ''You've had your last chance for a night on the town, Lenore . . . now I am going to make wild, passionate love to you until you beg me to stop.''

''I thought you had to be somewhere tomorrow,'' she answered him huskily between kisses. ''And how did you know my middle name?''

He set her down beside the bed. ''There are all kinds of things I know about you.''

''Such as?''

He held her face between his hands and looked into her eyes. Suddenly, deadly serious, he said, "Such as...in spite of every intelligent bone in your body, you fell in love with a man who—"

She pressed her fingers to his lips to stop him from saying anything more. "Careful, fella," she warned him lightheartedly, trying to postpone the time when they would have to face the last of the barriers that lay between them. "You happen to be talking about the man I love."

One by one he kissed those fingers. "Lenore," he began, ignoring her silent pleas to let this moment pass for now, "what I tried to do to you was so wrong. For me to say I'm sorry seems almost...almost absurd. My behavior was unforgivable. As much as I wish I could create one, I have no real explanation for the insanity that controlled me at the time. I only know that seeing Adrian again at Winchester after all those years made me feel as if I'd been a sleeping volcano that had suddenly erupted. Until that moment I honestly had no idea the hatred I had once felt for that man still festered in my soul. I had convinced myself that I had come to grips with my past and managed to leave it behind me.

"When I came back to Colorado and discovered the college was closing, and then finding out later that Adrian was to be the beneficiary of its demise— Well, it recreated everything that had transpired between us. And almost without my being aware of it, I found it brought that period of my life back in such critical focus that those events had developed polished edges so sharp, they had grown deadly. It was as if everything that had happened between Adrian and me had happened yesterday instead of ten years ago.''

Weary of the influence Adrian still seemed to have over his life, Mangas determinedly shoved thoughts of him aside. His voice softened, now sounding strangely hollow, as if he was speaking from a great distance. ''Something in me couldn't let the college close. Finding a way to keep it open had become my way of repaying a debt to someone—I realized too late—I had once loved dearly. A debt I had come to think of as impossible to repay.''

He gently stroked her cheek. ''You became involved almost by accident. From the moment I saw you, even from a distance, I knew you were incredibly special. When I thought you and Adrian.... It was like....'' He fought for words that refused to come. ''I can't explain it. I only knew that at the time a rage burned inside me. I couldn't let him—''

''Enough!'' Lenore said, again touching the tips of her fingers to his lips. She stared at him for long moments before she finally said, ''Since you first told me about all this, I've used it as a barrier between us. It created a convenient place for me to hide, where I could avoid facing a future that wasn't laid out for me like a road map. As long as I could summon the righteous indignation I was supposed to feel at the horrible way I convinced myself I'd been used, I didn't have to cope with emotions that couldn't be mentally catalogued or filed away into neat slots. As long as I didn't forgive or try to understand that what you had tried to do to me wasn't a true part of you, I didn't have to allow myself to become vulnerable again.''

Hesitatingly, with obvious effort, she went on. "I've changed, Mangas," she said, shaking her head expressively. "Little by little over this past year, I've finally grown up. And in the process I've learned that my talents are real, after all. I know now I can succeed without the security blanket of Mason, Langly and Mason. I also know that even if I give my heart to someone, I can still be me. It took me a long time, but finally. . . at last. . . I stopped being afraid.'' She reached up to brush his hair back from his forehead, letting the soft black waves pass slowly through her fingers.

"I love you," she whispered. "I hope you never get tired of hearing that, because I'll never stop telling you.''

He kissed her then, and all the pain that had been between them disappeared like morning dew on mountain grass.

With a lithe grace, he easily divested himself

of the clothing Lenore had started to remove. Turning back to her waiting arms, he caught her by the waist and slowly lifted her, raining kisses along the silk-covered flesh of her stomach. Without urging, as he lowered her and his mouth followed the lacy outline at the top of her breasts, she wrapped her legs around his waist.

Lenore let the straps of her teddy fall from her shoulders and shrugged her arms free to allow his mouth access to the tantalizing mounds that lay beneath. He paid homage to one exposed areola and its peaked center, giving a breathless pleasure with his teeth and with his tongue.

Gently he settled her across the bed and then joined her. His hand moved along the side of her face, down the curve of her neck with tender and loving strokes. When he brushed her cheek, she turned her face so that her lips touched his palm. Her tongue traced a moist circle before she again turned back to meet his mouth. As if they could deny the fire that burned inside both of them, a fire that would soon rage out of control and consume them, the kiss they shared was almost languorous. Slowly Mangas tasted the sweetness of Lenore's lips, her teeth, her tongue. Her response was almost shy as she dipped into the welcoming recesses of his mouth before leading him back into the sensuous cavern of her own.

As they kissed, his hand moved from her neck

to capture her breast, cupping the warm, pliant flesh as he returned the pressure that her arching back now created against his palm. He started to massage the nipple with his thumb, so that a deep moan came from the back of her throat. With deliberate slowness, his hand left her breast and moved to her waist, then on to her stomach, where it slipped beneath the filmy silk material. When the pressure of his hand was against the triangle of hair marking the passage to the core of her yearning, she could no longer hide the need that fiercely demanded satisfaction.

Still he delayed with teasing stroking touches that made her breath come in ragged gasps. Suddenly impatient with even the thinnest of barriers between them, he halted his sensuous massage to pull the flimsy scrap down over her hips. His mouth followed the apricot-colored silk as it slowly traversed her long legs. He made the journey back in passion-filled lingering kisses that had Lenore's hips moving in rhythm with the insistent contact of his mouth.

It had been so long and they had suffered so greatly that the gentle easy lovemaking Mangas would have shared with her was soon swept away in the burgeoning demands of their bodies. Abruptly their movements became more urgent, their soft cries to each other more filled with desire. And then at last, in the ultimate giving and the ultimate sharing, they joined and once again knew the perfect union of two bodies...of two souls.

Afterward, while Lenore lay in the loving shelter of his arms, she felt as well as heard Mangas release a deep sigh of contentment. Tenderly he brushed errant strands of her long silky hair from her cheek.

"I should have known..." he breathed contentedly.

She waited for him to finish, and when he didn't, she asked, "Should have known what?"

"What would happen between us. We were like two very separate and highly individual clouds in a tumultuous sky." He drew her closer, pressing a kiss to the top of her head. "The electricity that jumped between us from the moment we met was destined to produce a bolt of lightning powerful enough to light up the heavens."

"Spectacular, maybe...but over with so quickly. What happens after the lightning?" Turning to her stomach, Lenore propped herself up on her elbows and looked down at him. The loving smile that radiated from his eyes quickened her heartbeat.

"After the lightning, my beautiful Lenore, is the explosion of thunder that announces our coming together for all time."

And as she kissed him she heard the deafening roar of their love and knew it would be so for them for as long as they lived.

Almost unnoticed, the rose-colored evening drifted into a star-filled black night, and the night became the purple hues of early dawn. As he had never done with another person, Mangas gave himself to Lenore. All that he was, all that he had been, he shared with her.

All that she was, her hopes, her dreams, her aspirations, she shared with him, glorying in the giving, basking in the glow of his love for her.

ALTHOUGH THEY HADN'T SLEPT at all the previous night, neither seemed anything less than fully rested when they appeared at the courthouse the next morning. To avoid questions or drawing undue attention to themselves, they entered separately. Lenore took a seat at the back of the courtroom and waited for Mangas to take the stand.

After the preliminaries and rituals were over, Mangas was called and sat on the same wooden chair where Lenore had sat the previous day. Watching him, she shook her head in wonder. Had it really been less than twenty-four hours?

For an instant, as Roger Brown, the attorney for the defense, prepared his opening questions, Mangas's eyes met hers. The love, the warmth his fleeting glance imparted made her fears disappear. No matter how things turned out today, they would be together. Nothing else mattered. If Adrian should win through some obscene miscarriage of justice, if the amount of money he'd asked for was awarded to him, she knew she and Mangas would see it though.

It was time.

Roger Brown approached the witness stand. In a laid-back style of dress and a calm demeanor—dress that contradicted his fee and behavior that belied his well-deserved reputation for fierce cunning—he began his questioning. "Mr. Taylor," he said easily, conversationally, "would you mind telling the court a little about yourself?"

In an emotionless voice, Mangas gave the pertinent details of his background. It wasn't until Brown began to question him about his relationship with the Winchesters that reporters' notebooks snapped open and pens went to paper.

"So. . ." Roger Brown said slowly while tugging on his earlobe. "Let me get this straight. Long before you had any contact with Adrian Winchester, the son, you were acquainted with Adrian Winchester, the father."

"Yes, that's correct."

"Why don't you tell us a few of the details about this relationship?" Brown gently encouraged.

The memories brought a sudden softening to Mangas's features. His posture subtly relaxed as he began. "Mr. Winchester was one of the finest people I've ever known. He was a gentle man as well as a gentleman, someone who had inherited a harsh environment, in which he no more belonged than a field mouse belongs in a snake pit. He once told me he'd been unhappy for most of his life because of it. He also once told me that it had been a tradition for many generations, in the Winchester family, that the eldest son was supposed to double the fortune left by the father. It became a burdensome task for a man whose lifetime wish was to be a scholar.''

Mangas's voice was barely audible now. As if realizing what was happening, he glanced at the attorney and straightened imperceptibly in the chair. Clearing his throat, he began again.

''When Mr. Winchester discovered I was auditing classes at the college because I couldn't afford to register, I became something of a protégé of his. Over the three years it took me to get a degree, he became the closest thing I had ever had to a father. I left Colorado for personal reasons later; he was the only one here I kept in touch with. Then, after about a year had passed and several of my letters had been returned unopened, I learned he and his wife had been killed in a private plane crash.

''Soon after that I received a registered letter informing me I had been included in his will. A check arrived months later, a hand-written note from Mr. Winchester enclosed with it.

''He wrote me that. . . .'' Mangas stopped and took a deep breath, trying to find a way to say something he'd never spoken aloud. ''He told me he'd loved me like a son, that knowing me had made his years happier.'' Mangas glanced at Lenore and saw her reach up to wipe a tear from the corner of her eye.

Now, as the memories progressed, they brought a smile. "He also gave me a great deal of advice about how to use the money,'' he said slowly. "Very astute advice, I might add.''

In a gesture now so familiar to Lenore, Mangas reached up to rub the back of his neck. "It seemed like a fortune to me at the time, and even though it really wasn't, it was enough to let me turn my dream of building my computer company into a reality. Using the funds he'd left me as capital, I found banks were suddenly willing to loan me the rest of what I needed.'' He shrugged expressively. "In a nutshell, Apache Computers was born the day that check arrived.''

Gently the attorney nudged Mangas into telling the rest of the story.

"After a ten-year absence,'' Mangas went on, "I returned to Colorado for the first time...I learned from an article in the newspaper that the college was going to be closed. Because of all that had happened before, I simply couldn't let it happen. I owed Mr. Winchester too much to let the place he had loved so very deeply just disappear. I saw a chance to finally do something in return for all the old man had done for me and...I did it.''

Lenore blinked back the tears that continued to fill her eyes as the final piece of the puzzle that was Mangas Taylor slipped into place. A low rumble greeted Mangas's revelations. Several reporters left their seats. As far as they were concerned, the trial was already over. When the door was opened to let yet another of the notebook carriers exit, Lenore saw that they were running for the stairs. She didn't need to speculate on tomorrow's headlines.

When she again looked back at the raised dais where the judge sat, she saw that he and the attorneys were deeply involved in conversation. As soon as prosecution and defense returned to their seats, a recess was announced, and everyone involved in the case, lawyers and clients alike, filed into the judge's chamber.

Lenore anxiously waited for some indication of what was on. Pacing the hallway in front of the courtroom, she stopped periodically to peer through the door, afraid the proceedings would start without her. Despite knowing she would be informed when the trial resumed, she finally gave up and went back inside to wait.

At last they emerged. Immediatley Lenore's gaze sought Mangas's. The message he sent to her was one of love—but nothing else. Quickly she glanced at Charles Bingham. A smile had displaced some of the weariness but it failed to bolster Lenore's hope that the ordeal might possibly be over.

The courtroom was again called to order. Without preamble, without any dramatics, the judge calmly announced that the interested parties had reached a compromise.

After a second of stunned silence, a cacophony erupted. Immediately the aisle was jammed with spectators and the press as they rushed forward. A beaming Charles Bingham was surrounded by loudly cheering students, whose hugs and hearty handshakes he eagerly returned.

Ignoring the reporters who crowded around him, Mangas searched for Lenore. Spotting her standing at the back, he worked his way through the throng. Their hands met, and he pulled her to him, holding her in a bone-crushing embrace that told her more eloquently then anything else could have just how worried he'd been about the trial.

"A compromise?" she whispered anxiously.

Mangas grinned. "Adrian dropped the case on the condition no one talked about it."

Strobes began to flash around them when, oblivious to their surroundings, they kissed, deeply and wondrously.

When at last they became aware of the questions that assaulted them despite their obvious reluctance to answer, Mangas broke the kiss. Smiling broadly still, he slipped his arm around her shoulders, leading her through the crowd and out of the courtroom. They were joined by several intrepid reporters on their elevator ride to the ground floor.

Finally, in a moment of silence while the others paused to catch their breath, one crisp and efficient voice could be heard. "Now what, Mr. Taylor?" that voice prodded.

Mangas eyed the eager young woman, then turned to look deeply into Lenore's eyes. "You're asking the wrong person..." he said softly, meaningfully.

"Ms Randolph?" came the immediate question.

Her eyes never left Mangas's face when she answered. "Mr. Taylor and I have a lot of work ahead of us. Among other things, we have to decide how much time each of us can spare for a honeymoon." Happiness surrounding her like the special misty halo that sometimes surrounds the moon, Lenore glanced at the reporter and shyly added, "That is, if he says yes when I ask him to marry me...."

She looked back at Manges and was immediately lost in the loving world of his caressing eyes. Faintly, from what seemed a great distance, she heard the blond-haired reporter say, "I'll give anyone here one hundred to one odds on his answer."

ABOUT THE AUTHOR

After the Lightning is Georgia Bockoven's second romance. This time her wanderlust took her to Colorado Springs and Aspen, where in-depth research provided much of the inspiration for her characters' development. "During my week of roaming around the state," Georgia says, "Lenore and Mangas seemed like constant companions." In fact, her hero is named after an actual Apache chief.

With her father in the military, Georgia went to at least fourteen different schools while she was growing up, in as many different places. Her nomadic childhood gave her her love of travel and people, she says, but she always found it hard to leave the friends she'd made. Her father's last post was Sacramento—and she and both her brothers have lived there ever since.

Georgia is married to a marvelous man whose best traits tend to be reflected in her heroes' actions. She has two teenage sons.

THE GOLDEN CAGE

The first Harlequin American Romance Premier Edition
by bestselling author ANDREA DAVIDSON

Yours FREE, with a home subscription to
SUPERROMANCE™

Complete and mail the coupon below today!

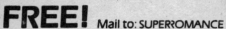

- -

FREE! Mail to: SUPERROMANCE

In the U.S.
2504 West Southern Avenue
Tempe, AZ 85282

In Canada
649 Ontario St.
Stratford, Ontario N5A 6W2

YES, please send me FREE and without any obligation, my **SUPERROMANCE** novel, LOVE BEYOND DESIRE. If you do not hear from me after I have examined my FREE book, please send me the **4 new SUPERROMANCE** books every month as soon as they come off the press. I understand that I will be billed only $2.50 for each book (total $10.00). There are no shipping and handling or any other hidden charges. There is no minimum number of books that I have to purchase. In fact, I may cancel this arrangement at any time. LOVE BEYOND DESIRE is mine to keep as a FREE gift, even if I do not buy any additional books.

NAME _____ (Please Print)

ADDRESS _____ APT. NO. _____

CITY _____

STATE/PROV. _____ ZIP/POSTAL CODE _____

SIGNATURE (If under 18, parent or guardian must sign.)   134-BPS-KAMJ
                                                          SUP-SUB-1

This offer is limited to one order per household and not valid to present subscribers. Prices subject to change without notice.

Offer expires August 31, 1984

LaVyrle Spencer
Sweet Memories

a special woman...a special love.. a special story

Sweet Memories is the poignant tale of Theresa Brubaker and Brian Scanlon, separated by Brian's Air Force officer training, but united in spirit by their burning love.

Alone and unsure, Theresa decides on a traumatic surgical operation that proves devastating for both her and Brian, a proud sensitive man whose feelings of betrayal run deep. Through the tears and pain, Theresa emerges from her inhibitions a passionate, self-confident woman ready to express her love.